THE
REUNION

Books by
Dan Walsh

The Unfinished Gift

The Homecoming

The Deepest Waters

Remembering Christmas

The Discovery

The Reunion

THE
REUNION

A NOVEL

DAN
WALSH

Revell

a division of Baker Publishing Group
Grand Rapids, Michigan

© 2012 by Dan Walsh

Published by Revell
a division of Baker Publishing Group
P.O. Box 6287, Grand Rapids, MI 49516-6287
www.revellbooks.com

Printed in the United States of America

Library of Congress Cataloging-in-Publication Data
Walsh, Dan, 1957–
     The reunion : a novel / Dan Walsh.
         p.   cm.
     ISBN 978-0-8007-2121-3 (pbk.)
     I. Title.
 PS3623.A446R48 2012
 813′.6—dc23   2012015814

This book is a work of fiction. Names, characters, places, and incidents are the product of the author's imagination or are used fictitiously. Any resemblance to actual events, locales, or persons, living or dead, is coincidental.

The internet addresses, email addresses, and phone numbers in this book are accurate at the time of publication. They are provided as a resource. Baker Publishing Group does not endorse them or vouch for their content or permanence.

12   13   14   15   16   17   18   7   6   5   4   3   2   1

To my son, Isaac, my inspiration for "Jake" in this book. With each phase of our relationship, I enjoy being your father more. And to all the military veterans who have served our country, now and over the years. Those of us who've never served owe you a debt we will never fully comprehend or ever be able to repay.

Some who seem least important now will be the greatest then, and some who are the greatest now will be least important then.

—Jesus (Luke 13:30 NLT)

1

Only a few scenes are more beautiful and tranquil than a forest of live oaks. They are not like the jungle, crowded with thick tangles of foliage that slap you in the face as you walk by. That mattered to Aaron Miller.

Even forty years later, Aaron was afraid of jungles.

The ground around live oaks is mostly bare. The trees give each other plenty of space. With massive trunks rising up from the earth, often several feet in diameter, limbs as thick as trees themselves. Sprawling outward, the limbs mingle with the branches of other live oaks, forming an intricate network of curves and arches. Spanish moss hangs from almost every bough, whispering when gentle breezes blow.

A hundred years ago, the place where Aaron Miller lived was just such a forest, splendid and majestic, untouched by man.

Aaron thought about all this during his quiet time that morning. Maybe it was the picture he had seen the day before, taken some sixty years ago. A black-and-white photograph of a simple farmhouse, built between two of the largest trees in the forest.

The house almost seemed to belong there, resting in the forest's shade, enjoying its protection.

Today, that farmhouse stood where it always had. But a few more rooms had been added. The biggest addition housed pool tables, video games, pinball machines, and a public restroom. Another served as a general store where any number of woodsy things could be bought. Citronella candles and mosquito spray, fuel for a Coleman stove, bags of ice.

From that time sixty years ago to the present, more than half the original oak trees were gone, the majority cut down to make room for trailer hookup sites and bumpy dirt roads. All of this to create Bentley's Trailer Park & Campground.

Aaron was the handyman at Bentley's, lived in a storage room just across the way from the main house. Mr. Bentley only docked his pay $150 a month for the privilege.

"Aaron, you out and about yet?" It was Sue Kendall; she managed the place. The black-and-white photograph Aaron had seen of the farmhouse hung on the wall behind her desk.

Aaron looked up at the clock hanging on the block wall of his storage room. Sue knew better than to bother him yet. He got up and took the walkie-talkie off the charger. "Not yet, Sue. It's only 7:50. I still got ten minutes."

"I know, but this fellow's in a hurry to check out of here." Normally Sue handled checkouts on her own. He'd go out to the site later on, straighten things up, if needed. "They need their LP tank filled up," she said. "He just paid me. He's heading to the big tank out front. Can you meet him there . . . now?"

"Suppose I can." He clipped the walkie-talkie to his belt, let out a sigh, and stretched his back muscles. He'd awakened just after sunrise, as always. Slept pretty well; these days that wasn't a given. He had the normal aches that came with age, but in recent months he'd begun to experience some new pains from old war wounds. Wasn't sure why they'd started up again. Hurt like mad right after the war. Then for years, it was like they'd just faded to the margins.

Sleeping good every night might go better if Aaron could afford a decent bed. He looked over at what he slept in—wasn't much more than a military cot. But it was way nicer than sleeping in cardboard boxes and underneath highway overpasses. He'd done enough of that years back.

Aaron walked over to his favorite and only armchair, closed his Bible, then went back to the workbench and unplugged the battery chargers for his tools. He glanced at the coffeepot, made sure it was off, collected his tools, and headed out the door. Not ten steps away sat his primary means of transportation inside the park: a beat-up golf cart parked under a palmetto palm.

As he rode toward the propane tank, he glanced at the clipboard he'd left on the front seat. That's right, today he had to take down all the Halloween decorations. He didn't mind that too much; he was tired of looking at them.

It was the second item on the list he didn't much like. *Sort out and set up all the Christmas decorations.*

Seemed way too early to him. Maybe it made sense for folks who lived up north where the weather was cold. In some places it had even snowed already. But in Florida in the first week of November, it was still getting into the low eighties some days.

He pulled up to the cyclone fence surrounding the propane tank, saw a man in a blue shirt about his own age standing by a minivan, a pop-up camper hitched to the bumper. Aaron recognized him; he and his wife had spent two nights in Lot 14. "Heading out already?" Aaron said as he got out of his cart. The man handed him his ticket, proving he'd paid the bill. Aaron lifted his propane tank and walked to the gate. He glanced at their pop-up. It looked pretty new, had a nice air conditioner on the roof. Aaron had lived in a tent a few years back. Would have felt like a king to have a pop-up then, especially one with A/C. "So you folks retired?"

"Almost," the man said. His cell phone started vibrating. "Excuse me." He flipped the lid, read a text, and started typing a reply.

Aaron finished filling the tank, disconnected it, and shut the big tank down. He looked back at the man, whose face was still glued to his phone. Aaron always felt awkward at times like this, didn't know how much small talk was appropriate. Some folks liked it; some acted like they had better things to do than talk with the help. "I'll just set this back in its stand there up by the hitch," he said. The man nodded, kept texting away.

Aaron had never texted anyone. Didn't even own a cell phone. Couldn't afford one. Really, who'd be calling him anyway? "You're all set," he said. The man nodded again.

As soon as Aaron got in the golf cart, the walkie-talkie squawked. "Aaron, you still on that LP?" Aaron waved at the man in the minivan as he pulled out of the park. "Just finished, what's up?"

"Need you to get back to that young couple that moved in here a month ago, but quick. Before someone calls 911."

"Lot 31?"

"That's the one. Got a call there's all kinds of yelling and screaming going on inside their trailer. Can you get back there right away? I don't want to scare off all the temps in here, make 'em think this park is full of lowlifes."

"This park *is* full of lowlifes." Aaron heard Sue's cousin in the background. "That's all we got in here."

"Now quit, Bobby." It was Sue, yelling back. "Don't mind him, Aaron."

"On my way, Sue." Among his many duties, somehow Aaron was expected to serve as the park's security guard.

He knew all about "that young couple" in Lot 31. Her name was Heather, if he recalled. Had a big friendly dog, mostly golden retriever. Aaron thought about her as the golf cart sped down the main road through the park. He'd been to Lot 31 twice over the last month: once to fix the lock, and again for a busted screen. On his last visit a week ago, he saw a red mark across the side of her face, like she'd recently been slapped. Her boyfriend had been nowhere in sight.

Before Aaron left, he'd asked if she was okay, and she insisted she had just tripped over a big oak root nearby, fell flat on her face. Aaron didn't buy it. She was way too nervous. If there was one thing he couldn't abide, it was a coward who hit women. Heather couldn't be more than sixteen or seventeen, had no business shacking up with that young man. He looked to be around twenty. Long dark hair, tall, wore baggy jeans pulled down halfway to his knees.

Aaron turned off the paved road onto the dirt path that led to the trailer. Mr. Bentley had about twenty of these trailers set up in the park. Income properties, he called them. Some vintage Airstreams and Fleetwoods and a few old twelve-wides. Aaron's plan was to wait one more year before going on Social Security, then he could afford to rent one and move out of that musty storage room. Had his eye on a nice little red one.

He heard a loud noise, looked ahead, and saw Heather's boyfriend coming out of the trailer, slamming the door behind him. He got in a blue souped-up Honda Civic, revved up the engine, put it in gear, and tore off, heading in Aaron's direction. The speed limit was fifteen mph in the park. In seconds, he was up to thirty or forty. Aaron had to yank the golf cart off the path.

He shot an angry glance at the young man as he sped by. The boy replied with an even angrier stare. Aaron's eyes followed the car as it raced through the park and peeled off down the main road. The boy was gonna kill somebody. Aaron released a pent-up sigh then turned back toward the trailer. The door hadn't latched after the boy slammed it, and it now drifted open.

The poor girl, he thought.

That young man better not have hurt her.

2

Aaron got out of his cart and walked up to the open door. He heard a girl crying softly inside. Walked up the three metal steps. "Hello, anyone in here?"

The girl kept crying, a little quieter. The sound came from his right. He stepped inside. The dog barked down at the other end of the trailer, behind a closed door. "Hello, it's me, Aaron, the handyman for the park." The drapes were pulled shut. It took a few moments for his eyes to adjust. Following the crying sound, he saw Heather lying in a corner by a couch, cradled in a fetal position. Aaron walked closer but gave her plenty of space.

"Are you okay, miss? Did that young man hurt you?"

She looked up. Her left eye was almost swollen shut. His anger started to boil. "He hit you, didn't he? You hurt anywhere else?"

She shook her head no.

"Well, let me get some ice on that eye before it gets worse. Why don't you sit up here?" He patted a couch cushion. She got up from the floor. "You just sit right there." Such a frail little thing.

He walked back to the kitchen and found a washcloth by the

13

sink. Then he opened the freezer, pulled three ice cubes from a tray, wrapped them in the washcloth. The kitchen wasn't that messy. The whole place was in fairly good shape. Heather was apparently a decent housekeeper.

"Here," he said, walking back. He handed the washcloth to her. "It'll sting a bit, but it should help reduce the swelling." The dog continued to bark and paw at the bedroom door.

"Thank you."

A box of tissues sat on the coffee table; he handed her a few. She wiped her tears then placed the ice on her eye.

"You're not going to tell me you got that tripping over a root."

She smiled and shook her head.

"And that red mark I saw on the other side of your face last week, he hit you then too."

She nodded.

"Your name's Heather, right?"

"Yes."

"Well, Heather, I need to call the police. It ain't right, letting him hit you like that."

"No, please don't," she said. "That'll just make things worse."

"It might, but it might scare him into thinking twice before he hits you again."

"I don't want the police. Besides, I think he's breaking up with me."

"Did he say he ain't coming back?"

She thought a moment. "Not exactly, but I'm not going to do what he's telling me to, so I don't think he's going to stick around much longer."

"Mind if I ask what?"

"I . . . I don't wanna say. But really, I'm okay now."

"Are his things still here?"

She sighed, nodded yes.

"Then he's gonna come back. I can't just leave you here knowing that. What if he starts in on you again? That young man's got a lot of anger, and he doesn't control it very well."

"I know."

"Then let me call the police."

"No, please. I'll be okay."

Now the dog added a high-pitched whine to its clawing and barking. "Want me to let him out? I've seen you walk him in the park. He seems friendly."

"It's a she. Her name's Tess. You better or she won't stop. But she's as sweet as can be, except when Ryan starts yelling." She looked down.

Aaron walked down the dark hallway and opened the door at the far end. Tess ran right past him. When he got out to the living area, she was all over Heather. She'd jumped right up on the sofa and lay across her lap. Heather was patting her, and Tess kept licking her hand.

Aaron saw a slight smile appear on Heather's face. "You mind I ask how old you are?" he asked.

"Seventeen, almost eighteen."

"Don't you have parents? That's pretty young to be out on your own."

"They . . . we . . . we don't really get along." Tears started welling up in her eyes again.

"When's the last time you talked with them?"

She thought a moment. "Maybe a year ago, maybe a little more. That was the last time we talked on the phone. I ran away when I was fifteen."

"Where do they live?"

"In Georgia, north of Atlanta."

"They know where you are?"

She shook her head no.

"I bet they care about you a lot more than you think. I could call 'em for you, if you want."

"No, don't."

"I won't tell them where you are, just see where they're at, you know? Might find out they're worried sick. You don't need to be with a guy like Ryan."

"I don't know. I'm pretty sure I know what they'd say. Especially now."

"Now?"

"Now that I'm—" She buried her face in her hands and started crying again. The ice fell out of the cloth onto the couch. The dog had calmed down and had backed off Heather's lap. She nudged her nose right under Heather's hands and licked them gently.

Aaron walked closer, scooped the ice up, and put it back into the washcloth. He stood there a few moments, wanting to comfort her somehow, but he didn't dare touch her. Instead, he patted Tess on the head. When Heather calmed a little, he handed her the washcloth. "Better keep this on that eye a little longer."

"Thanks, I will. But really, mister . . ."

"Just call me Aaron."

"I'll be okay, Aaron. I don't think he'll be coming back, for a few hours anyway."

"You have anywhere you can go, so you're not here when he gets back?"

"No, but I'll be okay. You've been very nice. But don't worry about me. I can take care of myself."

She didn't say this with a shred of confidence. He backed away. "Well, I don't feel good just leaving you here all alone."

"It's okay."

"Well, I'm going to go. But I'm going to keep my eye on this trailer all day. If I see his car back here, I'm coming back."

"I don't want any trouble."

"I don't want any, either. I'll just stay outside and listen. But if I hear any yelling, or if you even think he's going to hit you again, you just yell out my name, and I'll come on in." He waited a moment. "Look at me, Heather."

She looked up.

"I'm not going to let him hurt you again. You have my word on that."

3

After leaving Heather's trailer, Aaron stopped by the office to brief Sue. She was a big woman, with long hair she mostly wore tied up. Aaron figured she'd spent the better part of her life as a brunette, but half her hair was gray now. She could be nice, if you caught her at just the right time and said things just the right way. She had just thanked him in a roundabout way for handling the situation and agreed this Ryan fellow was nothing but trouble.

"Had a bad feeling about him when they first came in here," she said. "Should have gone with my hunches. Well, here . . ." She lifted a piece of paper toward him. "Here's a job you can do just across the way from that trailer. That way you can keep an eye on it, in case the boyfriend comes back."

Aaron read the note. *Replace rotting boards on wooden handicap ramp, Lot 28.*

"You've met the fellow lives in there last week. Billy Ames. 'Bout your age." She leaned forward and whispered the next part. "Got no legs, remember? Lost 'em in Vietnam."

Aaron remembered. He had listened to Billy for a few minutes, then had to answer a call for an LP tank out front. He'd excused himself but kept thinking about Billy the whole rest of the day. Such sadness in his eyes. Not the normal kind, like you get from a bad day or something you wanted that didn't happen. The kind of sadness that stacks up over many years. Billy seemed to mask it mostly by talking too much.

Sue leaned back and talked in normal tones. "Well, he called this in a few days ago, and I forgot all about it. He says that ramp is rotten in a few places. One place in particular creaks real loud every time he rolls that electronic scooter over it. He swears it's going to collapse on him another time or two. He demanded I fix it soon or else he'll sue. Imagine that. The guy's renting a trailer from us, been here less than a month, and he's threatening to sue us already? Anyway, why don't you get over there and fix that next. That way you can keep your eye out on Lot 31."

———————

Billy Ames sat on his electric scooter all alone in this miserable trailer, staring at his gun.

At first, he thought he should do it in his bed, but then those poor paramedics would have to lift his dead weight up onto the gurney. This way, they could just drape a sheet over him and wheel him right out to the ambulance on his scooter.

He also worried about the noise, didn't want the last sound he'd hear on earth to be a gunshot at full blast. He'd researched buying a silencer on the internet. Changed his mind when he realized no one would hear the gun go off, and his body might be stuck in that trailer for days.

No, he'd use a regular gun, but he thought of a way to muffle the noise. He'd wear a pair of headphones and listen to his Bob

Dylan CD. Had it in the player right now. All he needed to do was push the button.

Then, work up the nerve to pull the trigger.

He was so ready to leave this life. He just wasn't sure what he'd face on the other side, whether it was true what some church people said, that the Almighty didn't take kindly to folks taking things into their own hands. What if he'd spend eternity in a worse place than where he was now?

But he couldn't face it anymore. Nobody loved him, and he had no one to love. When he saw that handyman setting up Christmas decorations a little while ago, he knew . . . he couldn't face another holiday season alone. He had to take his chances with the Almighty. Seemed like most of the religious TV shows he'd watched lately talked all about God's love. Over and over again. If God did love him—which Billy found near impossible to believe—then God would know how sad and lonely Billy had been, for so many years now. He wouldn't punish him forever just because he wanted to put an end to all his suffering.

Billy wouldn't ask for much in heaven, knew he had no right to. They didn't even need to let him through the pearly gates or walk those streets of gold. He'd be happy just to walk again. They could stick him as far away from folks who deserved to be there as they needed to. Maybe in a section for people like him who'd taken the same way out.

Billy looked down at the gun again. Then over to the CD player. It was time to push the button, let Bob Dylan start whaling away on that old guitar of his and moaning through one of Billy's favorite tunes. He wasn't sure which song would be the one yet. Maybe "Like a Rolling Stone." Or maybe "Knockin' on Heaven's Door"; that might be a good one.

He smiled at the irony.

Just then, Billy heard a noise outside. He looked at the gun, then at the front door. Footsteps creaked up the wooden ramp, even louder in that one spot where the ramp was rotting. It scared Billy every time he'd roll over it on his scooter. Through the paper-thin walls of his trailer, he heard a man humming.

Three knocks.

He stayed put, didn't make a sound.

Four more knocks.

"Say, Billy, you in there?"

Sounded like the handyman. Maybe they were finally sending him over to fix that ramp. The trailer park manager, Sue-something, had introduced them. His name was Aaron-something. Aaron was a Nam vet like him. Judging by the deep creases on his face, Billy decided that Aaron's life may have been almost as hard as his.

Four more knocks. "Billy, it's Aaron Miller. We met at the general store last week. I'm here to fix this ramp leading up to your front door. Don't need to get in there. Just didn't want to scare you when I start sawing and hammering away out here."

Billy looked up at the door, saw Aaron peek in the window. He tensed up till he realized Aaron couldn't see anything through the sheers.

"Okay, maybe you're taking a nap. I'll do what I came to do then. Sure that'll wake you up. Maybe after, you could let me in for a soda. It's not supposed to be hot in November, but I'm actually sweating." He paused. "Felt bad running off after we met last week. Just the way this job is. Sue told me later you're a Nam vet like me, said you told her that's what put you in that chair. Just want to say, well . . . I'm here if you need someone to talk to. Us old farts need to stick together, you know? Well, I better get on this then."

Billy heard Aaron getting set up outside. A few minutes later, he heard him whacking away at the old plywood ramp, prying the rotted boards from their hold. Now what was Billy going to do? He hadn't planned on someone being right there when he pulled the trigger. It was just going to be him and Dylan.

He sighed as he put on the headphones, pushed the button on the CD player. Dylan couldn't sing worth a nickel, but when he sang, Billy felt like he was listening to an old friend rocking on the porch. He sometimes wondered if he and Dylan might have been friends, if they'd had a chance to meet, get to know each other a bit.

Anyway, he preferred listening to Dylan far more than the racket Aaron Miller was making outside. So maybe Billy would just sit there then, listen to Dylan till Aaron finished. Let him come in for a cold drink, talk a little while. Probably wouldn't stay more than a few minutes.

When the coast was clear, Billy could pick up where he'd left off.

4

The day was pretty much spent.

A two-hour job had taken the rest of the afternoon. Spending all that extra time with Billy Ames seemed like the right thing to do, but it left Aaron exhausted. The depth of sadness coming out of Billy frightened him. Aaron didn't get at the core of it in their chat, but he didn't have to think hard to come up with reasons why. Aaron had been that low in his life many times, and he had two good legs and things to do to keep busy all day.

Not good for man to be alone, he thought. Even the Bible said that. And it was never good for a man to feel he had no purpose, to just sit around all day, everyone else paying his way. By the sound of it, that pretty much summed up Billy's life for decades. Aaron could understand a temptation to end it all if that were his lot.

That was the look he'd seen in Billy's eyes.

He decided he'd better stop in on Billy at least once a day from now on, see if he could find a way to get him plugged in somewhere. Maybe hook him up with the local VFW or the folks down at his church. He'd seen a van pull up every Sunday with a hydraulic ramp for folks in wheelchairs.

Of course, it was clear the thing Billy needed most was a friend. It didn't help that Billy talked so dang much, once he got going. One thing after another, like he'd been sitting on a mountain of words and Aaron had come in and set off the volcano.

Aaron headed back to the storage room. Figured he better put his golf cart back on the charger now in case that boyfriend came back tonight. He knew he couldn't get over to Heather's trailer half as fast on foot. He went inside and set his plastic crate on the workbench and set about recharging his tools. He was really tired and thought about how nice it would be to wash the day away in a cool shower. But all that time he'd spent with Billy set him back on a few chores he was supposed to get to today. Maybe he should get everything he needed out now, so he could get a head start on things for the morning.

As he reached up to grab a tray full of electrical caps, he nearly knocked his special box to the floor. He caught it just in time but banged his elbow on the workbench. "Ow," he yelled. The pain was severe, almost caused him to drop the box again. He set it on the bench. "Don't know why they call it a funny bone," he said aloud. Nothing funny about it.

The box contained something he never talked about. To anyone. No one but him even knew what was inside. He didn't know why he'd kept it all these years, but he couldn't bring himself to throw it away. It was a plain gray metal box, about the size of a hardback book. After rubbing his elbow a few minutes, he carefully set the box back in its place.

He thought a moment. Maybe he should move it to a safer spot. Its contents had never touched the ground, not since the moment he'd received it back in 1970. He looked around the room.

It was such a small space. There just weren't any open places left to put it. Even the area under his cot was jammed with boxes.

He noticed the small picture frame, one shelf up from the metal box. *Yeah, that'll work.* He picked the frame up and carefully set it on top of the metal box. He wasn't likely to knock that over. And now he could see the picture better one shelf down. He paused a few moments. The picture in the frame had captured his attention. He picked it up and held it to the light.

It was his other prized possession.

These two things had been with Aaron through all the ups and downs these past forty years. The only two things he owned that he could say that about. He clung to them through the worst of it, even during his homeless years. The picture had faded a good bit and was even older than the contents of the metal box. It was a Polaroid photograph of his two kids, Karen and Steven, sent to him that last year in Vietnam by his wife Betty.

That Christmas Eve, swatting mosquitoes as rain poured down over his hooch, he'd held the picture for over an hour. One of the guys nearby had a radio playing all kinds of Christmas songs, one after the other. It was both wonderful and terribly sad. When this one song played, all the conversations within earshot of the radio suddenly stopped. Elvis Presley was singing "I'll Be Home for Christmas." Tears had rolled down Aaron's face when Elvis sang the last line of the chorus. The only way he or any of the guys could get home would be in their dreams.

Every year, Aaron repeated the same sad tradition. Wherever he was, he'd spend time on Christmas Eve holding that picture of Karen and Steven, listening to Elvis sing that song. His kids were just toddlers that first time; Karen was just a year old. They had to be in their early forties now.

Hard to imagine Karen and Steven in their forties.

He didn't even know what they looked like now, hadn't seen them since 1992, and then only from a distance. He'd sent them birthday cards for a few years after he and Betty had divorced. Never heard anything back from them, so he gave up. When he got off the streets and cleaned up in 1987, he tried to reconnect with them, gave Betty a call. She made it crystal clear. The kids would be better off if he just left them alone, for good. They had a new life now, a new dad. A big house, nice cars, a college fund. A real life.

Nothing like the horrible time he had put them through when he got back from the war.

He sighed, standing there looking at the picture. He'd messed it all up. Didn't blame Betty for shutting him out all those years ago. Not after what he put her through. They were better off without him.

He carefully set the picture frame on top of his metal box, then thought about poor Heather sitting all alone in that trailer in Lot 31, afraid that jerk boyfriend of hers might come back any moment. Aaron thought it was entirely possible Karen or Steven might have children Heather's age.

His grandchildren.

He liked to think if they did have kids Heather's age, and they got in some kind of trouble, someone like him might be there to look after them. He decided he'd do whatever he could to help Heather out. No way he'd let that young man hurt her again. He'd get the police involved next time or else take care of things himself if he had to.

Just then, the walkie-talkie crackled to life. "Hey, Aaron, have you clocked out yet?"

He picked it up off the charger. "I'm in the storage room, Sue. Whatcha need?"

5

They weren't thirty minutes into the date and Karen Miller already knew she wasn't eating with Mr. Right. He wasn't even Mr. Maybe.

Oh, Ken was handsome enough. More than handsome. He had just gotten up and excused himself to use the restroom. As she turned to watch him walk through the restaurant, words from a distant comedy floated through her head. Ken was "really, really ridiculously good-looking."

The problem was, he knew it.

They were eating at Haverty's, a fine dining establishment in Southlake, Texas, an upscale suburb in the Fort Worth area. The dining room had several mirrors mounted on different walls to enhance the décor. There were five of them between their table and the restroom. Karen knew this because she'd counted each time Ken had looked at himself as he walked by.

Even that . . . his name was *Ken*. Ken Morrow.

Karen remembered playing with Barbie and Ken as a little girl. Five minutes ago, she'd made a rather nuanced joke about his name, connecting it to that famous male doll.

Karen was the only one at the table who'd laughed.

She lifted her glass of Diet Coke to take a sip, wondering what her friend Gail had been thinking, setting her up on a date with this guy. He had to be in his early thirties, at least ten years younger than she was. Karen had always enjoyed the compliments that followed when someone learned her real age. In the rare moments when she felt good about herself, even she believed she looked years younger than her age.

But she had seen herself walking next to the ridiculously good-looking Ken in at least a few of those mirrors on their way to being seated. Her youthful looks didn't come close to shrinking the gap between them, and she wasn't about to become anyone's cougar story.

Karen looked up and saw Ken returning. She calmed herself with the thought that they both attended a solid megachurch in the Fort Worth area, and he really had been a perfect gentleman so far. There was a better-than-average chance he wouldn't make any embarrassing moves on her before the night was out. At least there was that.

"The food's not out yet?" he said as he sat down.

"Not yet, but I think they—"

Ken motioned to the waiter. Karen was about to say that she thought the pace was about right for Haverty's. It was known for its elegance and atmosphere, not speed. The waiter came over. Ken said something. The waiter nodded and walked off toward the kitchen. She guessed that was supposed to impress her; Ken was a take-charge kind of guy.

"The food should be here any minute," he said, turning his full attention back on her. "So, where were we? That's right, we were just starting to get to know each other better."

We were?

"So Karen, I've been dying to know something," he said. "Your last name is Miller—is that your maiden name?"

"Yes." What kind of question was that?

"I thought it was. So, you've never been married?"

Uh . . . duh, she thought. *That's usually what that means.* "That's right."

"I just find it hard to believe someone your age, who looks like you do, has never been married, especially in a church as big as ours. How is that possible?"

Was that an insult or a compliment? The phrase "someone your age" certainly stung a bit. "There's no great mystery behind it. I was in a long-term relationship with a guy named Greg. A ridiculously long time, to be honest. At first, we were both totally wrapped up in our careers. Then at some point, I started pressing the idea of getting married. After the longest time, Greg agreed we should, so we got engaged. Then we were engaged for another ridiculously long period of time, and he kept putting off the idea of setting a date. Then finally, after all that—"

"He left you, right?"

"Yes, for a younger woman." A woman just about Ken's age, she thought, give or take a year. Then it dawned on her why Ken wanted to clarify these things. He was making sure she was eligible for marriage in the church. Not that it mattered; Karen had no intention of marrying Ken, let alone going out with him again.

"I'm sure a breakup after all that time was painful."

"Yes, it was." His look suggested he had no idea.

He reached over and slid a breadstick out from a basket. "So Miller's your maiden name. Interesting. I thought your father's name was Rafferty?"

Ken would likely know about her father. He was a wealthy, influential deacon in their church. "It is," she said. "But he isn't my birth father. He married my mom when I was five and pretty much filled the father role for my brother Steve and me growing up."

Ken looked around the dining room. Clearly, he was hungry. He turned and faced her again. "Why didn't he adopt you?"

"I think he wanted to," Karen said. "He said he did a few times. But my real father—well, my birth father—is still alive, as far as we know. My mom didn't really want us to pursue finding him to get his permission. So we just left it alone. But I think of Mark Rafferty as my dad."

She wished the ridiculously good-looking Ken would drop this line of questioning. It didn't feel like they were trying to get to know each other better. It felt like an interrogation, like he was running through some kind of checklist, seeing if he approved of her pedigree. Then she remembered, Gail had said Ken was an attorney. A handsome young attorney.

Technically, it wasn't an exaggeration.

"So you don't know where he is?"

"Who?"

"Your birth father."

The waiter showed up with their main entrée. Karen whispered a quiet *Thank you, Lord*. "Oh look, our food."

The waiter now enjoyed Ken's undivided attention. Moments later, the food on his plate did. Karen was glad. And she was glad that he'd been raised right and would never talk with his mouth full. So for the next fifteen minutes, except for Ken's occasional delighted moans, she ate her spinach-stuffed tilapia with fire-roasted tomatoes in peace, while he ate his porcini-crusted filet mignon with herb butter.

She tried to think of questions she could ask when this chewing match was over. Not that she wanted to know him better; she just wanted to shift the focus off her. She wouldn't have minded it as much if he'd asked questions about her favorite movies or what kind of books she enjoyed. Maybe her favorite music, what she liked to do in her downtime. She didn't really want to tell him such things, but it would have been nice if he'd asked. No matter. After tonight, he wouldn't get the chance to know her better. She had just thought of a way to make sure this would be their first and last date.

"So Ken, I've got something I'd like to ask you."

He waited a moment, swallowed the last bite on his plate. "Yes?"

"Maybe you can help me understand something about dating. Something I'm having a hard time understanding lately."

"Oh? Uh . . . I guess I could try."

"What is it with guys nowadays wanting to go out with women way older than they are? You're a guy, I thought maybe you could explain it to me. Because I don't get it."

Ken's look was priceless.

"You seem really intelligent," she continued, "so I'm guessing you've figured out I'm at least ten years older than you are. Being so old, I can remember a time not too many years ago when this kind of thing hardly ever happened. I mean, you'd see older guys dating younger women, but not the other way around. I'm not trying to make you feel bad, I'm really just curious. Why would you want to date someone so much older than you are? Someone like me."

He gave her the look she was hoping for. It said, "I don't think I do want to date someone like you anymore." He looked around, clearly trying to find the waiter. She guessed it was time to order dessert. Ken wanted food in his mouth badly.

"Care for another breadstick?" she said, holding up the basket.

Tomorrow, she and Gail would be having a chat. Gail Washburn was her partner in a recovering real estate firm. Gail meant well and she was a great friend, but seriously.

She was a lousy matchmaker.

6

The next morning, Karen drove through the hectic morning traffic from her subdivision in Southlake to another subdivision in Keller, Texas, where she worked. Both were in the suburbs of Fort Worth. Fortunately, she only had to deal with the tail end of the rush hour, since she and Gail didn't start opening the model homes until 9:00 a.m. Even then, they generally didn't see many interested buyers till it got closer to lunch.

There was only one other car in the parking area: Gail's blue SUV. Gail lived closer, right there in Keller. Gail's first duty of the day—and they both believed her most important one—was to make the coffee. As she did, Karen would walk through the three model homes, turning on all the lights and, on this cold November morning, the heat as well.

A biting wind blew in from the plains north of town, making it feel fifteen degrees colder than the thirty-four degrees Karen had seen posted on a digital bank sign. The wind was supposed to die down in a few hours. She hoped so; they didn't need another excuse for customers to stay home. She opened the door of the nearest model home, which also served as their office. Thankfully, Gail had already turned the heat on.

Karen set her purse on her desk. Gail was already making the coffee in the kitchen.

"How'd it go last night?" Gail asked over her shoulder.

"Let me get the other models set up, and I'll come back and tell you."

"I can't wait to hear," Gail said.

"Actually, you can." Karen let that one linger in the air as she closed the front door and hurried to the home next door. As she walked through the other models, flicking on light switches and thermostats, she was freshly amazed at how beautiful these homes were. It was hard to fathom how low the prices had dropped. Buyers were starting to sneak back into the market, but it was nothing compared to the glory days a few years ago. Back then, they'd have lines stretching around the block and back if they'd let houses go at these prices.

After finishing the last house, she thrust her hands in her coat pockets and hurried back to the office. She found Gail sitting behind her desk, drinking her coffee. She'd already poured Karen's into her favorite mug.

"So . . . I'm guessing things didn't go so well with Ken last night."

Karen stirred her coffee and walked into what should have been the garage area of the home. "Let's say we maintained an attitude of Christian charity by the evening's end . . . and parted as friends."

Gail shook her head. "Am I going to be in trouble with Bill?" Bill was Gail's boyfriend. He and Ken were close friends.

"You shouldn't be," Karen said as she sat down. "I'm not

sure how Ken will describe the evening. I certainly wasn't mean to him. At least, I tried not to be."

"You weren't *mean*? It sounds even worse than I was thinking."

"It wasn't a terrible date." She paused. "Well, I guess it was. For me, anyway. I'm not sure how Ken will rate it. But I did my best to keep in mind he was Bill's friend, while also making it clear this would be our one and only date."

"He was that bad?"

"Oh, he's nice to look at. You certainly had that part right. But we had no business being out together. Other than attending the same church, we have nothing in common. Starting with our age."

"Did Ken make that an issue?"

"No, I did." She set her mug on the desk. "Gail, we've been friends for what, five years now?"

"Five or six."

"And I'm at least ten years older than you."

"At least," Gail said, smiling.

"In our friendship, it doesn't seem to matter that much."

"I don't think it does."

"But I really don't want to be going out with guys your age. It just feels . . . awkward. I'd say Ken is a very young thirty-three and I am a very old forty-four."

"You don't look forty-four," Gail said. "You don't even look thirty-five."

"Thanks," Karen said. "But looks can be deceiving. The point is, I *feel* forty-four."

Gail sat forward, her eyes lit up. "But that's why I wanted you to get out, Karen, start seeing some guys. It'll help you feel young. Our church is full of them. I always see them look at you, even the younger ones. But you don't seem the least bit interested. I know Greg hurt you terribly, but it wasn't your fault, and it was four years ago."

The worst year of my life, Karen thought. It was the year Greg left *and* the year her mother died. "But Gail, we've been friends all this time, and my dating life hasn't been an issue before. You haven't even dated that much until recently."

Gail sighed. "That's just because . . . I wasn't getting asked by the kind of guys I wanted to be with. Not guys like Bill. A year or so ago, I started really praying for the right man to show up."

"I didn't know that. But . . . I'm real happy you've found Bill. You guys seem great together."

Gail looked up, her eyes beaming. "I am happy, Karen. I think he might be the one."

"Well, I really am happy for you. You know that, right?"

"I do. It's just . . . I want you to be happy too. And I'm a little worried, to be honest."

"That I'm not happy?"

"Yes, but not just that. I'm concerned about what's going to happen to our friendship if Bill and I get more serious. I know you would never go out by yourself with Bill and me, and I'm starting to spend a lot more time with him."

"So . . . you're trying to set me up with someone so we can still be friends . . . as couples?"

"Well, we'll still be friends no matter what. We'd just get to spend more time being friends if you were . . . you know . . . with someone. Besides, I hate seeing you alone."

"Gail, that's very sweet, but I doubt any of Bill's friends would be a good match for me. And neither of you probably know a guy at church my age."

"None that aren't already married."

"Exactly."

"You know, Karen, plenty of women are married to much younger men, and they're perfectly happy."

"I'm sure that's true."

"But it bothers you."

"It looks like it does," Karen said. But she didn't really know why. Maybe it had something to do with Greg leaving her for someone so much younger. She sighed. Why did all the men in her life end up leaving her? Her biological father left when she was five, leaving her only a meaningless last name. Then Greg. She'd be spending yet another Thanksgiving and Christmas alone. Sure, she had her brother and his family. And the dad who raised her, Mark Rafferty. They loved her. But it wasn't the same.

"Are you going to be okay?" Gail asked.

The front door opened. The wind rushed in behind whoever it was. "Hello?" a woman's voice called out.

"I'll get that," Gail whispered.

"No, let me," Karen said. "I could use a distraction right now."

7

Dave Russo was taking a sick day from his regular job as a wire editor for the local newspaper. He didn't like being sick, but it gave him some time to spend the day doing the kind of writing he really wanted to do. A book about the heroes of Vietnam, in honor of his father, who died when Dave was only three.

The hardest part about writing the book was closing the door on all the memories it stirred. They didn't shut down as easily when he closed his laptop. The memories that bothered him the most weren't even things he planned to put in the book. It was all the personal stuff, like seeing his mother cry every Christmas and every anniversary. This went on well into his teens.

The book wasn't even about Dave's father, Joey Russo. It couldn't be. There wasn't enough information about his death to fill a few chapters, let alone a book. And his father hadn't died in some heroic fashion. He had just blown up in a mortar barrage in one of the last battles of the war. There wasn't even a body to ship home for a funeral. So Dave had decided to write a book about some of the heroes of Vietnam whose stories could be told, and dedicate the book to his father's memory.

What he did know about his father came mostly from his mom, Angelina Russo. But Dave was concerned this project was becoming too hard on her. He did his best not to talk about it, but she still kept drifting down memory lane, just from seeing all the Vietnam books and resource material he'd have out on the kitchen table while he worked. Dave lived in her condo in a little town in north Florida with his son Jake. He'd been living there the past four years.

He looked up from the table toward her closed bedroom door. She was in there now, just getting over another good cry. She had come up behind him ten minutes ago, reading over his shoulder.

"Your dad was so handsome, Davey," she'd said. "And funny. Boy, could he make me laugh. And he was romantic too, your father. And a great singer. And strong. He had these broad shoulders and big muscles in his arms."

Dave had listened quietly. He didn't know what could have gotten her thinking about him; it wasn't anything Dave had just written. It was probably just the lingering emotions from this past Sunday. It would have been their forty-fifth wedding anniversary.

He'd looked up at her and smiled, watched her eyes drift toward the ceiling. She was seeing Joey Russo's face, hearing something he'd said. She smiled. Then tears filled her eyes, rolled down her cheeks. He had gotten up and grabbed the box of Kleenex, tried to think of something else to talk about, something in the present.

He reached over now and grabbed a few Kleenex for himself, blew his stuffy nose. Then one of his own memories stirred, something that happened when he was nine years old. Two kids at school were arguing. One had just bragged that his dad was a war hero, because he'd won the Silver Star in Vietnam. The other boy said it didn't count because his dad had told him Vietnam was a scum war, the first war we'd ever lost.

That angered Dave. Without even thinking, he slugged the kid right in the face, gave him a bloody nose. The teacher had sent him home for the rest of the day. When he'd gotten home, he ran into his room and cried into his pillow so his mom wouldn't hear. He didn't understand much about the Vietnam War then. Just enough to know something was wrong with it. He knew the whole country had turned against it—even against the soldiers who'd fought in it. And because they had, Dave never felt like he'd gotten the chance to grieve properly for his father. He didn't know anyone he could talk to about it, anyone who'd understand.

He remembered as a kid how he used to envy people who'd lost fathers in other wars, especially World War II. Those men were all considered heroes, because that was a "good" war. A war we had to fight. But when Dave was growing up, no one ever talked about the Vietnam War that way. It was the scum war, the war his father fought in and died in for nothing.

He was so glad things were different now. And as painful as it was, writing this book was good for him. For some reason, it helped him feel closer to his father, helped his father seem more real than just a smiling face in a few fuzzy Polaroid photos.

8

An hour later, Dave's mom was back in the kitchen, making dinner. She seemed totally over it. His cell phone rang. It was Harry Warden, his boss at the newspaper.

"Okay, Dave, I got the funding for the Houston trip approved," Harry said.

It took Dave a moment to track with what Harry was saying; maybe it was the cold medicine. "Oh, thanks, Harry. You remember I'm taking a vacation day tacked on the end."

"For your book thing, right?"

Dave nodded. "I have to confirm it, but I'm hoping to interview this oil company executive who won the Silver Star in Vietnam, lives right there in Houston."

"And you remember the expenses for that extra day aren't included," Harry said.

"I do." Of course, the per diem the newspaper gave Dave was way more than he'd need. It wasn't hard on these trips to stretch the food allowance. He couldn't do anything about the hotel expense, but—

"How's this book project coming?" Harry asked.

"I've still got a ways to go," Dave said. "I'm not even close to shopping it out yet. Just gathering info. I've got a ton of Vietnam veterans left to interview. Since I'm having to pay my own way, it's taking forever. That's why trips like this one to Houston are so great."

"Can't you just interview these guys over the phone?"

"I could. I've tried that a few times, but it's just not the same. The stuff I'm trying to get these guys to talk about is heavy stuff. Stirs some bad memories, lots of emotion. I've found it works better if we can meet in person. Take it slow. I can read how they're doing a lot better face-to-face."

"I can see that. It was a horrible time. How many people you going to interview before you're done?"

"A lot more than I'm putting in the book. I'm going to select about seven or eight men from dozens of interviews—the ones that affect me the most—and tell their story with lots of details. I'm hoping to make it read like a fiction novel."

"So, what's with this guy in Houston?"

"I've only talked with him briefly, so I haven't heard very much. From what I read, he got his medal defending a Huey that crash-landed. Knocked the pilot out. He kept the Viet Cong at bay until help arrived. Something like that."

"Well, hope you heal up in time for your trip."

They hung up. Dave had two other calls to make. His son Jake was on the local high school basketball team. They'd had an incredible season last year. On the strength of that, they'd been invited to a big preseason tournament in Houston. That's what this trip was all about. He decided to give Jake a quick call, then Mr. John Lansing, the oil executive/war hero in Houston.

He dialed Jake's number but got his voice mail. "Hey, Jake, it's me, Dad. Just got word that the paper's sending me with you guys to Houston. I'm calling to see if your team already made flight arrangements. If so, can you give me the info for the way there? I'd love to ride with you if there's any seats left. But just on the way there, not the flight home. I have to stay an extra day in Houston. Well, call me when you hear this. Love you."

There was at least a fifty-fifty chance Jake would call him before the day ended. They had a good relationship, on the whole. And Jake was a good kid. High school is a scary time for any parent, but Jake hadn't given Dave too much cause for alarm so far. He was a little concerned about Jake pulling away now that he'd made the basketball team. Seemed like he was. But they had talked, and Jake had convinced Dave it was just the schedule, not anything going on in his heart.

Keeping their hearts connected was the main thing for Dave. Meant more than anything else in his life. Certainly more than this job at the newspaper. Or his book project.

Jake's mother had died four years ago in a commuter plane crash.

That's what had brought Dave here to Florida from Atlanta. Dave's mom had moved down from Chicago years ago; really to be closer to Jake, her only grandson. She and Dave's ex-wife, Anne, had stayed close after he and Anne divorced. That happened back when Jake was seven. From then until four years ago, Anne had primary custody. Dave saw him at fixed times in the year, because he lived out of state.

They hadn't been all that close. Dave now believed this was totally his fault.

Just like the divorce. He was an idiot. A selfish, ambitious fool. It took Anne's tragic death for him to see it. Didn't come in time to help their relationship but hopefully in time to give him and Jake a second chance.

It seemed to be working.

Dave sighed, tried to push these thoughts aside. He looked up John Lansing's cell number and dialed. He expected to get his voice mail too. He already knew Lansing was an extremely busy man. And obviously, a multimillionaire.

"Hello? Mr. Lansing?"

"Hey, Dave. How are things? You're in Florida, right?"

He was surprised Lansing even remembered him. They'd only spoken briefly two other times. He must have kept Dave's name and number on his caller ID. "Pretty nice, actually. November's a great month here. I'm guessing it's a little chilly there."

"Chilly and windy."

"I've never lived in Houston, but I did live in the Dallas–Fort Worth area a couple of years. Do you have a minute?"

"A few," he said. "This about the book you're writing?"

He remembered that too. "It is. I don't know if you recall this, but I work for a newspaper here in north Florida. They're sending me out your way to cover a basketball tournament our local high school is participating in. I was hoping I might get with you while I'm out there, see if I could interview you about your experiences in Vietnam. Particularly, what happened that led to you getting that Silver Star."

"Funny you should bring that up. Since the last time you called, I got an idea that won't let me go. I called two of my best Nam buddies and talked it over with them. We get together every few years to reminisce. They liked the idea. Liked it a lot, in fact. So, yeah, I'd definitely like to talk with you."

"Were these men with you in that battle, the one where you got the medal?"

"No. I got that during my first tour in '67. I was stupid enough to sign up for a second. That's when I met the friends I'm talking about."

Dave was having a hard time following him. What could these guys tell him about John Lansing's Silver Star if they hadn't even been there? "Do you want these men there for the interview?"

"No, they live in different states."

"I guess I don't follow what—"

"No, I don't suppose you do. But I'd rather explain all this when you're here in person. You have my office number?"

"I do."

"Well, you hang up and call my secretary, Ellen. I've already told her a little about this. You tell her when you're coming and tell her I want to block off the better part of that day. Tell her to call mc if she runs into any snags."

"Well, that . . . that's great, Mr. Lansing. I really appreciate it."

"Guess you better start calling me John."

"So the interview's all set."

"Interview? Well, sure. You can still interview me, I guess."

Still?

"But the real reason I want to meet is not quite what you're expecting."

"It's not?"

"Son, it's like that old *Godfather* quote. I'm about to make you an offer you can't refuse."

9

Aaron was glad that the past several days at Bentley's Trailer Park & Campground had been relatively quiet. He'd been checking on Heather every day. So far, her boyfriend had not returned to get his things. She didn't seem to know what he was up to or when he'd be back, and she didn't care, either.

Aaron was pretty sure she was pregnant, and pretty sure she needed money. Before she drove off for work this morning, she'd asked Aaron if he wouldn't mind stopping by on his lunch hour to walk Tess. She hoped to talk her boss into letting her work the dinner shift too, which meant poor old Tess would be stuck in that trailer till after 7:00 p.m.

The other person Aaron had been keeping his eye on was Billy Ames. He stopped in on Billy every day after he clocked out. Billy had tried out the new ramp Aaron built a time or two, but for the most part, he stayed holed up in that dingy little place all day and night. Aaron had been trying to get him to get outside, get some fresh air. Always did Aaron some good when he was feeling low.

On most days, especially now that the weather was nice, Aaron spent his lunch hour outside at this little hideaway he'd found on the back end of the park. It was available to everyone who lived at Bentley's, but Aaron had never seen another soul make use of it. He liked to pretend the place was his. It was a wooden deck built out on a curve along the old Suwannee River, a section where the river faced mostly west. The tree line on the far side didn't block the sky much. Made for some beautiful sunsets. No properties had been developed along the water's edge as far as he could see in either direction. Made it nice and quiet. He was sure it would do Billy Ames a world of good if he'd get out there every now and then.

But getting to the deck took a little effort. It was at the edge of the property, and you had to walk a block through a marsh across a winding wooden walkway. The walkway and deck were pretty old. Over the last two years, Sue had given Aaron permission to fix it up. He'd replaced all the rotten boards, made it as solid as he knew how. But folks in the park still didn't take to it. Aaron figured they were afraid they'd run into snakes and spiders or the wasps who built nests under the wood railings. To Aaron, this wooden deck on the Suwannee was just a little closer to heaven than most places on earth.

Aaron looked at his watch. Still had thirty minutes left on his lunch hour. He stopped off at Heather's trailer and put Tess on a leash. Then he walked up Billy's ramp and knocked on the door of his trailer. He waited a few moments then knocked again.

"Who is it?"

"It's me—Aaron."

"Be right there."

Aaron patted Tess on the head. She sat beside him, looked up at him like they were best friends. A moment later, Aaron heard Billy's scooter humming toward the front door.

"What are you doing here this time of day?" Billy said as he opened the door.

"I got some time left on my lunch hour, wanted to show you something."

"You got a dog?"

"No, not the dog."

"Then what is it?"

"You gotta come out here to see it."

"Outside?"

"Well, of course, outside." Aaron walked Tess down the ramp, hoping Billy would follow. He turned to find Billy sitting on his scooter half in and half out the door. "You coming?"

Billy looked around. "Where?"

"There's a place I want to show you. It's not far. Won't take ten minutes to get there on your scooter."

"Is that dog friendly?"

"Well, look at her, Billy. She's smiling, wagging her tail. She's part golden retriever."

"I can see that."

"Then you know she's friendly. C'mon. She won't hurt you."

"Why you walking a dog?"

"It's just a favor for a friend. You coming?"

"This place, is it down the main road? 'Cause I don't want to take this thing down that road. They don't have a sidewalk, and I don't want to get stuck in the dirt."

"We're not even going to leave the trailer park."

"So where is it?"

"It's kind of a surprise. I'd rather show you than talk about it. C'mon. Don't you trust me?"

"Now why should I trust you, Aaron? You been real nice to me these last few days, but I don't know you all that well."

"I think you know me well enough to know I won't hurt you. You don't like this place, you don't ever have to go back. But I think you might like it. It's a place I go almost every day." Aaron turned and walked Tess in the right direction. He heard Billy's scooter heading down the ramp.

"As a rule, I don't like surprises," Billy said.

"I think you'll like this one." Aaron slowed his pace to let Billy catch up. When they were side by side, he said, "You ever have a hiding place when you were a kid? A place you liked to sneak off to when you wanted to be alone?"

"I'm not sure. I don't think so." They walked in silence a few moments then turned left on the paved road. "Actually, I do remember a place like that," he said. "There was this old orange orchard a few blocks from our home. I used to like to head there sometimes. Mainly to get out of doing chores or when I got in some kind of trouble."

"A place of refuge?" Aaron said.

"I guess you could call it that."

"Well, there's this spot on the back end of this property that's become my place of refuge. No one ever goes out there but me. It's right up ahead here. I thought if I showed it to you, you could go there whenever you wanted."

Billy gave him a puzzled look, but he kept following. Tess's head was just about even with Billy's hand. She walked right next to his wheelchair. "Hey there, girl." Billy patted her head. "What's her name?"

"Tess."

"Kinda fits. She's got a nice face."

They got to a place where the paved road curved to the left, around one of the larger oak trees in the park. About fifty feet ahead, across a grassy area, the oak forest gave way to a border of scrub and cabbage palms and much thicker brush. Cypress trees began to show up too, because they were close to where the marshy area began. As Aaron and Tess stepped into the grass, he heard Billy's scooter stop. "It's all right, Billy. I keep the grass mowed real good here. The ground's nice and hard."

"Where we going?"

"See the sign?" He pointed to it up ahead. It said: Nature Trail & Lookout.

"I can't go in there."

"Sure you can. It's got a strong wooden walkway, goes all the way to this deck right on the river."

"I don't . . . I don't go in jungles."

"It's no jungle. It's just a marsh, and it's pretty much—" Just then Aaron remembered. Billy had a major fear of jungles, even worse than his own. That's where Billy lost his legs in Vietnam, walking through jungles so thick you couldn't see a man ten feet in front of you. He had been walking point and stepped on a mine, something they called a Bouncing Betty. Blew him twenty feet in the air. When he came down, his legs were gone just past the knees.

Aaron walked back to Billy and bent down to eye level. Tess came right over. Her expression changed to something that looked like genuine concern. She seemed to know Billy was struggling. "I know what you're thinking, Billy. And we don't have to go back there if you don't want. I haven't told you too much about my time in Nam, but I got the same fear of jungles you have. But this place ain't anything like the jungles in Vietnam, I promise. That's part of the reason I love it back there."

Billy looked at him a few moments.

"Really, it's okay." Aaron stood up and walked a few steps toward the river. "Once we get down that walkway a bit, you'll see. Just low-lying marshes, as quiet and peaceful a place as I've ever seen. It turns and winds a little, maybe fifty yards. Then it opens up to a nice big wood deck, right on the river. And the scene there? Well, sometimes it takes my breath away. Besides the beauty of the river, you see all the best things that grow in Florida, just the way God meant them to be seen. And no people around, just you and me."

He looked back at Billy. He was smiling a little.

"And the wildlife," Aaron continued, "I see all kinds of things back there, especially birds. You'll see all different ones wading in the water here and there if you're quiet. Like white egrets and blue herons. Even storks on occasion. Sometimes bald eagles will fly right by, ospreys too. Like your own nature show, except you're seeing it with your own two eyes. What do you say?"

"I don't know," Billy said. "I'm not sure I'd feel safe riding this thing over water, and I ain't been an outdoorsy guy, ever since I lost these." He pointed down.

Tess walked over to Billy and sat beside him. She leaned up against his wheelchair and rested her head on his thigh. Billy looked down. "Would you look at that?" He patted her on the head.

"Seems like she's taken to you." Aaron looked at his watch. He only had about twenty more minutes. He wasn't thinking he'd be spending so much time having to talk Billy into this, and he needed to put Tess back up in the trailer. But he could tell Billy was softening up to the idea. "That wood out there is solid, Billy. You'd be as safe as riding on pavement, but I tell you what. We'll head back and you think on it awhile. I don't want to force you into doing something you're not comfortable with. But if you'd like to try it again tomorrow, I'll take you out there on my lunch break or after I clock out. Will that work?"

"I think I'd like that better." He spun his wheelchair around.

"I understand," Aaron said. When they got back to the curve in the paved road, they heard a roaring sound up ahead. Aaron looked up to see that souped-up blue Honda racing into the park entrance then fishtailing around the curve leading up to Heather's trailer.

It was her no-good boyfriend. Aaron tensed up till he remembered Heather wasn't home. They walked a little farther, and his heart skipped a beat. "Uh-oh." Heather was opening the front door of their trailer.

"What's the matter?"

"Heather is home."

"Who's Heather?"

"Tess's owner. That boyfriend of hers likes to beat her. I better get a move on it. You'll be all right if I leave you here?"

"I'm fine. I know my way back."

"Can you keep Tess with you?"

"Sure. You go on," Billy said.

10

Aaron did his best, running through the park toward Lot 31. As he neared the trailer, he saw the boyfriend's car parked at an odd angle. He listened but didn't hear any yelling. When he caught his breath, he called Sue on the walkie-talkie. "Sue, I'm outside Lot 31. Stay near the phone, will ya? You might have to call 911."

"I know," Sue said. "I saw that blue car whiz by my window. Don't you keep a pistol in your room? Maybe you better go get it, just in case."

"I don't want to leave here to get it, in case something happens while I'm gone."

"Your call, Aaron. Just say the word if you need me to call the cops. But let's don't do anything unless you think he might get violent. Don't want to stir a big mess if they're just talking. They get loud, you can step in for the park's sake. Tell them we can't have them yelling like that around here."

"All right, Sue," he whispered back. He walked a little closer till he was between Ryan's car and the front door. He heard them talking through the open window.

"Don't you tell me what you're *not* going to do. You'll do what I tell you."

Aaron understood that. So did anyone else within a hundred yards. Heather said something quiet in reply.

"The most you're getting outta me is a few hundred for an abortion. That's it! I told you, I ain't stickin' around to be no kid's father."

Heather said something back.

"Love you? We were having fun, least I was. But it ain't fun no more."

Heather said something else, but now she was crying.

"You crying don't change a thing. I'm serious. You *will* be getting an abortion, that's all there is to it."

"I am not!"

Aaron heard that. Then some banging noise, sounded like from the kitchen. Drawers being pulled out.

"Stop . . . Ryan, what are you doing?"

"You ain't keeping that baby, then telling folks it was mine. I've been asking around. They got tests that can prove it's mine, then you can start hitting me up for money. I can't have that. Someone told me they could even put me in jail because of your age."

"Ryan, put that down."

There was terror in her voice. That was it.

No time to call Sue. He had to move now. He scrambled up the metal steps and pushed open the front door. "Hey!" he shouted. Heather was backing up against the living room wall. Ryan was moving toward her, a kitchen knife in his right hand.

He turned.

"You put that thing down, right now."

Ryan's face filled with rage. "Oh, you gonna be a hero, old man? Guess I gotta take care of you first."

"Well, come on then," Aaron said. "Let's see what you got." He braced for the attack.

Ryan took a short step, faked one direction then lunged forward, jabbing the knife at Aaron's middle, like a sword. Aaron deflected Ryan's arm upward and grabbed his wrist, then shoved his right knee full-on into the boy's face. Heard a crunching sound. Ryan dropped the knife and fell back on his rear end, crying out in pain. Aaron jumped down on him, started pounding him in the face with his fist, two or three times. "How's that feel?" he yelled. "Feel good getting hit?" He smacked him again. "You like hitting girls?"

"Stop!" Heather screamed.

Aaron stopped. He looked up at her then down at the boy.

Ryan covered his bloody face with his hands. He looked confused. Aaron stood up, then bent over and grabbed Ryan by the collar, lifted him to his feet in one motion. All the while, Ryan covered his face. Aaron pushed him toward the front door. "Not so tough when you're fighting a man, are you, punk?"

The boy didn't answer. Nothing but fear in his eyes. Aaron walked him to the front door and shoved him out, over the steps. Ryan fell to the ground. "You get out of here and don't come back. I ever hear that you laid a hand on Heather here, I'm coming after you. I'm faster with a gun than my fists. I'll make sure you don't ever hurt her or anyone else again. You got that?"

Aaron looked around. A small crowd had gathered beyond the outskirts of the trailer.

Ryan looked up at him, then at the people. "What about my stuff? It's still in the trailer." There was no anger in his voice now, only fear.

"You just made a donation to the Goodwill."

Ryan nodded then rose to his feet.

"And you're not going to go tearing out of this park when you leave. You drive out of here going fifteen miles an hour. You understand? The whole way."

Ryan wiped his face on his sleeve and walked to his car. He got in, turned it on. Some people backed out of the way, and he drove off. Aaron watched, and so did everyone else, as he drove slowly through the park toward the front entrance. Aaron saw Sue coming out of the office, looking his way.

She held up the walkie-talkie, pointed to it. "Aaron?" she said. "Everything okay over there?"

He picked his up and said back, "Everything's fine now, Sue. Had a little ruckus, is all. But I think I scared that young man off. Maybe for good."

"I need to call the cops?"

"Don't think so. Let me talk to this young lady here a minute, see what she wants to do. Then I'll come over there and fill you in."

"All right then."

Aaron looked up at the folks standing around. "Sorry about that," he said. "Everything's okay now. Just had to get rid of a troublemaker." He waved, then backed inside Heather's trailer.

He turned and saw her sitting on a nearby armchair, holding her head in her hands. She was trembling. "You gonna be okay?" he said softly.

A few hours later, Aaron was back in his place in the storage room, trying to calm down. Heather felt pretty sure Aaron had scared Ryan off for good. She gave him a big hug and said, "You saved my life, Aaron. Me and my baby." She still wasn't sure what she was going to do in the days ahead.

Sue could tell he was pretty upset, and his knuckles were scraped up, so she'd given him the rest of the afternoon off. He'd taken a long, hot shower and was getting ready now to head out to his quiet place by the river.

He needed some time out there after a day like today.

His hands were still shaking. He didn't know when that had started, sometime after all the fuss settled down. He wished he could make them stop. Probably just the adrenaline. Still it bothered him, the level of violence that arose in his heart while he was hitting that boy. Aaron hadn't felt anything like that since Vietnam. It was like his training was right there below the surface.

Along with the instinct to kill.

He didn't like how it felt. Not one bit. That's not who he was anymore.

11

The next morning after his quiet time, one theme kept running through Aaron's mind. It had started yesterday evening, out by the river. He kept dismissing it as just an aftershock from the tension he still felt over his confrontation with the boy. But the way it kept coming back this morning made him start to wonder if it wasn't God trying to warn him about something. He needed to fix the lock on Heather's door, so he made Heather's trailer his first stop.

As he stood at the base of the steps, he looked at his watch. Hoped it wasn't too early. He knocked gently, just enough so she'd hear if she were in the kitchen or the living room. He heard footsteps.

"Hi, Aaron."

He turned toward the voice coming out the screened window to his right. "I came to fix the lock on this doorknob."

"I'm glad. It sure needs it." She unlatched the chain and opened the door.

He stepped up inside, looked at her face as he walked by. The dark rings under her eyes told him she hadn't slept much last night. "How are you making out?" Tess ran up to greet him, wagging her tail.

"Not very well," she said, relatching the chain across the door. She stepped into the kitchen, picked up a mug of coffee from the counter. "I don't feel very safe in this trailer anymore."

"That's really what I've come to talk to you about. Did you hear from that boy?"

"Not yet. I know I was saying yesterday that I thought you scared him off for good. Last night and this morning, I'm not so sure."

"He's an angry young man," Aaron said. "I'd judge him to be real unstable."

"Believe me, he is."

"You know you can't stay here, not in this trailer anymore." She paused, took a sip of coffee. "I know."

"You have any place to go?"

"I called a friend who works at my restaurant and explained what happened. She said I could stay with her a few days. I'll probably go there. But I don't know what I'm going to do with Tess."

"Then where will you go after a few days?"

"I don't know. I don't even feel good going there. Ryan's met her before. I wouldn't put it past him to come looking for me over there."

"He knows where she lives?"

"No, but it wouldn't be too hard for him to figure out."

Aaron just needed to say what he came to say. He knew she hadn't been open to the idea before, but it was what he felt

God wanted him to say, the real reason he was there. "Can I sit down a moment?"

"Sure." She walked into the living room, sat on the edge of the sofa. Tess followed, jumped up beside her.

He sat on the armchair nearby. "This won't take a minute, but I'd like you to hear me out. I know it ain't something you're too keen on."

"What is it?"

"See, I know you said you're . . . having a baby. That's what got all this going, isn't it?"

She nodded.

"And I take it you're set on keeping it, right?"

"Well, I know I'm not getting an abortion. Whether I keep the baby or not . . . I don't know. I was raised in a church, and I know right from wrong. I've been doing nothing but wrong since the day I ran away. And look where it's got me. But I can't make this baby pay for my mistakes."

"I'm glad to hear that," he said. "About the baby. I wasn't raised in a church, and I spent a whole lot more years doing everything wrong than you. More years than you been alive. But I got right with God some years back, started going to church myself. And one thing I know for certain, God loves little babies something fierce." He took a deep breath. Had to come at this slow. "So you thinking maybe about adoption?"

"Maybe. I don't know." She took another sip of coffee, set the mug down on the coffee table. "I'm so confused. All I do know is, I can't stay in this trailer."

"Well, see, Heather . . . I think part of the reason you're confused is, God doesn't mean for someone your age to be going through all this by yourself, making these kinds of big decisions on your own."

"But I don't have anyone else."

"I think you do. Or at least, you might."

She looked at him, trying to figure out what he was getting at. Her eyes said she got it. "You mean my parents."

Aaron nodded. "After what happened last night, and the predicament you're in right now, I'm thinking you should try calling them, or at least let me try."

She sighed loudly and looked away. "It's too late. I've been gone too long."

"See, I don't think that's probably true. Those are feelings you're having. My preacher might even call them lies of the devil. All's I know is, I keep getting a strong feeling God wants them involved. Won't you at least let me call them, see what they say?"

She didn't answer for the longest time. He decided it was best not to speak.

Finally, she turned and faced him. "They probably hate me." Tears streamed down her face.

"There's a chance they might," he said softly. "Folks can be hateful sometimes. But you know God doesn't hate you, right? Even if they do?"

She shook her head slowly.

"If you were raised in church, you must have heard how Jesus treats folks that have done wrong and then turn back to him. He's all about forgiving people, taking back sheep who strayed. And if your folks are still church folks, there's a good chance they know they're supposed to forgive people who've done them wrong, especially if . . . if those folks are sorry for what they've done. Sounds to me like you are sorry."

Tears poured down her face. "I am." It was all she could say.

He saw the tissue box and pulled some out, waited a minute

to give them to her. When she calmed down, he said, "How about you let me call them? I could do it right now. You know how to reach them?"

"I know their number. I've called them a few times, even recently. From a pay phone, so they couldn't see the number."

"So you have talked with them?"

"No, I never said anything. I just wanted to hear their voices. Then I'd hang up." The tears were welling up again.

"Well, let's get up, and you write that number on a piece of paper. I'll go right over to the office and call from there. Won't matter if they see that number, you're leaving this place anyway, right?"

"I guess."

"Have you ever talked about your parents with Ryan? He know where they live?"

"No, I've never told him anything about them. Of course, he never asked either."

"That's good," he said.

She stood up and walked toward the kitchen, then pulled out a drawer and fished around for a pen. She grabbed a pad from a little tray next to the refrigerator. "I guess it can't hurt to try," she said.

"If it goes sour," Aaron said, "you're just back where we started, right?" But he didn't think it would go sour. Wouldn't be like God to stir up this idea and keep stirring it, if he knew there weren't any point.

"But that won't work." She looked at Tess, then reached over and hugged her around the neck. "I can't go home. I can't bring Tess if I do. My mom's allergic to dogs. And I can't bring her back to the humane society. She was just two days away from being put down."

Aaron stopped and thought a moment. Then an idea came to him, a good one. "Let's take one thing at a time. You let me worry about Tess. Whatever happens, I won't take her back to the pound."

As Aaron walked toward the park office, he was aware of something else stirring inside him, something Heather had said that bothered him. But for some reason, he couldn't quite get a bead on it.

12

Sue, I got a favor to ask you."

Sue looked up from the counter. "What is it, Aaron? I'm pretty busy."

"It's about what happened yesterday, with that young girl in Lot 31."

"I saw you heading over that way this morning."

"Well, that door's busted again."

"She change her mind about calling the cops?"

"Not exactly, but that's why I'm here. We got to talking, and we're both thinking she's not safe to stay in that trailer anymore."

"I agree. That's why I think we should call the cops on that fella. The way he came at her with that knife, then came at you too? They'd lock someone up for that in a heartbeat."

"I know, but she's not wanting to take that route. It gets her having to deal with the guy for months. You'd have a trial and all that. She wants to be free of him once and for all. That's how I read it. Anyway, there's something else." He looked over toward the back office in the corner, the one where she did all her paperwork. "Could I use that phone a few minutes? She gave me the number of her folks in Georgia."

"She's had enough then, ready to go home?"

"Seems that way, if they'll take her back. I told her I'd call for her. Might be hard for her to hear it herself if they said no."

She sighed. "I guess it's all right." Aaron lifted a part of the counter up and walked past it. As he laid it back down, Sue noticed the bruises on his knuckles. "You put ice on that hand?"

"I did yesterday and part of last night. It still hurts pretty good, but I'll be all right." There was that nice side of Sue, asking him how he was doing. She went back to whatever she'd been writing, and he walked back to her office. He set the piece of paper on the desk and dialed the number Heather had given him. It rang three or four times.

"Hello?" It was a woman's voice.

"Hello, ma'am. I'm hoping I got the right number here. Would you know a young girl named Heather, about seventeen years old?"

"Oh no, Heather? Is she all right? Is this the police?"

"No, no. Nothing like that. She's all right. Just spoke with her not a half hour ago."

"Oh thank you, Lord," the woman said. "I'm so relieved. We haven't heard from her in so long, I . . ." It sounded like she had started crying.

"Are you her mother?" he asked.

"Yes. Can you hold a minute? I want to get her father in here. Can I put you on the speaker so he can hear?"

"Sure, I guess." He heard a bump, then nothing, then a few clicks.

"George is here, Heather's father."

"Hello, sir, do you know where our daughter is?" George said.

"I do. She actually said it would be okay if I called you."

"Can't she call us herself? Is she all right?"

"She's all right," Aaron said. "She's been through a pretty bad time, but she's not hurt. But I'm not feeling too good about her staying here in our trailer park after what happened yesterday."

"Oh no, what happened?" her mother said.

"Maybe it would be best if I took a minute or two and explained things. But from hearing you already, would I be right in assuming you'd be okay if she came home?"

"Oh yes!" her mother said tearfully. "We most certainly would."

"Definitely," her father said. "We've been praying for her every day since she left. It's . . . it's been tearing me up inside." Sounded to Aaron like he was choking up. "It's partly my fault . . . mostly my fault. She was causing all kinds of trouble, wouldn't listen to a thing we said. But I was too hard on her."

"We both were," her mother said.

They took turns explaining to Aaron what had happened, but he knew Sue wouldn't be okay if this went on too long. He jumped in and interrupted them as nicely as he could. "That's you folks' private business," he said. "I ain't here to judge. But you need to let me tell you what happened. I'm sure when I do, you'll agree, we need to get her home as quickly as possible."

"Sure, go ahead . . . I'm sorry. We don't even know your name."

"It's Aaron. Aaron Miller. Okay, well, here's what happened." Aaron laid it out pretty straight over the next five minutes. They both gasped several times. He left out the part about him beating on the boy, only mentioned he was able to stop him and put him out. Heather's mom started crying again when Aaron got to the part about her being pregnant.

As soon as he was through, Heather's father said, "Thank you so much for calling us, Aaron. I'll get in my car right now and drive down there to pick her up. But I don't even know where you are. You said north Florida?"

"Yeah, it's a little trailer park along the Suwannee River, about thirty miles east of Gainesville. She said you live a little north of Atlanta. I'd give you the address, but I'm thinking it's going to take you six or seven hours to get here, and I don't want that boyfriend coming back while she waits. What I'd like to suggest is, let me call my church, tell the secretary what happened. The church is only fifteen minutes from us. They'll probably send someone over to pick her up, let her wait for you at a church member's home. No way that boyfriend would find her there, and once you get her, she'll be safe for good. She told me she's never told him anything about you."

"That's a good plan, Aaron. I don't know how we can ever thank you for what you're doing here."

"Well, I'm happy to help. I'll feel a whole lot better when she's on her way back home." As soon as he said it, he felt that troublesome feeling inside, the one he'd been feeling since his talk with Heather a little while ago.

"Can we talk to her?" the mother said. "You think she'll talk to us?"

"I think she will now," Aaron said. "I'll go right over and tell her what y'all have said, soon as I call my church and set that up. She'll need to get her things together, but I'm sure she'll want to talk to you now. She'll probably call you on her cell phone."

"Thank you, so much," the mother said.

"You've been doing the Lord's work, Aaron," Heather's father said. "I wish I could meet you and thank you in person. Will you be there at the church when I arrive?"

"No, I don't think so. Got way too much to do around here. Fact is, I better get back to it now before I get in trouble with my boss."

They said a few more nice things to each other, and Aaron hung up. He called his church office next, and they were more than happy to help Heather out. Then he briefed Sue and headed over to tell Heather the good news.

As he strolled across the park toward Lot 31, that disquieting feeling was there again. This time he knew what it was. A scene replayed in his head of Heather telling him she was sure her parents hated her now, and him assuring her they probably would forgive her and take her back. Turned out, he was right.

He was thinking about how much he wished he could say the same thing about his own family situation. Wishing there was some way he could get back with Karen and Steven again. But it was no use; it wasn't the same thing. It was too late. He was no teenage runaway. And he hadn't been gone just a couple of years. He'd been gone a few decades.

And the way his ex-wife Betty talked when he'd tried to come back the last time, she'd made it clear they wanted nothing more to do with him. They had brand-new lives now. The kids had a real dad, even called him Dad. Had a normal family life going for many years.

"It's too late, Aaron," she'd said. "Much too late. I'm glad you're feeling better about yourself now, and you finally got off the streets. But this isn't your home anymore, and this isn't your family anymore, either. It's best you leave well enough alone. The kids don't even ask about you anymore. Haven't for years."

Tears rolled down his face as the scene and words replayed in his head. It had happened over twenty years ago. Still hurt worse than anything he'd ever felt.

13

Karen Miller pulled into a local Tex-Mex restaurant to grab a late lunch with her older brother Steve. She loved him probably more than anyone else on earth. He was only eleven months older, but throughout their lives he'd been all that an older brother could be. Especially after their mother had died and Greg left her.

As she pulled in beside Steve's white Lexus, Karen wondered why he'd asked to meet with her. Steve was a business attorney and usually extremely busy during the day.

She walked through the restaurant doors and informed the smiling hostess that her party was already here. It didn't take long to find him; they'd met here many times, and Steve always sat in the same area, just like at church. He smiled and waved her over. She took off her coat but left her sweater on, then slid the coat and her purse into the booth and sat beside them.

"I already ordered the chips and salsa," he said. He barely got the words out when the waitress walked up and set a big bowl of chips and salsa down. Then two large glasses of soda.

"These are both Diet Cokes," the waitress said, looking at Karen. "Is that all right? Your husband said you liked yours with lemon."

"Husband," Karen said. "You think I'd marry this guy?"

Steve laughed.

"I'm sorry, I just thought—"

"Don't apologize. He's my brother. But he knows what I like to drink. Diet Coke with lemon is just fine, thanks."

"Do you need a few minutes to order?"

"You mean he didn't do that for me?"

"I would have," Steve said. "But you get two or three different things here."

"He's right," Karen said. "But I don't need any time. I'm in the mood for that chicken strip salad today." She handed the menu back to the waitress.

"Nothing for me, just the chips and salsa," Steve said. The waitress walked away.

"You already ate, didn't you?"

"Had lunch with a client. Sorry. I know you hate eating alone." He reached for a chip. "But I'll keep eating these."

Okay, Karen thought. *He's not even eating lunch.* "Is everything okay?"

"What?"

"Is Aileen okay, the kids?"

"Yeah, everyone's fine."

"Am I in trouble?"

"What? No."

"So why are we here?"

"Can't a brother take his little sister out for lunch?"

"But you're not eating lunch."

"Okay, that's—"

"And you're a busy attorney who gets paid an obscene amount per hour."

"It's not obscene." He smiled. "Well, maybe a little. How does that even matter?"

"You're taking time away from your busy day, losing money, to meet with me. And it's not even for lunch. Something must be up." She sipped her Diet Coke.

"Nothing is up, honest." He reached for another chip, dipped it in the salsa. "These are *so* good."

"Steven, tell me. Why are we here?"

"It's just . . . Gail called, told me about your lousy date the other night and . . . she thought you could use a little TLC. After asking her a few questions, I agreed. That's all this is."

"That's all?"

"Really. I just wanted to see how you're doing. Aileen and I've been talking about it, and so I decided I should just ask you myself."

Karen was so relieved. Now she could eat. She reached over and dipped a chip in the salsa, then in a small bowl of ranch dressing.

"So, how are you doing?"

"I don't know how I'm doing. And the date, by the way, was no big deal. You might even know him. He's an attorney too. Ken Morrow."

"Ah, a young guy. I don't know him personally but know of him. Seems nice."

"A nice *young* guy."

"Well, Karen, you know that kind of thing doesn't matter so much anymore."

"No, I guess it doesn't. But it bothers me. Not what others do so much, it's just . . . I don't know. It didn't feel right to me."

"You think it bothers you more because of Greg? Since he left you for someone younger?"

"I don't know. Maybe," she said. She sat up in her seat as the waitress stopped by and dropped off her salad. "This looks delicious. I'm so hungry." After a quiet prayer of thanks, she cut up the chicken strips. "I don't think it really matters, because I couldn't see myself with someone like Ken if we were born two days apart."

Steve laughed. "Okay, so he's not your type, I get it. But I have to tell you, it was encouraging to hear you went out with anyone. It's been a long time."

Karen nodded, finished chewing. "Dates like that are the reason why. Spent the whole day preoccupied over it, went home, got all dressed up, redid my hair . . . and for what?"

"I know," Steve said. "It can be a messy business, finding the right one. Aileen said the other night how glad she was that we're not still out there, searching. We get to just sit on the couch and look at each other. No work, no fuss."

"Is that supposed to be helpful?" she said, smiling.

"Sorry, guess not. I was trying to empathize."

"I know you were."

"Aileen's had her eye on this guy who's just started volunteering in the church bookstore."

Karen laughed. "And you're okay with that?"

"What?" Then he got it. "No . . . I don't mean she's interested in him herself. She was thinking about him for you. She said he seems about the right age. No ring on his finger. So she—"

"Please, Steve, no. Thank her for thinking about me but . . . no. I'm not interested in people trying to set me up on dates. Not Gail, and not you guys."

"But Karen, it's been four years since Greg left—I really do wish you would have let me kill him, you know." He was smiling. "We haven't seen you show any interest in anyone since."

"I know it's been four years," she said. "I just haven't met anyone that interests me yet."

"Are you even looking?"

"No. I guess I'm not." She took a bite of her salad so she wouldn't have to elaborate.

"All right, I get the hint. New subject. Thanksgiving. You're still coming over, right?"

After she swallowed, she said, "Have you heard anything about Stevie? Any chance he'll be coming home from Afghanistan?" Stevie was Aileen and Steve's oldest son.

"Karen, you're the only one who still calls him that. He's been going by Steven since high school."

"*Steven* then," she said.

"No, he won't make it home for Thanksgiving. But we got an email from him yesterday. He's getting over two weeks at Christmastime. He'll be home on December 16 and won't have to head back till January 3. And this time he won't be heading back to Afghanistan but North Carolina."

"Really? That's wonderful. I pray for him all the time, you know."

"Thanks. We do too."

"He looks so much older in those pictures."

"He does," Steve said. "We're so proud of him."

"Well, I'll definitely be spending Thanksgiving with you guys."

"Good," he said. "Then it's settled." He took a long sip of his Diet Coke. "You know . . ." He got a mischievous look on his face. "You can bring a friend with you if you want."

14

One week later, Dave Russo got on a plane to Houston, along with his son's high school basketball team. Jake had ridden to the airport on the team bus; Dave followed behind them in his car.

On the plane, it still felt like he was following them. He could see Jake's head fifteen rows in front of him, sitting with his friends. Because Dave had booked his flight later, there weren't any seats even close. But that was okay. He was glad Jake had made the team and that he'd made some good friends. The depression Jake had been fighting ever since his mother died seemed firmly in the past.

Dave knew he was just feeling sorry for himself. But knowing this didn't make it go away. He wanted to get closer to Jake. And they had been, right up until Jake made the team. But Dave knew what came next. Jake would get even tighter with the friends he'd made on the team and keep making new ones. He'd finish high school this year then head off to college. Four more years would go by. Somewhere in there he'd meet the woman of his dreams and go nuts over her.

Of course, none of this was wrong. It was all good and healthy stuff, the kind of things a parent wants to see. Jake wasn't on drugs or running with a bad crowd; he got decent grades at school.

So why was Dave depressed?

The plane hadn't reached its cruising altitude, which meant they couldn't turn on their electronic devices yet. He waited for that announcement so he could pull out his laptop and distract himself with work. He tried to care about an article on the best places to ski in New England, but every few minutes he'd look up the aisle at Jake.

Had it really been four years since Anne died? When he'd gotten the call from his mom, Dave had been stunned. It didn't seem real. He'd booked the next flight down from Atlanta, worried sick about Jake the whole while. They had talked a few times on the phone, but after only a few sentences, one of them would start crying and they'd have to end the call. When he talked to Jake, the last thing Jake had said was, "Just get here . . . soon."

Anne, Jake's mom, was the woman Dave had met in college and went nuts over. If he'd had any sense, he'd have stayed nuts over her. She was a great lady, a good wife, and an even better mom.

He didn't know who cried more at her memorial service—Jake for all he'd lost, or Dave for what a fool he'd been. He sat there in her church, listening first to the pastor then to one friend after another get up and tell him all the things he'd already known about her but had taken for granted.

It tore him up inside.

He'd let their marriage slip away. Sitting in church that day next to Jake, he knew he was through choosing his job over his family. Jake was all that mattered now. Finding a way back into his life.

One day, maybe a week after the memorial service, a breakthrough came. They had been talking about things that barely mattered for so many years, Dave didn't know how to talk heart-to-heart with Jake. He could see how much Jake was hurting, and all he kept thinking was how he wished Anne were there to talk him through it.

Dave said, "Let's take a walk, get some fresh air."

"Where?" Jake said.

"How about down by the creek, where we used to go fishing?"

"I don't feel like fishing."

"Me neither, but maybe the fresh air will do us some good."

"I guess."

It was about two blocks away. They didn't say much at first, but Dave could tell Jake was warming up to him being home. He knew Jake had some good talks with a few people already; a couple with his grandmother and one with the youth pastor at church. Those talks seemed to do Jake some good. Dave had expected him to be mad at God for taking his mom. If he was, Dave couldn't see any sign of it. "How you doing today?" he asked as they navigated the path through the woods toward the creek.

"Okay, I guess. I still feel numb mostly."

"I know what you mean."

"You feel that way?" Jake asked.

"Mostly, yeah," Dave said. "It doesn't seem real."

"Will it ever?"

He put his hand on Jake's shoulder. "I think so, Jake. It'll take some time, I guess." But he didn't know. How could he?

His father had died, but he was too young to even remember. He'd never lost anyone close to him before.

When they got to the spot, they sat down on the same flat rocks they'd always sat on when they fished. The water flowed around and over the rocks as strong as it always had. The same trees stood along the banks where they had always stood.

Everything was familiar, and nothing was.

"Can I ask you something, Dad?" Jake was looking down at the water.

"Sure, Jake, anything."

"It's kind of personal."

Dave sighed. He had wanted this, to get personal. But he was afraid at the same time. "That's all right."

Jake looked up. "You seem to be crying since Mom died, almost as much as me."

"I guess that's true."

"Can I ask you why? I mean, I know why I'm crying. But you and Mom, you've been divorced a long time."

"We have, but you know we got along pretty good. All the years since."

"I know, but . . . did you still love her?"

Dave couldn't help it. Tears filled his eyes.

"See, you're doing it again."

"I know. You're right." Dave let out a sigh, hoping it might give him some control. "I did still love her. But not the way I should have. You did. You were a great son. And she loved you so much." Tears escaped down his cheeks. "But see, I wasn't a great husband. No . . . I was a lousy husband. I should have never left your mom."

"Is that what happened? She said it was mutual, that you both had just grown apart."

"She was being nice. We did grow apart, but it wasn't her fault. I let this stupid job take over my life." He picked up a stone and threw it hard at the water.

"Which job?"

"All of them, really. I just wanted to make it in the big leagues, become the best reporter working at the best paper making the most money. But your mom, she didn't want that. She just wanted to live here. Raise you here, have a few more kids here. She got tired of moving every few years, and me never being home."

"She still loved you, you know?" Jake wiped the tears with his sleeve. "She never even dated anyone else all those years."

Dave lost it then. He had never dated anyone else, either. Not seriously. It never felt right. He always thought he and Anne would get back together somehow, and he wanted to be able to say he'd always stayed true to their vows. But here he'd wasted all those years they could have had together. He just hung his head and sobbed.

After a few minutes, he felt Jake's arms around him. Jake was crying quietly, resting on his back. When Dave got control of himself, he wiped his tears and looked up. "Jake, I want you to know something. I am so sorry I left you and your mom. It wasn't her fault. It was all mine. I can't do anything to get her back, but if you'll let me, I'll try to be the best dad to you I can be. For all the years we have left."

A pinging sound interrupted Dave's thoughts, then a male voice came over the plane's intercom. "We've reached our cruising altitude. Feel free to use any approved electronic devices. The captain has turned off the seat belt sign, so you can move about the cabin if you'd like. But please keep them fastened while in your seats, in case we run into any unexpected turbulence."

This announcement came just in time. He was bent down, wrestling his laptop from the case under the seat, when he heard a familiar voice in the aisle. "Hey, Dad, how's it going back here?" It was Jake.

"Doing okay, I guess." He looked up and smiled. "I guess you guys are having a hard time squeezing into these seats."

"Especially Tommy Haynes. He's our center."

"He's six-five, isn't he?"

"Six-six now. His knees are literally up by his face."

"You doing okay? I mean . . . with the flight?" He and Jake had talked this through already, how Jake felt about flying since his mother had died in a plane crash. Jake nodded. "So where you going," Dave asked, "to the restroom?"

Jake looked down at the empty seat next to Dave. "No, I came back here to be with you. I figured once we landed, we wouldn't get much time together. You know how crazy it's going to get."

"Oh."

"Is that okay? I see you reaching for your laptop. Do you need to get some work done?"

Dave looked down at his laptop bag then up at Jake. "Are you kidding? Here, I'll move over."

15

Four days later, the basketball tournament complete, Dave saw Jake off at the airport for his return trip to Florida. Jake's team hadn't actually played at all that final day. The Panthers had won their first game, lost the second, then were eliminated on day three. It was hard for Dave to even write about that third game.

After the first quarter, the Panthers never got closer than twenty points. Jake got to play seven whole minutes there at the end. He'd only made the second string, which meant he only got in the game when his team was twenty points ahead or twenty behind. At the buzzer, Jake looked into the stands and found Dave. Seeing the smile on Jake's face, you'd never know his team had just been thoroughly trounced and eliminated from the tournament.

Because they had, Dave and Jake got to hang out together on day four. They'd stayed with the team the whole time, watching the finals, but no one seemed to mind Dave tagging along. He suspected the guys had known he was there reporting for the newspaper back home; they wanted to see their names in print.

Dave had all their names woven into the stories he'd sent back to Harry, and quite a few pictures as well. That was the real purpose of the trip, for the paper, anyway. So the folks back home would buy up all those extra copies of their sons, grandsons, and cousins playing basketball in Houston. But for Dave, it was about spending time with Jake. It still affected him, days later, thinking about that moment in the plane when Jake chose to sit with him over his friends.

Today, Dave started Phase II of his trip.

He was still in Houston, driving south down the I-610 loop for an interview with John Lansing, the former Vietnam War hero and present oil executive. The GPS on Dave's rental car led him off the interstate, through an upscale business zone, then through the exclusive Bent Oaks neighborhood where John and his family lived. Some of the homes on this gorgeous oak-lined street were extremely nice; the rest were mansions.

John Lansing's house was just ahead on the right. As Dave pulled into the driveway, he got the sudden impression that he had rented the wrong car. The green Ford Fusion didn't deserve to be parked in front of a place such as this.

He stood a moment, gawking. The house was bigger than most of the yards in the subdivisions back home. A banner of ivy draped across the front, neatly trimmed around the French windows and over a double front door made of polished bronze. After ringing the doorbell, Dave half expected to be welcomed by an old English butler.

Instead, it was Mr. Lansing himself, wearing a big Texas grin, a plaid long-sleeved shirt, and dark blue jeans. He was taller than Dave had imagined. "There you are, Dave. Right on time. I like that. Come on in, come on in. Any trouble finding the place?"

"No trouble at all, sir. Just followed the GPS."

"You're going to have to find a way around calling me sir," he said, "if we're going to be spending the day together. It's the house, isn't it? A little intimidating to some folks. I've lived here so long, I don't even think about it anymore. But you work on calling me John, okay?"

Dave looked around the foyer. Shining marble floors, dueling staircases on either end circling upward to a balcony that wrapped around the room, bordered by a black ornamental iron railing. A crystal chandelier hung suspended from the ceiling.

Just the foyer intimidated him.

"Follow me," John said. His boots clicked as he walked across the floor away from the front door.

"You don't mind if I record our conversations?" Dave said. "No one will see them but me. It'll just allow me to catch everything you're saying better, including your expressions. Make it easier to put the story together later."

"Ah, I don't care. Not planning on sharing any state secrets." They walked through the foyer then through a wide hallway lined with family pictures. On either side, doorways opened to massive rooms. They turned left at the last one. Dave guessed it was the library. A wide stone fireplace occupied the far wall.

"I thought we'd meet in here," John said.

Dave looked down at an array of dark leather sofas and armchairs centered in the room.

"Sit anywhere. Doesn't matter."

Dave waited until John sat, then picked an armchair nearby. A thick wooden coffee table stood between them.

"Evelyn's out shopping for the day. I let the staff have the day off. All our kids are married, so it's just you and me. There's some iced tea there in that pewter pitcher. Help yourself."

"Thanks." Dave poured himself a glass. That's when he noticed something else on the coffee table, right in front of John. A box of tissues. John didn't seem to have a cold. He saw Dave looking at it.

"Guess you're wondering what that's here for. They're for me. I hardly ever talk about the story I'm about to tell you, except with my two war buddies. We just got together a few weeks ago for a reunion. We do that every couple of years. I told them about your book idea. We thought it would make sense to go over the story while we were together, make sure we got the details right. The thing is, try as hard as I might to keep it together, there's just certain parts that get to me."

Dave set his video recorder on the coffee table between them and pulled out his pad of questions. The questions were all based on the assumption that he was there to interview John for winning the Silver Star in Vietnam in 1967. He got the impression John had other plans for their time.

"So how's the book coming along?" John leaned back on the leather sofa.

"So far, so good. I haven't actually begun writing it, though. Just an outline."

"I've read a few good books on Nam in recent years," John said. "Problem is, the better ones take me right back to things I spent a whole lot of time trying to forget."

Dave knew from interviews he'd already done that this was going to be a challenging time for John. He reached down, took a sip of iced tea. He wasn't sure how to ease into his first question. "It was your first tour where you got the Silver Star, right?"

John nodded. "My first tour was between 1966 and '67. But really, Dave, you don't want to interview me about that. It's a decent story, but I've got one you need to hear that's way better. It happened during my second tour. The fellow I'm talking about did way more heroic things than me. Actually, I wouldn't be alive now if it weren't for him. Me or my two friends."

"Really?"

"He saved our lives during this one firefight in 1969. Almost got himself killed doing it."

"So, who is this guy? What's his name?"

"His name is Aaron Miller. He won the Congressional Medal of Honor for what he did that day."

"Really? The Medal of Honor." The man's name rang a faint bell. "I think I've heard of him." Dave took out his interview list and scanned the pages. "Here it is, halfway down page three."

"You've interviewed him?" John was almost yelling. He leaned forward in his seat. "You know where Aaron is?"

"No, I haven't talked with him yet. He's just on my list of hopefuls." As Dave looked back at the page, he saw he had almost nothing on the man. Which was probably why he was on page three. "So, he's the guy?"

"Yes, he's the guy. Aaron Miller." John sat back again. "I'm going to tell you his story, Dave. Because that's the story you want to write about. And when I'm through, I guarantee he's going to move from page three to the top of page one."

Dave was definitely intrigued. "Does he have anything to do with the offer you're going to make me? The one I won't be able to refuse?"

He smiled and nodded. "Yeah, but that will have to wait until after I tell you his story."

16

Fear.

In a word, fear was what John Lansing remembered most about that day. Not just that day but all the days back then, for months leading up to that day. He was afraid all the time. He didn't know why he didn't drop dead; the fear was so intense some days. If they'd stuck guys his present age in situations like that, you'd see men dropping dead every hour or so from a heart attack or stroke.

No, war is a young man's game.

And John was young then, twenty-three years old. But at that age, he was older than most of the men in his platoon. Nineteen was average. They were all part of the 3rd Battalion, 9th Marines. A few weeks earlier, they'd been airlifted into the area to set up Fire Support Base Cunningham on a ridgeline overlooking the valley. A firebase was essential to any combat operation in

Vietnam. It was a high, level place where the helicopters could land and drop off men, equipment, and supplies.

But even more important, a place Marines could set up their artillery guns, so when patrols in the jungles below got stuck in a firefight, radiomen could call in a fire mission. When they did, the artillery at Cunningham would rain a firestorm of shells down on the enemy. These artillery fire missions had saved John's hide more times than he could count in the last few years.

Few years.

What an idiot he'd been to sign on for a second tour. He could have been home over a year ago. All the John Wayne, Green Beret crap he'd bought into was long gone. No fighting for God and country running through his veins anymore. John had just one thought in mind when he woke up every day, one thought when he went to sleep.

That morning, the thought was "thirty-six."

He only had to survive thirty-six more days and he'd get sent home. Every soldier in country (what they called time in Vietnam) started their combat tour knowing they had to make it through thirteen months. No hope of it being shorter, unless you went out in a body bag or stretcher.

John thought about that as the loud, staccato thumping of a Huey helicopter faded in the distance. It had flown in at first light to medevac out two Marines wounded last night in a firefight by their listening post. The company set up three LPs every night, two-man teams just beyond the perimeter defenses, hoping to hear any enemy movement in time to warn the rest of the unit before an attack.

Sometime just after 3:00 a.m., John awoke to chaos as the night sky filled with gunfire. All around him men shouted and swore and grabbed their weapons, bracing for battle. But within minutes, it was over. The VC patrol who'd stumbled on this LP quickly disappeared back into the jungle. The only sound after were the agonizing screams of the two men who got jumped.

At dawn, John watched the Huey disappear over a hill on the opposite side of the valley. It was the first day in nine that the fog had lifted enough to see that far. Despite their injuries, he envied those two men. They still had arms and legs, and it didn't look like their wounds were fatal. The perfect ticket out, he thought.

"Bet you wish that was you, Tex." John looked over at Hammer, one of his two best friends in the platoon. John got the nickname Tex for obvious reasons. Hammer got his because he'd been a carpenter's helper before the draft. His real name was Allan Summers.

Tex didn't answer, just kept putting on his gear, getting ready for the patrol.

"I wish it was me," Hammer said. "Those guys are outta here for good. But hey, you're getting close, right? You only got, what, thirty days?"

"Thirty-six," Tex said.

"I got more than double that left." Hammer picked up his M-16, looked down, and kicked the dirt. "I don't see myself making it home now, since they dropped us out here. I mean, look, right off the bat, we got VC probing our LPs at night. And now we're getting sent out in the jungle to hunt 'em down. Who knows what we're gonna run into."

"You'll be fine, Hammer. Redman and me will look after you." Redman was John's other friend. His real name was Paul Patterson. He made the mistake once of bragging he was one-fourth Cherokee Indian.

"Redman's only got a week more than you. Wish I was a short-timer."

Overhearing all this was an Italian guy from the Bronx named Sardelli. He was short but built like a tank. They hadn't picked a name for him yet, since he'd only been in country two weeks. "You guys are talking like this thing's gonna go on forever. Nixon just got sworn in back home. He said he's gonna end this thing soon."

Tex and Hammer looked at him. "You're kidding, right?" Tex said.

"No, I'm not. The whole country's against the war now, and Nixon said he was gonna find a way to end it . . . with honor."

Tex bent down and opened an ammo box. Technically speaking, they weren't allowed to say anything negative about their commander-in-chief. "I wouldn't hold him to that campaign promise," Tex said.

Hammer said something a little more colorful.

"I don't know," Sardelli said. "You guys are just messed up from being over here so long. We might get the VC cleaned out of this valley a few weeks from now. This could be the last big battle of the war."

"How much time you got left, Sardelli?" Hammer said.

He thought a moment. "Three hundred and forty-two days. But—"

"Thought so."

"Why?"

"That's why you're talking that way," Hammer said. "If that helps you sleep better at night . . ."

"That's not why I said it."

Hammer didn't reply.

After getting all the ammo clips he needed, Tex straightened up. "You better get something straight, Sardelli," he said. "This ain't like other wars we fought in, where guys like us win a few big battles, force the enemy to give up his ground, and then he surrenders." This was one of the hardest lessons Tex had learned once he got here in '66. "See, the battles we fight out here aren't about beating the commies back to North Vietnam. Our commanders don't even talk like that *might* happen someday. It's all about how many VC we kill today versus how many of our guys they kill. We kill more of them, we won the battle."

"Then the next day, we start all over again," Hammer added. "It's a numbers game. It's all about body counts. Last year the whole battalion fought over a week to take this one hill and the jungle around it. We lost thirty-eight guys, but hey, we killed over four hundred Viet Cong. So, we won big-time, right? We owned that hill. But did we stay on it, make sure it stayed out of enemy hands? No, they took us off the very next day. Headed out to take some other nameless hill."

Sardelli just stared at them, a deflated look on his face. *But hey*, Tex thought, *the guy's gotta be told*. Just then, Redman walked toward them. He'd been talking with their CO, Lt. Mann, this whole time.

"Guys," he said. "I gotta be on point for the patrol this morning." His face was white as a sheet.

"What?" Tex said. "But last night Cracker said he'd do it again."

"I know," Redman said. "But the lieutenant said no. Cracker's been volunteering to take point too much, and he's putting a stop to it. Cracker was standing right there next to him. The lieutenant looked at me and said, 'Redman, you know it's your turn. Now get ready. We're moving out in ten minutes.'" Fear was all over Redman's face. "I got a bad feeling about this."

Everyone knew, the point man was the first to get it on patrol. Most of the time, anyway. First to get shot in an ambush. First to cross a trip wire and set off a mine. First to step in a punji trap—sharpened bamboo stakes that stuck straight up from a hidden hole.

Something was wrong with Cracker. For some reason, he'd been volunteering to take other guys' places as point on patrols. Maybe he was fearless. Or maybe he had some kind of death wish. Tex wondered if that was it.

"Well, don't worry, Redman. Hammer and I got your back. I bet ol' Sardelli here will stay close, right, Sardelli?"

Sardelli looked away.

"Forget him," Hammer said. "We'll get through this. You'll see."

Tex saw Cracker walk toward them.

"Sorry, Redman, you know I tried."

Redman just nodded back. Cracker turned and walked away. He was mostly a loner, did what he was supposed to do, but didn't talk much. A lot of the guys made fun of him. Sometimes he, Redman, and Hammer joined in. He'd heard Cracker was from some no-name town in Florida, talked with a strong Southern accent. That's how he got the name.

His real name was Aaron Miller.

17

As the sun rose over the Song Da Krong Valley, it made everyone in the platoon forget this was supposed to be a winter month. It wasn't nearly as stifling or muggy as the monsoon season, maybe up around seventy degrees. But with all their gear on, it felt twenty degrees hotter. The men descended the hill into the shade offered by the thick canopy of trees running down the eastern half of the valley. The heat eased up a little, but there was almost no wind coming through.

Tex wished the weather was all they had to worry about. He made his way to the front of the line to join Hammer and Redman, who was now on point. Every few steps, Redman looked back. "We're here," Tex said. He tried to sound reassuring, but there was no truth in it. With each step farther into the jungle, Tex's own fears went up another notch. What he wanted to say was, "You're on your own," and slip to the back of the patrol.

They called these missions "Search and Destroy," the idea being they went out searching for VC and, once found, destroyed them. They should've been called "Search and Get Ambushed" patrols, because that's what really happened. Everything about these missions played to the enemy's hand. They were in his backyard. He knew these jungles, and he was out there hiding, waiting for them to come his way. No matter how quiet they tried to be, he could always hear them coming.

It was steep going down the hillside, at times hard to find a foothold. A thought flashed into Tex's mind: maybe he should just let himself fall the next time he slipped. Take his chances. He'd probably get cut up real bad, maybe even break a bone or two. But he'd be alive. Sarge would lay into him when they found him down the hill, hurl every four-lettered insult he knew. But then he'd send some guys to drag him back to Cunningham. If he was hurt bad enough, they'd medevac him back to Vandergrift.

"Watch it, Tex." It was Hammer.

A large fern whipped around and slapped Tex across the face. "Sorry, you gotta stay closer, man."

Tex didn't want to stay closer. The others looked to him as if he was tougher than they were, so he played along with it. He was the one who'd signed on for a second tour, got the Silver Star. He was from Texas. He'd even thought he was tough . . . a few years ago. Or was it a few months ago?

All he knew was, something clicked inside when counting down his days and he got to the number thirty-nine. *Thirty-nine.* Wasn't too far from a month. In just over a month, he'd have all his days in, then he'd hightail it out of here on that big Freedom Bird back to the States.

But only if he stayed alive.

For the last eleven months, he'd spent his days and nights doing every awful, hateful thing he'd been asked to do. Killing VC a dozen different ways, zipping friends up in body bags, sleeping in muck and swamps with artillery fire pounding in his brain, eating cold rations and living in the rain for days on end, picking off leeches, swatting mosquitoes, dodging bullets and booby traps. So many close calls. More than he could count. He was sure he'd never make it to the end. He'd almost stopped hoping he'd survive. But here he was, just over a month away.

The last place he needed to be today was up here near the point with Redman and Hammer.

"Here it is," Hammer said. "Here's where the fight went down last night." They had reached the LP.

Tex looked around at the scarred and broken tree limbs and branches. The twisted vines and palm fronds blackened by grenade explosions. He saw blood splatters in the grass and leaves in two places. *Those two guys were sitting right there*, Tex thought. *Right there*. Could have been him and Hammer. Or Hammer and Redman sitting there, not making a sound.

Pitch black. Listening for crackling leaves, a breaking twig. He remembered the last time he was at an LP. Got to where he could hear his own heartbeat.

"Okay, guys, look sharp. We're in no-man's-land now. Hand signals only from here." It was Sarge, maybe ten yards back.

Hammer turned and whispered to Tex, "Sarge said there's a better than fifty-fifty chance we won't see any booby traps out here. From what he heard, this whole operation is about those trucks the North Vietnamese been driving on that highway south of here, you know, coming in from Laos. He doesn't think the VC have been out here long enough to set any traps."

Tex nodded and kept following Hammer deeper into the brush. It was damp, and the whole area smelled like a cellar. He wasn't buying the news about the traps. For two reasons. First, Tex had been a sergeant last year, until he got busted down to private for insubordination. He'd routinely said hopeful things to his guys that he didn't believe. And second, it didn't take long to set some of those traps, especially those punji spikes and trip wires they hooked up to mines.

"Redman," he said in a loud whisper. "You hear me?" The jungle was so thick here, he couldn't even see him, though he was only a few feet past Hammer.

"I hear you, Tex."

"You still keep an eye out for those traps."

"Oh . . . I am. But . . . can't hardly see a thing." Tex heard a tremble in his voice. The three of them were close enough that if Redman did blow up, both he and Hammer would get some of it too. They weren't supposed to bunch up like this. They were taught to keep a certain distance between them, to minimize casualties should the point man walk into an ambush or set off a trap. But they always stuck close together. Hammer had said they were like the Three Musketeers. One for all and all for one.

It's a bunch of crap is what it is. For something as stupid as that, Tex was up here with Redman and Hammer, about to get maimed or killed. He could feel it coming.

He looked behind him, saw Cracker, no expression on his face at all. Sardelli was close behind him. None of the guys stayed the right distance apart in jungle this thick. They were all as afraid as he was. In a place like this, there was plenty to fear. Forget the Viet Cong waiting to kill you. Deadly snakes and spiders were all over the place, lurking about. Disease-carrying insects. And the darkness. It wasn't even nine-thirty in the morning, and it was dark enough to be well after sundown. And it wasn't like they were treading along some nature trail marked out with signs. You lost sight of the guy in front of you, even for a minute, the jungle could swallow you whole.

They continued their downward descent for the next twenty minutes in silence. Finally, they reached a place where every now and then there'd be a slight break in the trees. Tex looked up and saw parts of the valley, far off in the distance, lit up by the morning sun. It was almost scenic. A few minutes later, he heard the sound of trickling water.

A few minutes after that, Redman stopped dead in his tracks. So did everyone else.

He put his finger to his mouth then pointed to the ground. They had just reached the base of the hill. Before them, a narrow creek flowed through a winding path of rocks and fallen limbs. Tex looked down to where Redman pointed.

Footprints in the mud along the creek bank. Dozens of them.

He looked around for any sign of their owners. So did Hammer and Redman. The men behind them waited to see what came next. The other side of the creek was lined with tall bamboo and elephant grass. Anything could be hiding in there, Tex thought.

Redman looked at him. Tex could see in his eyes: Redman was asking him what he should do. He didn't want to take another step.

But he had to. You couldn't stop when you were on point. Tex nodded for him to keep going, slowly. More fake bravado. Everything inside him wanted to turn and run back the way they came.

But Redman obeyed. Short, quiet steps. Hammer followed after, stepped gently onto the muddy bank. Then Tex. Within a few minutes, the entire patrol walked along the bank. No one said a word. Here, the creek was about the width of a wide hallway. They had to duck in spots to clear the brush overhead, which created a tunnel effect.

About fifty yards farther, the creek opened wide to a section about forty feet across, littered with fallen trees and rocks. The water branched out and swirled in little pools behind the bigger boulders until it escaped on either side. Except for the tropical vegetation, it reminded Tex of creeks he'd visited as a boy at his grandparents' property in the Carolinas.

Redman looked back. Tex nodded for him to stay to the right. They continued walking until they reached the halfway point in this open area. Tex didn't hear Cracker behind him anymore, so he turned. Cracker had stopped. He was squatting about thirty feet back in the water behind a dead tree. Tex had moved past that same spot moments ago. Cracker didn't have a look of fear on his face. It was something else. His eyes scanned the creek beds on either side, then downstream. His eyes peered into the bamboo and tall grass.

Cracker's face suddenly changed, a different look.

The whole area exploded with machine-gun fire.

18

Redman went down, screaming, "I'm hit! I'm hit!"

Tex and Hammer dropped to the mud. A wide spray of bullets flew past, not ten inches overhead.

"Get down! Everyone down!" Lt. Mann shouted. No one needed to be told. "Return fire, return fire. But stay down." The familiar sound of M-16s entered the space, as every Marine in the patrol fired wildly down the creek in the other direction.

Boom! A B-40 rocket shot past, exploding into a tree behind Tex, Hammer, and Redman. The top half of the tree sheared off and fell into the creek, cutting the three men off from the rest of the patrol. VC machine guns tore into the trunk of the tree.

"We're trapped, Tex. We're gonna die here," Hammer said.

Tex looked behind them. The rest of the men had taken cover anywhere they could, except Sardelli. He froze for a moment, confused, then dashed toward the fallen tree. "Get down!" Cracker yelled. Too late. Three machine gun rounds raked across Sardelli's chest. He dropped dead in the water.

Tex looked away. Redman was groaning up ahead. Tex wanted

to look, see how he was doing, but the gunfire was relentless, now just a few inches above their heads. "Redman, you okay?"

"My leg. Hurts bad. Bleeding something fierce."

"Hammer, can you tie it off?"

"I can't move, Tex."

"He'll bleed out." He wondered why Redman didn't make his own tourniquet. Was he hurt too bad or just in a full-blown panic?

"Help me, Hammer," Redman pleaded.

"I want to, Red. I can't."

The gunfire back and forth was deafening. This was no small band of VC, Tex thought. Might be an entire platoon. Over the noise, Tex heard the radioman request permission to call in a fire mission.

"They're too close," Lt. Mann shouted back.

He was right. Tex guessed the VC set the ambush no more than twenty yards down creek from this open area, then waited for them to walk right into it.

"I'm bleeding out," Redman said. "Somebody do something!"

"Lieutenant," Hammer shouted. "Get us out of here!"

"Fire the LAAW!" the lieutenant shouted. "Both sides of the bank. And M-79s. Pour it on." The men obeyed. Rockets and grenades from the M-79 grenade launchers flew overhead, followed by explosions downstream. But there was no letup in the AK and machine-gun fire coming from the VC.

"We're still pinned down, Lieutenant," Tex said.

"Tex, can you help Redman?" he shouted back.

"Can't move. I lift my head up, they'll shoot it right off."

"Let me down there, Lieutenant." Tex recognized the medic's voice.

"Stay put, Doc," the lieutenant said.

"But he'll die."

"Stay put. Keep pouring on the fire, men."

Thump-thump-thump. A familiar sound came from the VC end of the battle.

"Oh no," Hammer said. "We're dead."

"Mortars!" someone shouted. "Get down."

Tex buried his face in the mud and waited for death.

Explosions ripped through the air all around him. One, then another, then another. The ground shook, they were so close. But the VC had overshot; the mortar rounds landed on the far bank of the creek. Tex knew they must have preset this location, preparing for the ambush. More rounds would come. They had minutes to live before the VC got the math right. Hammer was saying Hail Marys over and over again.

"God, please make it quick," Tex prayed quietly. "I haven't been walking with you like I should. Forgive all my sins."

"Cracker, get down!" It was the lieutenant's voice.

Tex looked back. As the smoke from the mortars cleared, he saw Cracker running low through the water for the cover of the fallen tree. Tracers flew inches above his helmet. He carried two M-79 grenade launchers. They looked like sawed-off shotguns. "They don't have any more time," Cracker shouted.

A B-40 rocket boomed. Flashed over Tex's head, right for the tree. He huddled in the mud. A roaring explosion sent water and wood splinters high in the air. He looked back. Cracker had to be dead. The biggest part of the tree was still there. In a little space between the tree and waterline, he saw Cracker lying in the water on his back. Cracker rolled over slowly, then got up. He repositioned himself against the thickest part of the tree, aimed the M-79 straight and level and fired, right where the VC rocket came from, maybe thirty yards down creek. Boom! Tex heard high-pitched screams. Marines cheered. Cracker had taken out the VC rocket man and maybe a few of his friends nearby.

For a moment, the enemy fire halted. "Pour it on!" Lt. Mann shouted.

Cracker moved down to where the fallen tree lay buried in the water and hopped over it. He ran toward them along the far side of the creek, where the three mortar rounds had just exploded, then ducked behind a large rock. Tex realized he'd picked that spot because the VC wouldn't fire there again.

The enemy gunfire began again, and once more, thump-thump-thump. "Mortars! Incoming!" someone shouted. Men scrambled for cover.

Tex buried his face for another mortar shower. This was it. No more chances.

"I'm cold," Redman said.

Three quick explosions. The center of the creek erupted. The mortars had made a direct hit on the fallen tree, sending chunks and pieces flying through the air. Limbs and branches rained down all around; several hit Tex and his friends. But none were that big.

Somehow, they were still alive.

When the smoke cleared, he looked back to the rock that Cracker was hiding behind. He was still there. One side of his face was covered in blood, but he was standing, still holding the M-79s. Tex watched as he reloaded and aimed the first one, angled it slightly upward, then fired. He tossed it in the creek, aimed the second in the same direction, and fired again. The grenades arched into the air. Moments later, two explosions down creek. After the second one, high-pitched shouts and cries of pain came from the same direction.

He did it! He'd taken out the VC mortar.

Again, the enemy gunfire halted. Bending over, Cracker ran across the creek right at them, leaping over rocks and tree limbs, water splashing all around. "Get up!" he shouted.

Tex got up on his hands and knees. Then stood in a crouch.

"I can't move," Hammer yelled, his face still buried in his hands.

"You gotta move," Cracker yelled. "I ain't going back without you." He quickly reloaded his grenade launcher, ran toward the enemy, and fired downstream. Then came back to the three men.

Tex helped Hammer to his feet. "We're okay, but Redman is hit. It's his leg."

"You guys fall back, then, I'll tie it off." Cracker dropped to his knees beside Redman.

Tex and Hammer scrambled back to join the others. But the lieutenant and the rest of the patrol were rushing out from their positions, firing everything they had down creek. Tex and Hammer turned around and joined them.

It reminded Tex of some Civil War scene.

"Cracker's got them on the run," the lieutenant yelled. He turned to the radioman. "Call in a fire mission, 125 meters up creek."

The whole patrol ran together, back toward Cracker and Redman, Doc leading the way. He split off when he reached the two men and dropped next to Cracker. Tex stopped a moment, to make sure Redman was okay.

"I think I got it stopped," Cracker said. "But he doesn't look good."

"Scoot over," Doc said. He looked at Cracker. "You don't look so good, either. Your face, it's covered in blood."

"My right side hurts a little, but I'm all right."

"Pull your flak jacket back," Doc said. Cracker's shirt was

covered in blood. "You're hit, Cracker. You got shrapnel wounds all over. Lie down."

While the Marines continued down creek, pouring fire in the enemy's direction, Lt. Mann walked back to take stock of the situation. "What do you need, Doc?"

"Redman needs to get back up to Cunningham ASAP. We need to medevac him out. Cracker too. Not sure how bad he's hit, but he's cut all over his right side."

"Take as many men as you need to haul them up that hill."

"I'll help," Tex said.

"Gonna need at least four men on each guy," Doc said, "considering how steep that hill is."

"Okay," Lt. Mann said. "Tex, round them up and get going." He bent down next to Cracker. "How are you making out, Aaron?"

"I'm okay, sir. My side hurts a good bit."

The lieutenant stood back up. "That was an amazing thing you did back there."

Cracker smiled through the pain, laid his head back on the muddy bank, and passed out.

19

When John had finished, Dave could tell he had more to say, but he was exhausted.

He stood up, so Dave did too.

"Say, Dave, you and I both know everything I just told you . . . that's the cleaned-up version. We weren't so careful with our language in those days. Fact is, the only adjectives any of us used back then were four-letter words. But that's not who I am now, so I—"

"I understand, John. No need to explain. I've talked with a lot of vets and read a lot of books on Vietnam."

"Well, I figured you'd understand," John said. He stretched then started walking toward the doorway leading back to the kitchen.

Dave thought this might be a good time to remind him of something. "You mentioned something about wanting to offer me some kind of deal I'd find impossible to refuse?"

"That's right, I did. How about I tell you that over some pulled pork sandwiches?"

Over the next ten minutes, John heated up some tasty pulled pork he'd taken from the refrigerator. He and Dave piled it high between slices of thick Texas toast, grabbed a bag of potato chips, refreshed their iced tea, and sat at a glass-topped dinette table in a little nook just off the kitchen. It had a great view of John's patio. From this angle, Dave could also see a swimming pool, a guest cottage, and an elaborate garden beyond that.

The break seemed to do John some good. After a few bites of his sandwich, the intense emotions that came out as he told the war story had subsided. "So, what'd you think?" he said.

"An amazing story, but I've got to know what happens next. I'm guessing Hammer and Redman are the two war buddies you've talked about."

John nodded as he chewed. When he swallowed, he said, "We stopped calling each other by our nicknames years ago, but we've stayed in touch pretty much ever since."

"How'd things turn out for them after the war?"

"They've both done very well. Paul, the one we called Redman, is a retired high school principal. Lives over in Louisiana. Allan, or Hammer, is still working some, but he's semiretired. He made a good deal of money in Dallas in the construction business."

"So Redman's leg, I mean Paul's leg, did it heal up okay?" Dave took a quick bite of his pork sandwich.

John looked down at his. "I'll tell you what, we're not going to get very far with this lunch here if I have to keep talking and using my manners at the same time. I've had enough lunch meetings over the years to know, the one asking the questions gets to eat his food while it's hot. You mind if I eat while I talk? I'm starving."

"You go right ahead," Dave said with his mouth half full.

"Paul's leg healed up fine, no permanent damage. He bled a

good bit that day, but the bullet didn't hit any major arteries. He'd have eventually bled out if something wasn't done, but he wasn't hurt as bad as we'd thought. We were all just scared. Hard to think straight with mortars coming at you." He swallowed and looked right at Dave. "We were all going to die that day. We've talked about it a number of times. One more mortar round and we'd have been blown to bits. And it was coming, there's no doubt in our minds. That bullet in Paul's leg would have been the least of his problems. Aaron saved our lives. I wouldn't be here today if he hadn't done what he did. None of us would."

"Seems like he earned that medal for sure."

"But there's more." He took a large bite, chewed a few moments. "See, we didn't know it then, but Aaron was way worse off than Paul. His shrapnel wounds alone were far more serious than Paul's leg. He had over a dozen pieces of metal stuck all up and down his right side and back. He'd tucked himself behind that big rock as best he could, but he was way too close when those mortars landed." John sat back, looked off to the side, like he was seeing it right now. "But it was like . . . he just ignored the pain. Fought right through it. Here we were, cowering in the mud like scared little kids, and he just decided he wasn't going to let those gooks get us."

He shook his head. "I'm sorry. I shouldn't have called them gooks. That's just a name someone came up with. Made it easier to shoot at 'em if you didn't have to think of them as real people."

"I know guys do that in every war," Dave said. "Come up with nicknames for the enemy."

He sighed. "We did. But I don't want to be calling those people names anymore. They didn't want to fight that war any more than we did."

A few moments passed in silence. Dave figured John had a right to them. When it seemed he had pulled himself together, Dave said, "You were talking about how Aaron came to your rescue when you guys were pinned down, about his injuries, I think."

"Right." He reached over, took the last bite of his sandwich, cleaned up with a few napkins, then continued. "We found out later that Aaron not only had shrapnel wounds but that somewhere in there he'd taken a bullet right through the midsection. Went clean through, somehow missed his vital organs. But word got back to us a few days after the medevac choppers got him out. He and Paul. They went back to a field hospital in Vandergrift, a bigger base not too far from Fire Base Cunningham. Lieutenant Mann pulled us all together and filled us in. He couldn't stop talking about what Aaron had done. All the guys were going on about it. Hammer said—I mean, Allan—'You need to put him in for the big one, Lieutenant.' He was talking about the Medal of Honor. The lieutenant said he'd already started the paperwork headed in that direction."

"What did the after-action reports say about the firefight?" Dave said.

"Well, turned out our guys had chased the VC out of the immediate area. They left in a hurry after what Aaron started. We searched the jungle, counted eleven enemy dead. We'd only lost poor Sardelli, and two wounded. Paul and Aaron. But Dave, that's not what was *supposed* to happen that day. Except for what Aaron did. Which he didn't have to do. I mean, it's not like we were good friends. If anything, we treated him pretty badly most of the time, or else ignored him altogether." A look of disbelief came over his face. "He came after us anyway. Paul, Allan, and I should have died that day in a nasty firefight, along with a dozen more of our guys. Of course, the three of us didn't need to read that in an after-action report. We knew we were dead men."

John looked back at Dave. "That's why we've got to find him. If he's still alive. We've got to find him, to thank him properly for saving our lives."

"You didn't get to see him again after that?"

"Only once. I've got a picture of the three of us at his bedside, Paul still on crutches."

"You do? Can I get a copy of that?"

"Sure. All three of us have a copy. The picture was taken in a bigger hospital about two months later in Quang Tri. A few years after the war, Paul saw a picture of Aaron getting the Medal of Honor at the White House. It happened a year after that hospital picture, in 1970."

"Were any of you there?"

"No, but we heard about it."

"Could I get a copy of that picture too?"

"I'll see that you do."

"You said things didn't go well for Aaron after that."

"From everything we heard, he had to stay in the hospital several more months. They shipped him back to the States. One of the guys heard he'd gotten addicted to painkillers. Like a lot of guys, he really struggled with all the head stuff. The guilt, the nightmares, the depression. He couldn't pull out of it. He became an alcoholic. Lost his family and eventually started living on the streets." John looked up and said, "That's where you come in, Dave."

"Is this the part where you make me that offer?"

"It is." He took a swig of his iced tea. "The guys and I talked about this, and we're all in agreement. We want to see Aaron again, if he's alive. And we want him at our next reunion to thank him properly for saving our lives. None of what I have here . . . my wife and kids, grandkids, my business, this big house. I wouldn't have any of it if it weren't for Aaron Miller and what he did for us that day in February of '69. The guys feel the same way. We've got to find him, if we can. After you called a little while ago, I got to thinking. You're researching this book, and you're a journalist. If anyone can find Aaron Miller, Dave, we think it's you."

"Me? But I'm not—"

"Hear me out. Here's the deal. I know you're trying to write this book here, and we think that's an honorable thing. And I want to help fund your research. Call it a research grant. We came up with an amount. Twenty thousand dollars. Use the money however you need."

"What?" Dave couldn't believe it.

"I'm not finished. Twenty thousand dollars to research your book and another twenty thousand to find Aaron Miller."

"You're going to pay me twenty thousand dollars just to find Aaron Miller?"

"The thing is," John said, "we want you to make finding Aaron job one."

That is not a problem, Dave thought. "I . . . I don't know what to say."

"Say you'll do it. I'm ready to start whenever you are."

"I'll do it."

"That's great, Dave. If you can find Aaron Miller for us, give Paul, Allan, and me a chance to see him again, thank him in person . . . well, you can't put a price tag on something like that."

"But what if . . ." Dave almost didn't want to say it.

"What if what?"

"What if I can't find him? What if he can't be found?"

"You mean . . . what if he's dead?"

Dave nodded.

"We've thought about that. So how about this . . . do the best you can, and if that's where the trail leads? Well, that's where it leads. We'll still give you the research grant, either way. So what do you say?"

Dave did his best to look professional and mature, but inside he was jumping up and down. "Sounds like an offer I can't refuse."

20

A few minutes past quitting time, Aaron Miller was in his storage room. He'd just put up all his tools, put the ones on chargers that needed it. At lunchtime, he'd gotten Billy Ames to agree that Aaron could come by after work, and they'd take another stab at visiting the wood deck, Aaron's little hiding place on the river. But he needed to get over to Billy's trailer right away. At this time of day the sun was already setting, and it would be totally dark in an hour. Didn't need to give Billy another reason to fear.

Once again, they'd be accompanied by Tess, Heather's mostly golden retriever. Only now, she was Billy's dog. On a trial basis, anyway. But knowing how sweet she was and how much Billy needed the company, Aaron felt pretty certain the arrangement would become permanent.

As he hurried toward Billy's trailer, he thought about the tearful farewell, when Heather had to leave Tess in Billy's care. When Aaron first asked Billy about it, Billy had flat-out refused.

111

But he'd softened right up when Aaron said what would happen if they had to bring Tess back to the animal shelter.

"You mean they'd put her to sleep?" he'd said. "A dog as pretty as that?"

"Good chance," Aaron had said. "From what Heather told me, Tess was just two days away from getting that needle when she picked her up. They just don't have the room to keep all the dogs folks drop off."

"They wouldn't put Tess down, would they? Seems like a fine dog."

"You and me both know life ain't always fair."

After that, it wasn't hard to get Billy to consider a trial basis. Aaron promised he'd help Billy however he could, but from what Heather had explained, Tess was pretty low maintenance. Aaron had checked in on the both of them the last few days, and Billy had no complaints. In fact, Aaron had never seen him smile so much.

Tess just had a way about her. If Aaron had even a little extra room in his storage room, he'd have taken her in himself. Of course, Sue wouldn't have approved, so this worked out for the best.

He'd turned down the path that led to Billy's trailer when he saw Mrs. Irene Hamlin wrestling with her screen door, right there on the corner lot. She was making quite a racket. Aaron wasn't worried about the noise so much as about Mrs. Hamlin toppling to the ground. She was in her late eighties and barely got around behind an aluminum walker. He ran up to help her. "Let me get that for you, Irene."

"It's been sticking lately," she said. "I know it's not locked, but it won't open."

"Let me take a look."

She backed her walker off to the side. "I was just out here enjoying this nice weather on my chair, then figured I better get in before it gets dark."

Aaron jerked it a few times, lifted it a little, and the catch broke free. "You shoulda called me or Sue. I'd have fixed it for you real quick."

"Well, you're always so busy, and it wasn't acting this bad till now."

He opened it wide for her then stood out of the way. "I've gotta get with a fellow now a few trailers down, and I don't have what I need to fix it. Are you going to need to get out here anymore tonight?"

"No, once I'm in, I'll be in for the night."

"Well, when I'm done with my friend, I'll go back to my place and get some WD-40 and a few tools. That's all it needs, some oil and a few adjustments. Should be good as new."

"Thank you so much, Aaron. But it can wait till morning, or even anytime tomorrow."

"No trouble," he said. "Won't take me ten minutes." He stood there to make sure she got in okay. A few months ago, he'd built her a nice ramp so she could get up in her trailer better. Well, safer anyhow than those old metal steps. He watched her as she made her way up. It still made him nervous, the thought of her falling backward before she reached the top.

Irene was such a sweet lady. She and her late husband, Moe, had lived here for years. Aaron had forgotten how long. Moe had actually passed away a year before Aaron got here. But Aaron almost felt like he'd known the man from all the stories Irene told. As she made it to the top, she turned and said, "Well, if you're set on fixing it tonight, I'll leave this porch light on for you, so you can see."

"Thanks, Irene. Appreciate it. So will you be having Thanksgiving here this year or with your family?" He wished there was some way he could talk her into moving in with them instead of living here all alone. She'd mentioned they brought it up all the time.

She made it through the doorway. "I'll be in Tampa with my kids and grandkids again. I don't much like the drive down there, but I do enjoy the company. But I told them, if I'm coming down there, I need somebody to drive me back home the next morning. Can't leave my cat shut up in this place by herself all those days. And of course, I'm already bracing myself for another round of them pressuring me to move down there for good." She looked around a moment at all the stuff on the screened porch and the property just beyond it. "But I don't want to leave here. It's the last place me and Moe were together."

She looked out toward the front. "We'd spend almost every evening sitting out on those chairs under Big Bertha there, sipping coffee till sunset, watching everyone walk by." She and Moe had named the huge, ancient oak tree on their corner. Its thick limbs spread all across their trailer, covered almost the entire lot in shade. "So how about you?"

How about him? No chance Aaron would spend Thanksgiving with family. "I'll probably be eating Thanksgiving down at the church again. That's my tradition. Around one, I serve Thanksgiving dinner at the street outreach center in the old downtown area, then around four I head over to our church and eat with a bunch of folks in the social hall."

Which reminded him, he better get over to Billy's. "You have a good evening, now." He closed the screened door. She waved and closed the trailer door.

One of his goals was to try and talk Billy into joining him this year for Thanksgiving. He knew it wouldn't be easy. From one of the many opinions Billy had already shared, Aaron knew he wasn't too fond of church, church people, or, as he put it, "the man upstairs."

21

Aaron walked up the ramp leading to Billy Ames's trailer. Before he even knocked, he heard Tess barking on the other side of the door. Then the hum of Billy's scooter. "All right, girl, I know you're excited we got company," he heard Billy say, "but you need to back up. That you, Aaron?"

"It's me."

The door opened. There sat Billy in his scooter, Tess smiling, beating him with her tail. "I was beginning to think you changed your mind. Gonna get dark before long; you still think we have time to do this?"

"Now's the best time," Aaron said. "We'll get to see the sunset. It's either now or first thing in the morning."

"Then we better go now," Billy said. "I ain't a morning person." He had Tess on a leash. Not that she'd run off; it was just park rules. As Billy rolled down the ramp he said, "Aren't we going to get eaten alive by mosquitoes?"

"In the summer it's bad. But it's been nice the last few weeks when I go. We should be all right."

They rolled along toward the back of the property, same way as before. Only this time, it was pretty clear Tess and Billy had become fast friends. She walked right beside him. Every few steps, she looked over to make sure he was all right. He talked the whole while, mostly telling stories about things Tess had done that he found amusing.

When they got to where the pavement gave way to grass, Billy didn't even pause. He just rolled that scooter right up and past the nature trail sign.

Aaron stepped onto the walkway. "It's not far to the deck from here." He walked a few feet and looked back. Billy had paused at the ramp, gave it a look of concern. But Tess walked past him, straight onto the deck till she got to the end of her leash. Billy didn't even let the leash get tight. He revved the scooter up and followed.

"If we're quiet through here," Aaron said, "we could start to see some wildlife." He looked up. The deep blue sky overhead gave way to a dark orange, then shifted toward lighter hues of pinks and reds as he gazed toward the west. Clouds blocked most of the sun, just inches above the horizon. But Aaron didn't mind; clouds at sunset gave God more canvas to paint on. "Isn't that something?" he said quietly to Billy as they walked along. Billy didn't answer. Aaron looked back. The expression on Billy's face said plenty.

They wound their way through the wooden walkway till they finally reached the deck on the Suwannee. Here the beauty of the sky was joined by the sky's reflection off the water, as well as an amazing variety of palms, cypresses, and oaks. As if on cue, an osprey came swooping past them downriver, then soared overhead, disappearing a few moments later over the darkened tree line.

"Nothing to be afraid of back here, is there, Billy?"

"No. This is . . . very nice."

Billy sat in silence a few minutes. Aaron realized it was the longest span of time they'd been together that Billy hadn't filled with chatter. Aaron looked down at Tess; her gaze was focused on Billy. Billy kept his right arm around her shoulder, and she sat there next to him. Finally, Aaron worked up the nerve to talk about the thing he wanted to get to. "There's another place I'd like to take you sometime soon."

"Oh, where's that?"

"Where I go to church on Sunday." He was talking quietly. Out here on the deck, it seemed fitting.

"I don't have any way to get to church."

"Well, our church has a bus that picks up people who need rides. And a special bus for folks in wheelchairs. I've seen quite a few vets on that bus. You can tell by the clothes some of them wear and their baseball caps. I'd ride in that one if you'd go with me."

"You know I don't like church or church people, Aaron." He was looking straight ahead. "I don't even believe in God, not really. I wonder, considering how your life has turned out, how you could believe in him, either."

Aaron wished he knew the right thing to say. He wasn't any good at this sort of thing. "The way I see it, I don't have a choice."

"Course you have a choice. That's what makes us different from the animals. Why the world's so screwed up. Humans got the power to choose."

"What I mean is," Aaron said, "if there was no God, then who saved me? Because somebody sure did. I didn't save myself."

Billy looked up at him. "What do you mean, 'saved you'? That's just a dumb cliché religious folks say. 'Are you saved? You need to get saved.'"

"It may be a cliché," Aaron said. "And I don't know about anybody else's life. But I needed saving. I got no doubts on that." He leaned up against the wood rail. "I was a mess when I got back from Nam. Some guys seemed to snap out of it, at least to where they could function. For some reason, I never could. I was all tore up inside. The guilt, for one thing, was killing me. All those terrible things we did. Didn't matter that we were just following orders, or doing things that had to be done. Those were the dumb clichés, you ask me." He released an involuntary sigh. "Horrible scenes would just keep replaying in my head. I took all the drugs and booze I could, trying to shut them down, find some peace. But nothing worked. Years went by. Couldn't keep a job. Lost my family. Wound up out on the streets." He looked down at Billy. "I sank to the bottom and stayed there, Billy. Should have been dead at least a dozen times."

"So . . . how'd you get out?"

"That's the question, isn't it?" Aaron said. "I was stuck, all right. Then about this same time back in '87, I went to a Thanksgiving dinner at a church. Course, I did that every year. Figured I could sit through one more preacher sharing about God's love if it meant a good turkey dinner with all the fixings. But something happened that year, can't explain it. For some reason, everything the man said made sense, like God was saying it all to me. Something broke in my heart, like some kind of drain opened and all the crud poured right out of me. That's why I love Jesus, Billy. Ain't a cliché for me, being saved. If Jesus didn't exist, then who saved me back in '87 from all that emptiness? And who's saved me at least a hundred times since then?"

He looked back toward the sunset. The sun had fallen below the horizon now. "Truth is, I need him every day. 'Bout just as much."

22

There was a big splash in the water. Aaron turned in time to see a largemouth bass zipping away. Tess stood up and pressed her head through the railing to get a better look. "So, Jesus . . . or God, is like your crutch," Billy said.

Aaron was a little surprised. Seemed Billy wanted to keep talking on this subject. "I guess so," he said. "But talk about using a cliché. People always talk like anyone who turns to God just needs a crutch. As if their lives were going so well on their own." He looked at Billy again. "Everybody's weak, Billy. Nobody's got their act together. They just act and talk like they do in front of other people. Somebody who says they need God, to me, is just being honest."

Aaron thought he better wrap this up since Billy was starting to get edgy. He looked up at the sky. "See, I'm wondering how people can see all this beauty and *not* believe in God. That doesn't make sense to me."

"But look at what he's done to me!" Billy was getting more than a little edgy. "Look how my life's turned out. I got nothing. I never had nothing. And now my life is over, and I still got nothing. I hate him."

"The Bible says only a fool can believe there is no God. Hating him at least gets you one step up from that."

"So how come you don't hate him?" Billy said. "Except for the fact you still got legs, you're as bad off as me. Worse in some ways. I never had a family. You had one and lost it. I never lived out on the streets like you did. At least I've had a disability check come in every month, sorry as it is. It's still better than what you have. And look at you now, you still got nothing, living in that old garage back there. I can at least afford that stinkin' trailer."

Some of what Billy said stung a little. Especially the part about Aaron losing his family. "Sounds like you got at least a few things you should be grateful for."

"What? No, you're missing the point."

"The point being . . . I should hate God like you do?"

"That's right. What good's he ever done for you, or for me?"

Aaron thought a minute. It was some question. He could hardly believe Billy asked it. Like he just lobbed a softball right over the plate. "He sent his Son Jesus to earth, Billy. Let him die on the cross to pay for all the bad things I done and all the bad things people done to me. I may have lost everything, but God didn't take them. Not the way you mean, anyhow."

"Then who did?"

Aaron smiled.

"What are you smiling at?"

"I said almost the exact same words back in '87, after years of living on the streets, totally strung out on drugs and booze. I had nothing, lost everything. Didn't see a way to ever get any of it back. I only believed in God long enough to hate him."

Billy looked at him like he didn't know what to say. "So . . . what happened?"

"I was eating my Thanksgiving dinner after that preacher got done. I was talking to this young man at least half my age. It wasn't as if he'd said something no one ever said before. Maybe it was just my time to hear it."

"What'd he say?"

"He asked me a question. He said if I had a teenager that was about to go out with his friends, and I loved him and worried about what might happen to him, I would tell him all these things not to do, so he would stay safe. And then if he went out and ignored everything I said, did whatever he wanted and whatever his friends talked him into, and they got into all kinds of trouble, would my son blame me for everything that happened to him?" Aaron let the question sit out there a moment.

"Guess he wouldn't," Billy said.

"Who should he blame?"

"I guess himself, maybe his friends."

"Why shouldn't he blame his father?"

"I get your point."

"That's what I was doing back then. What you're doing now. Most of the people who blame God for everything never even try things his way, so how can they blame him when it all goes wrong? But they do. I did. For years, till eating that meal. That day, the lights came on. And I saw that all I ever did was do things my way, my whole life. And all it ever did was get me in trouble and more trouble. That young man went on to explain the mercy God had for me, even though I hated him. The things Jesus did to make it right. That's why I'm inviting you to church, Billy. So you can hear about this stuff for yourself. I'm no good at explaining this sort of thing."

Billy sat there a few moments. Aaron couldn't read him. Tess seemed to know he was a little tense. She leaned on him, laid her head on his knee.

"You don't gotta come to church with me, Billy. I'll still be your friend. And if you want me to, I'll stop asking."

Billy looked down, past the legs he didn't have to the wooden deck. "No, I don't want that."

"You don't want to come, or you don't want me to keep asking?"

"You can keep asking." He looked up at the water and the tree line across the way. "As long as you're not too pushy."

"Was that pushy just now?"

"A little bit."

The three of them stayed put a few minutes more, no one saying anything. Aaron finally suggested they get back before it got too dark. As they stepped off the deck, down the ramp, and onto the grass, Billy said, "I suppose I might even go with you to that church. Maybe not this week. But someday."

23

It was Saturday morning. It worked out that Dave's Houston trip ended on a Friday, so he was able to take the weekend off. A hungry, ambitious reporter named Jeremy Arlo took over Dave's wire editing job on weekends and whenever Dave was out of town. Jeremy's regular job was writing local stories, human interest mostly. He was going to love this new development.

Dave sat at the breakfast table in his mother's condo, waiting for her and Jake to join him so he could share his big news. He smiled as he read his name on the gold debit card John Lansing's accountant had given him. Dave had checked—all the money John had promised was already in the account.

The debit card only weighed a couple of ounces, but Dave felt a much greater weight on his shoulders because of what it represented. He'd come to care about John, and he didn't want to let him down. He really wanted to make this reunion happen for him and his two veteran friends. If Aaron Miller was alive somewhere, Dave would find him.

Dave set the debit card on the dinette table then said another quick prayer of thanks. This opportunity was amazing. It was like God had answered a prayer Dave didn't even have the faith to pray. He was actually going to be able to write this book now, something that had been brewing in his heart for almost twenty years.

He remembered the exact moment the idea came, just a few weeks after the first Gulf War. The troops had won an incredible victory—in two months' time. He and his mother lived in Chicago then. The city threw a parade to honor the returning troops. They both stood in front of the television, watching the whole thing unfold down Michigan Avenue. Crowds cheered and waved banners, expressing their patriotism and gratitude.

Then an amazing thing happened.

His mom had just finished saying, "Our boys didn't get this, you know. Your father's friends, when they came home from Vietnam. They got treated terrible."

Dave looked down at her. Her lip was trembling. He put his arm around her. As they watched, a large group of Vietnam vets began marching in procession right behind all the Desert Storm troops. And the crowds cheered and waved at them just as loudly. Dave saw tears streaming down many of those old soldiers' faces. He started choking up; so did his mom.

Something seemed to change in the country then. A healing had begun. The nation that had turned its back on these troops when they were young now realized the terrible injustice they had inflicted upon them. It was time to welcome them home, time to honor them for the valiant sacrifices so many had made.

That was the moment Dave had decided to write his book, to honor the heroes of the Vietnam War, and to try to connect more with his father, with the war that had parted them.

"Okay, Davey, I'm here. What's up?" His mother's voice jolted him from his thoughts. He turned. She was walking down the hall from her bedroom, still in her bathrobe. She set her coffee mug on the dinette table.

"I really want to tell you and Jake together." He stood up and walked toward Jake's bedroom. "Jake, you almost ready?"

Jake's door opened. He was dressed in his sweats, holding his Panthers duffel bag. "This going to take long, Dad? I've got to be down at the gym for practice by 9:30."

"Won't take five minutes, I promise. Just some news I want to tell you and Grandma."

Jake followed him back to the dinette table. "Is it about your book?"

"Yeah."

"C'mon, Davey, the suspense is killing me," his mother said. "I could hardly pay attention to my devotional."

He and Jake sat beside her around the table, and Dave told them the whole story. Afterward, he picked up the debit card. "Here's the golden card."

"Davey, that's wonderful. It's like you won the lottery."

"Not quite, Mom. But it's a pretty big deal."

"Wow, Dad. That's sweet. It's almost like he's hiring you to be a private detective. You have any idea how you're going to find this guy?"

"I've done some investigative journalism before. I have a few threads I can pull."

"I'm so happy for you, Davey. I been praying for your book thing every morning."

"Thanks, Mom, I appreciate that."

"So when's this thing start?" Jake said.

"Right away."

"What about your job at the paper?" he asked. "Can you do both at the same time?"

Dave sighed, shook his head. "That's where it gets a little sticky. I don't see how."

"You're going to quit the paper?" his mother said.

"Not quit, Mom. I'm hoping Harry won't freak out when I tell him. I'm going to ask for a leave of absence."

"For how long?"

"I'll start with three months. But that's just a guess. I figure I'll need at least two months for my book."

"You think you can find this Vietnam vet in a month?" Jake said.

Dave shrugged. Jake looked at his watch, then stood up. "This is so cool, Dad. Can I tell the guys?"

"Not just yet. I need to talk to Harry first. I'm hoping I can reach him today. I'll call you when the coast is clear."

"I'm real happy for you." Jake came over and gave him a shoulder hug, then pecked his grandmother on the cheek. "Gotta go." He hurried out of the kitchen and out the front door.

Dave's mom got up from the table. "I'm going to make some more coffee. Want some?"

"I don't think so. I'm going to call Harry, see if I can meet with him this morning."

"You think he'll be mad, maybe let you go?"

"I hope not. I have no idea where it's going to end up, though. I've got plenty of money for the next few months from this." He held up the debit card. "But when I'm through, there's no telling how long it'll take for me to get a book deal. Or *if* I'll get one. Publishing is tricky. I'm probably going to still need my job at the paper when I'm done."

"Don't you worry about that. I just know you're going to get your book published. You're such a good writer."

"Hope you're right. But there's already a lot of good books about it on the shelves."

"But there's none of them written by Davey Russo. Those people are going to love your book."

Dave smiled. He had at least one guaranteed fan. "There's one thing I need to mention. I didn't want to say it in front of Jake just yet. I may be doing some traveling on this project. Are you going to be all right with that?"

"Me? Don't worry about me. I'm all set here. I got Sally and Mary to keep me company, and the other ladies at the church. And Jake is here."

"You think Jake will be okay with this? I didn't tell him yet, but he seems like—"

"Jake will be fine. He's doing real good now. And he's so busy with all his friends and his basketball games."

"Well, I'm going to make sure I schedule my trips so I don't miss a single one."

"He'll like that. You're not going to be gone for Thanksgiving, right?"

"Not a chance."

"Well, you go do this. We'll be fine."

Dave put the debit card back in his wallet, got up, and gave his mom a hug. "I'm going to call Harry, then get a shower. I'll let you know how things turn out." As he walked down the hall, he started tensing up.

He was dreading the call to Harry Warden.

24

Dave walked through the newsroom, winding through the cubicle section. He saw Harry up ahead in his office, staring at his computer.

"Hey, Dave." It was Jeremy Arlo, the reporter who covered for Dave when he was away. "How was the trip?"

Dave stopped by his cubicle. "It was good."

"Read your stories about the basketball team. Too bad they got knocked out of the tournament so early."

"They didn't seem too shaken up. I think they were jazzed just to be there. It was pretty exciting."

"Will you be back at it Monday?"

What should he say? No, he wouldn't be back? "Actually, I'm not sure yet," he said. "I better get in there. Got a meeting with Harry." Jeremy nodded then turned back to his computer. Dave walked up to Harry's glass door, knocked twice, then entered.

"Have a seat, Dave. Just let me clean up this last paragraph."

Dave sat in the office chair closest to the window and watched Harry peck away with his index fingers. A few moments later, he sat back in his chair. "Now that was a piece of junk. I might have to let that new girl go. She's fresh out of college, can't stand to just write what I tell her. Wants to turn everything into a masterpiece."

"Maybe she'd be better off writing for a magazine."

"That's good. I'll use that when I give her the bad news. So . . . what's up? I've only got about twenty minutes."

Dave didn't know where to start. He leaned forward, put one arm on Harry's desk. "Something unexpected happened on my trip." It was straightforward, a decent headline.

"Which part?" Harry said. "The basketball tournament part or the Vietnam hero part?"

"The Vietnam hero."

"Oh?"

"You know this was just supposed to be an ordinary interview, one of dozens more I had planned."

"Yes."

"And I told you it would be months before anything came of this, because I'm having to do this in my spare time, using my own money."

"I know this too." Harry's eyebrows drew close together.

"Well, something's come up that's changed all that."

"What do you mean?" He sat up in his chair.

"The Vietnam hero I interviewed, I told you he was a millionaire oil executive, right?"

"I think I remember that."

"You should have seen his house, by the way. It was . . ." Dave could tell Harry wasn't in the mood for side stories. "Well, I didn't actually even hear his war story while I was there."

"What did he do, offer you a job?"

"Not exactly."

"You're leaving me," he said. "I mean, the paper."

"Not exactly."

"Well, c'mon, Dave. What are you saying?"

"I thought I had twenty minutes. I've only been talking two."

"I said twenty minutes when I thought you wanted to talk business as usual."

"All right, I'm sorry, Harry. I didn't plan on this. Nobody could. It's actually pretty crazy." Dave told Harry the whole story. He tried to put it as gently as he could, hoping to leave the door wide open after his leave of absence.

"When's this thing supposed to start?" Harry said.

"If we can work it out, I'd like to start on it right away."

"You can't even give me two weeks?"

"If you need it. Of course I will. But you and I both know, Jeremy out there is chomping at the bit to do my job. He's been working out okay, filling in for me, hasn't he?"

"He's all right. He doesn't have your instincts, still have to review everything he does. If I give him the wire desk, I'll need to get someone to take his place."

"Maybe. Maybe not. He's single. It'll stretch him, but I bet if you ask him, let him know it's only for a few months, he might be willing to do both jobs and just pocket the extra money. You might have to pawn off some of his smaller assignments on others, but I don't think it would be anything close to a personnel crisis."

Harry sat back in his chair again. "You sure this is only going to be a few months?"

"Not totally. But I think in a month, I'll be able to give you a firmer time line. I know how much time I'll need to finish my book research. The variable is finding this guy, Aaron Miller."

"And I can take you completely off the payroll?" Harry said. "I'm going to need to pay Jeremy more if we do this."

"You can take me off starting Monday." Dave knew Jeremy Arlo would jump at this thing. He just hoped Jeremy didn't learn the job too well and leave Dave stranded when his leave of absence was up.

"Well," Harry said, "I guess that's it then." He shook his head. "I knew when I hired you it was only a matter of time before I'd lose you to something better."

"You're not losing me, Harry. We're talking a few months."

"We'll see."

Dave stood up; so did Harry. Dave stuck out his hand. Harry shook it. "You're still my boss, Harry."

"Not exactly," he said. "If I were still your boss, I'd say get back in here Monday, first thing."

25

Over the next several days, Dave worked through a check-list of search ideas; some he'd created from his days as an investigative journalist, some from things John Lansing had said about Aaron Miller.

But every lead he'd followed led to a dead end. He was sitting now at a Panera Bread not far from his mother's condo.

The problem wasn't finding an Aaron Miller; the problem was there were hundreds of them nationwide. Before hearing John's war story, Dave had never heard the name before. But there were fifty-eight Aaron Millers in Houston alone, fifty more in Atlanta, forty-five in Miami. Every major city in the southeast had about that number.

But who was to say his Aaron Miller was even living in the southeast? All John knew was that Aaron had a Southern accent. Dave had assumed he might live in a major city, because John said Aaron had been living out on the streets at some point. More homeless people lived in big cities than small towns.

But who was to say which city? Most homeless people didn't have a listing in the White Pages. Or carry a cell phone. Or have an address. And John's information was over two decades old.

And who was to say Aaron Miller was even alive anymore? Dave had read a study that said the average life span for a homeless man was forty-five years. Aaron could be dead right now.

Is that what Dave should be searching for? Evidence of Aaron's death?

He got up to refill his coffee for the third time then looked at his watch. Houston was an hour back in time. John had given him his private cell number, with permission to call anytime. But John said he'd better get comfortable leaving voice mails. Dave pulled out his cell phone. If John could remember what city Aaron was from, that would narrow down Dave's search from hundreds of people to possibly a few dozen.

But he wasn't that optimistic. He remembered a conversation he'd had with John, standing in his massive foyer. "Aaron was a private kind of guy," John had said. "He never opened up to anyone. And to be honest, we didn't work too hard at getting him to share. We weren't exactly touchy-feely types."

Dave decided he had to try, see if he could flush out a few more details without irritating his benefactor too much. He dialed the number and waited for the voice mail message.

"Hello . . . Dave? Is that you?"

"Mr. Lansing, I didn't expect to reach you."

"Then why'd you call?"

"No, I meant I expected your voice mail."

"Well, you got the real deal, but I only have a minute. What's up? Make any progress?"

"Not exactly," Dave said. "I'm mostly eliminating the counterfeits."

"There a lot of Aaron Millers out there?"

"A ton of them."

"He's the only one I ever knew."

"Me too," Dave said. "I'm thinking if I could narrow down the scope of the search, get a fix on what city he might be from, that would eliminate a mountain of wasted time."

"I'm not sure I can help you with that, Dave. Like I said, I don't recall Aaron ever mentioning where he was from."

"Could you tell me at least what part of the South he might be from? There's different kinds of Southern accents."

"He wasn't from Texas, I know that. But I'm not sure I know enough distinction between the others to be of any help."

"Did he ever talk about his family? Did he have a wife or any kids?"

There was a long pause. "Hmmm."

"Is that a yes?"

"I do recall Aaron talking about his wife once. Yeah, I remember now. It was near Christmastime. Aaron was holding on to this photo he'd just gotten in the mail of his two kids, real young, from what I remember. But that was in '68 or '69, so they've gotta be about . . ."

"Probably my age," Dave said.

"Yeah, sounds about right. Anyway—I can't believe I didn't tell you this—about twenty years ago, after one of our reunions, I hired this private detective to try to find him. But I wasn't doing as well then, and he charged an arm and a leg. I had to cut him loose. But before I did, he found Aaron's son. It didn't go anywhere, though. The kid was in college then, law school, I think. He said he hadn't seen his dad since he was five and had no idea where he might be. I think that's when I found out Aaron had been living out on the streets. His boy told my private eye that. But he made it real clear, he wasn't interested in helping us find Aaron and he couldn't help even if he wanted to. His mother told him his father was just some homeless drunk and they had no idea where he was."

Dave sighed. Then he thought of something. "Did your private detective say where he found Aaron's son or what his name was?"

"He did, but kids go out of state for college all the time."

"I know, but at least it's something."

"Well, he was going to Baylor. I remember, because that's in Waco, about three hours north of here. I was surprised, because I was pretty sure Aaron wasn't from Texas. But then I let it go. Like I said, the boy wasn't living with Aaron, hadn't seen him for years. So Aaron could be anywhere."

"You're probably right," Dave said.

"Well, I've got to be going. Call me if you need me, any time," John said.

"Oh wait, the name," Dave said. "Do you remember what his son's name was?"

"Uh . . . yes. Steven, or Steve. Steve Miller. I remembered because of that rock band by the same name. Keep in touch."

———————————

Dave had stayed long enough at Panera Bread to get close to the dinner hour. He called his mother to let her know he wouldn't be home.

"That's okay," she said. "Sally called an hour ago. She asked if I'd like to go out shopping with her. I'll call her back and tell her to come get me. Then we'll just get something out, the two of us."

"What about Jake?"

"He's got a late practice, then some of the guys are going out for pizza after."

That worked out. "I shouldn't be out late, but I did want to mention, I might be flying to Texas tomorrow."

"Really?" she said. "To meet that oil man, the one who gave you the money for your book?"

"No. I'm working on a lead for the man I'm trying to find. This time I'll be flying into Dallas."

"President Kennedy got shot there."

"I know."

"You need me to drive you to the airport?"

"No, I'll be fine. I'll just leave the car in the parking garage till I get back."

"But you have to pay for that."

"I got that gold debit card, remember?"

"That's right."

He could almost see her smiling on the other end.

"Well, just let me know your plans when they're steady. You're coming back in time for Thanksgiving on Thursday, right?"

"I definitely am. This might just be two days. Leave on Tuesday, back on Wednesday."

"It'll be expensive buying tickets at the last minute," she said. "Especially on a holiday week."

"It's not a problem, Mom."

"Okay, then. You have fun."

"I'll try. But I'll see you tonight. Probably get home before you will. But I might not see you in the morning. I'm going to try and book an early flight."

"See you then."

He hung up as he walked to the counter. He ordered a bowl of soup and a sandwich. After refreshing his drink, he picked up his food and went back to the same booth. As he ate, he checked flight times from Gainesville to the Dallas–Fort Worth area.

After talking with John, Dave had decided to search for attorneys named Steve Miller practicing in the larger cities in Texas, starting with those closest to Baylor University. Houston was three hours away, but Dallas and Fort Worth were only an hour and a half. There were only a handful of attorneys named Steve Miller to wade through.

He could try calling them, but he had the money to make the trip and thought he'd get better results if he was there on the ground. So tomorrow, he'd fly in, rent a car, make some calls, and see what turned up. It was a long shot, but a long shot was better than no shot.

Even if his efforts proved futile by the end of all this, he'd have a month's worth of expenses to show how hard he tried.

26

Karen sat back at her desk in the main model home. She had just walked a middle-aged couple through all three models. They seemed pretty excited. But then, most of them did at this stage. They'd asked some decent questions, taken the brochures. The woman said they were still looking but would definitely keep their subdivision on the list of ones to consider.

Not exactly signing on the dotted line.

It was Thanksgiving week, and she was trying to remain thankful. But so far, she had no sales in the last three weeks. And the last one had been Gail's, not hers. It was almost six o'clock, time to close up. Gail had already left a few minutes ago.

Karen's cell phone rang. It was Steve. What could he be calling about?

"Hey, Karen. You're never going to guess who I just got off the phone with."

No one came to mind. "Who?"

"A writer researching a book about Vietnam heroes."

"Okay . . ." What could that have to do with her . . . or with him?

"He was asking about our dad."

"Dad? He didn't fight in Vietnam."

"Not our dad, Mark. Our . . . *other* dad. Our first dad."

"Aaron Miller?"

"Yeah, can you believe it? I wasn't going to take the call, but my secretary said this guy was in town trying to locate the son of a Vietnam War hero. All he knew was that this man had a son named Steve Miller and that he was an attorney. She normally wouldn't have put something like this through, but she thought I might want to speak with him. She didn't know our dad was a war hero."

"Neither did I," Karen said.

"You and me both."

"How did he find you?"

"Sounds kind of like a needle-in-a-haystack sort of deal. Anyway, you've got to hear the best part. Our dad—our birth dad—won the Congressional Medal of Honor in Vietnam."

"What!"

"I'm not kidding. That's what the man said."

"Are you sure this is legit?"

"It piqued my curiosity, so I took the call. The writer's name is Dave Russo. He said this is no joke. He's trying to locate a war hero named Aaron Miller."

"Good luck with that," she said.

"I know. Anyway, he'd picked up a lead that Aaron Miller had a son with my name who was an attorney, and he's been contacting Steven Millers all day. I was the last one on his list in the Fort Worth area. He couldn't believe it when I told him Aaron Miller was our father. He got really excited and wanted to know if we could meet this evening or tomorrow morning. But Aileen and I have this dinner party tonight, and tomorrow my day is packed. I couldn't squeeze him in anywhere. I'm trying to get everything done so I can take Thursday and Friday off for Thanksgiving."

Karen knew where this was going. "You didn't tell him about me."

A long pause. "I'm sorry, but I did."

"Steve . . ."

"Karen, you should have heard him. I was just so stunned by what he said, I didn't even think. I said there was no way we could touch base before Thursday, and before I knew it, I blurted out—"

"'But I have a sister . . .'"

"Pretty much. Look, I'm sorry. He's going to call you in about five minutes."

"You gave him my cell?"

Another long pause. "Karen, just tell him no. Really, I wasn't thinking. I just found myself wanting to help this guy. He sounded really nice. I wish I could meet him myself, find out more about this Medal of Honor thing."

"But we don't know where our birth dad is."

"I know, I told him that. But he still wanted to meet. He said you'd be surprised how little details can make a big difference in something like this. He used to work as an investigative reporter in Atlanta. He thought if he interviewed one of us, we might shed some light on our dad's whereabouts."

Why would she want to shed light on the whereabouts of this man . . . Aaron Miller? She sighed. "I don't know, Steve."

"Look, I'm sorry for putting you in the middle of this. So, really, just tell him no, you're not interested. He'll probably try to talk you into it, but just say it was a long time ago and you don't want to get involved. Tell him that if he's still interested, he can call me back after Thanksgiving, and I'll try to make a time to see him myself."

"I guess I can do that."

"Well, I've got to go. Sorry, Karen. But if you do wind up meeting with him, I want to hear all about it at Thanksgiving on Thursday."

"I don't think I'm . . . well, we'll see."

This was not how Karen wanted to end her day. After ending the call, she got up from her desk, kept her cell phone, and walked over to the two other model homes. After she'd gone through the normal lockup routine for all three, she looked at her watch. She had no energy to go home and cook. If she left now, she could probably beat the crowd at Chili's.

Her phone rang. She didn't recognize the number, which probably meant it was that writer. It rang again. She thought about letting it go to voice mail but decided a guy that had come all this way on some kind of manhunt would just keep calling again and again. "Hello?"

"Hi, is this Karen? Karen Miller?"

He had a really nice voice. "It is."

"My name is Dave Russo. I was just talking with your brother, Steve, a little while ago."

"I know, he called to let me know."

"He did. That's great. Did he tell you what this is about?"

"He did. Something about our birth father, Aaron Miller. And him winning the Medal of Honor."

"He won it back in 1970."

"That's . . . really something." Her father hadn't walked out on them until 1973. Her mother had never told them about the medal.

"Say, I know this must sound a little crazy and totally out of the blue here. I'm almost in a state of shock that I made this connection with you guys. You have no idea how many Aaron Millers there are in the world."

She didn't, and she didn't care.

"But I was wondering if we could meet and talk for a little while."

"I don't think so . . . what did you say your name was?"

"Dave."

"I don't think that's a good idea, Dave. There's really nothing to talk about. Aaron Miller was responsible for the biological side of things for Steve and me, but that was about all. He walked out on us when we were just little kids. We haven't seen him since."

"I know. I'm sorry."

Was he apologizing for their father's neglect or just feigning compassion here? It seemed like genuine sympathy.

"How about this?" he said. "I flew in from Florida this morning, so my body clock is one hour ahead. I'm really starving. How about you let me take you out to dinner? Any place you like, my treat. We can talk there. After that, I'll never bother you again. I promise."

She really was hungry, and he really did have such a nice voice. "Do you know how to get to Chili's?" *What am I saying?*

"I love Chili's. But I'm not sure where the one you have in mind is."

"Where are you now?"

"I'm on Southlake Boulevard, not far from your brother's law office."

"You're closer than I am." She started giving him directions. He said he could just put it in his GPS if she told him which location. So she did. They agreed to meet there in twenty minutes. "Could you get us a booth as soon as you get there?" she said. "I'll look for you."

"Sounds great."

"So . . . what do you look like?" she said. "How will I know how to find you?"

"Right. I've got brownish hair. I'm forty-five years old. I'll be wearing a brown leather jacket and blue jeans. Well, if they've got the heat on, I'll probably take the jacket off. So you'll see my long-sleeved green shirt. If you have any trouble, just dial my cell and we'll use them like walkie-talkies till we connect."

"Okay," she said. "I'm heading out the door now."

"Great. And Karen, really, thanks so much for doing this. I can't believe I've found you. Wait, that sounds a little weird." He laughed.

"I know what you mean," she said. "I just hope you're still excited when you hear how little I have to say." She said goodbye and locked the model home. As she made her way to the car, she still couldn't believe she'd let herself get talked into this.

Then she thought, *If his looks match his voice . . . this could be interesting.*

27

Dave sat at the booth in Chili's, enjoying the aroma of a sizzling plate of steak fajitas passing by. *Steak faji-tas it is.* He looked toward the door, saw a number of couples and four college kids, but no women his age yet. It had been almost twenty minutes since the call, so Karen could arrive any moment. He wondered what she looked like. He'd forgotten to ask.

He looked down at his notepad at a list of possible questions to ask her. "Karen Miller," he mumbled aloud. Was she married? She couldn't be, or she'd have corrected him when he'd called her by her maiden name. And if she was married, she wouldn't have so readily accepted a dinner invitation without mentioning the need to call her husband. If Dave were the husband, he'd struggle a bit if his wife had dinner out with another man. Even if it was just business.

Anne, his ex-wife, wasn't a professional and never had an occasion to go out to dinner with any man but him. But half the people Dave interviewed in Atlanta were women, and half the time the interviews took place in restaurants. Nothing had ever happened, but he knew that part of his job often irritated Anne. Especially when she'd see what some of the women Dave had interviewed looked like when their pictures accompanied his articles.

Anne never felt like she measured up.

But she did. She was beautiful, even without makeup and spending forty minutes fixing her hair. But he hadn't told her she was. Not nearly enough.

He reached for his iced tea then looked up as the front door opened again. An attractive brunette walked in, wearing a navy blue wool coat. Some people partially blocked his view, but she looked like she could be the right age. She said something when the hostess greeted her then glanced over toward the booths and tables. She hadn't seen him yet. She unbuttoned her coat. He modified his initial assessment of her.

She wasn't merely attractive. She was stunning.

Please let that be her.

He didn't know why he thought that; this wasn't a date. It might not even be her. She scanned the restaurant again. He had the impulse to wave, but what if it wasn't Karen? He'd taken his jacket off. He'd told her he was wearing a green shirt, hadn't he? Finally, her eyes settled on him. She looked him over for a moment, smiled, and waved.

He waved back as she made her way toward him. Her smile, the way it matched the brightness in her eyes, only added to her beauty. *Now you're being silly*, he thought. But he couldn't take his eyes off her. He looked at her hands, both of them.

No wedding ring.

He stood up. Suddenly he felt nervous. *Calm down.* He'd only ever felt this way after seeing one other woman in his life.

Anne. He still remembered. She was sitting across the room in their English literature class at DePaul University.

Karen reached the table. "Dave?"

"It's me," he said.

She took off her coat and purse, set them in the seat across from him. She held out her hand. "It's nice to meet you."

Dave fought an urge to cling to her hand a few moments longer. He'd suddenly forgotten all about his Aaron Miller questions.

"Is everything all right?" she said.

"What? Yes, everything's fine. This is a little embarrassing though. I need to go wash my hands. I didn't want to do it until you got here in case I missed you." He held up his left hand; it had an ink smear on it. "Feel free to order if the waitress comes, anything on the menu," he said.

"Do you mind if I start with the chips and salsa?"

"I love their salsa here, just the right kick." He smiled. "I'll be right back."

He walked into the men's room. The double sink was clear. He walked up, leaned both hands on the counter, and stared at himself in the mirror. *What are you doing? Get ahold of yourself. It's just an interview*. It was so unsettling. It felt like much more than an interview, something surreal. But it was probably just some kind of misfire in his brain. He'd been thinking about Anne. That's what it was. Thinking about her had stirred some deep feelings inside him.

But an image of Karen standing there in the foyer a moment ago flashed back in his mind. The moment when she finally looked right at him and smiled. The irrational feelings began stirring inside him all over again. It wasn't about Anne.

It was Karen. Something about *her*.

It was more than physical attraction. When Dave saw Karen

just now, he experienced so much more than mere physical attraction. It was as if he instantly knew they would get along well. As if he could already anticipate a thousand wonderful conversations with her, see years of memories they would make together in the future.

All in that one moment.

It was the exact same thing he'd experienced with Anne twenty-five years ago in that English lit class.

The restroom door opened. A tall young man wearing a cowboy hat walked in, looked at Dave, and nodded. Dave nodded back, pulled a paper towel out of the holder, and rubbed his hands with it. After tossing it in the trash can, he walked out. He stopped in his tracks just before clearing the foyer. He looked down at the ink smear still on his left hand.

You idiot. He turned around and headed back into the restroom.

Okay, Karen thought as she nibbled on a tortilla chip. *He's the right age, he's got a great voice and . . . he's in great shape. I like his face, a lot. And . . . no wedding ring.*

And, she reminded herself, he was here to interview her about her deadbeat father who walked out when she was just a small child. In less than two hours, Dave would be out of her life, flying back to wherever he came from. She dipped another chip in the salsa and looked over her shoulder.

Here he comes.

This is just an interview. You don't even like the topic.

As soon as Dave sat down, the waitress returned. "Have you had enough time to figure out what you want?" he asked Karen.

"Yes. I'll have the buffalo chicken salad."

"Are you sure you don't want a steak? Some ribs?" Dave asked. "I'm buying."

Karen smiled. "That's really what I want. But if you're dying to part with your money, there's this gorgeous emerald ring I've been coveting in a jewelry store not far from here." Dave laughed but didn't say anything. *Ugh, why did I say that?* she thought. *He must think I'm so weird!* "I'm totally kidding," she said, feeling embarrassed.

"I know."

"How about you, sir?" the waitress said. "You still want the steak fajitas?"

"Even more now."

"I'll go put your order in then be back to refresh your drinks." She turned and walked away.

Dave was looking at Karen in a funny way. "What is it?" she said. "It looks like there's something you want to say."

"It's nothing. It's just . . . the word you used just then. *Coveting*. You hardly ever hear that word anymore. Except with . . ."

"Christians?"

He nodded.

"Well, you caught me. I'm a church girl, have been since high school."

He smiled. "I'm glad."

Now why would that make him glad? "Are you . . . do you . . ."

"I'm a Christian too," he said. "But not for very long, just four years."

"Four years is pretty long," she said. She wondered what had happened four years ago and whether she should ask. "Four years ago was the worst year of my life." Why did she say that?

"Really?" His face showed instant concern. "Mind telling me

why?" He looked down at his pad. "Totally off the record." He dipped a chip in the salsa and popped it into his mouth.

"Two pretty awful things happened. Not that far apart from each other. My mother died, then my fiancé left me . . . for someone else."

"I can't imagine that."

"You mean both things happening the same year?"

"No, but I can see why that would be horrible. I can't imagine someone leaving you for another woman."

The way he said it, the look in his eyes. So full of care and, it seemed, something else. It was obviously meant as a compliment. She loved it but didn't know what to say. She wanted to shift the focus off her. "So what happened to you four years ago that caused you to become a Christian?"

He looked away and sighed.

"Usually, people don't get depressed telling that story," she said. "Don't feel like you have to tell me."

"No, I don't mind talking about it, a little. I guess God used it to wake me up. It's just . . . my wife died. In a plane crash."

"Oh my." Her heart sank.

"Yeah, it was pretty awful." He looked back at her. His eyes looked moist, like he was holding back tears. "But I don't want to give you the wrong impression. We were divorced at the time. Talk about long stories. And it was all my fault."

Karen didn't know why, but she tensed up. Had Dave left his wife for someone else like Greg had left her?

"I wasn't unfaithful, at least not to my wedding vows. The other woman was my stupid career. I didn't realize how foolish I'd been till her funeral, sitting there next to my son Jake. I got so wrapped up in what I was doing, where I wanted to be next." He looked down. "I left Anne and Jake for a job, a stupid job."

He sighed again and looked up. "Well, I didn't mean to go into all that. I'm sorry. I won't let it happen again."

Karen didn't know how to reply. But one thing she knew for sure: she was suddenly in no hurry for this dinner to end. And she didn't care whether they ever got around to talking about her deadbeat dad, Aaron Miller.

She wanted to know whatever she could find out about David Russo.

28

After the waitress brought their dishes, they spent the next twenty minutes getting to know each other better. Karen told Dave about life as a realtor in today's sad housing market. She'd talked a little about Gail and about her church, which Dave realized was at least ten times larger than the one he attended back home. She'd started to talk about her father a few times—her real father, as she called him, not Aaron Miller—but then stopped. Dave detected she was struggling, but he didn't want to pry.

Dave started asking questions about her favorite music (country western, but she also liked Coldplay), the kinds of movies she enjoyed (romantic comedies and anything set in the 1800s), favorite places she'd visited (New York City, the Disney theme parks, and Rome). She'd stopped him then, insisting he talk for a while.

Dave told her what life was like growing up in an Italian family on the south side of Chicago, living with a Vietnam War widow who'd never remarried. It really seemed to affect Karen when she'd learned his father had died in Vietnam. Dave talked about how his mother had moved down to Florida to be near Jake after Anne had died. He'd spent the rest of the time talking about Jake and how much closer they'd become since he'd quit his job in Atlanta and moved back to Florida.

This felt much more like a date than an interview. He didn't want the evening to end.

The waitress returned to clear their plates. "Would you folks like any dessert or coffee?"

"I'm not ready for dessert, but I would like some coffee," Dave said.

"Me too," Karen said. "But how about we head over to a Barnes & Noble down the road? It's at an outdoor mall. We could get some coffee there and keep talking."

"I'd like that." He looked up at the waitress. "Guess we just need the bill."

"I'll be right back."

Karen looked at Dave. "So where were we? You were talking about your son Jake. That's great you guys are so close. Usually it's just the opposite. Kids tend to pull away when they hit the teen years. I never had any children, but my brother Steve and his wife have had all kinds of ups and downs when their kids reached that age."

"I'm really grateful for the way things are going between Jake and me. But lately, it feels like he's pulling away a little. Not in a rebellious way. I think it's just life. He's a senior in high school, on the basketball team, making friends." Dave paused, wondering what Jake was doing now. He looked at his watch; he needed to remember to call him. It was an hour later in Florida. "I'm kind of dreading next year."

"When he goes off to college?" Karen said.

"Yeah." He sighed.

"Did he get a basketball scholarship?"

Dave laughed. "No . . . that's not likely to happen. But he's got a 3.9 average, so we're hoping he might get some kind of academic one." He took a sip of his drink. "So, were you and your fiancé engaged very long before you broke up?" As soon as he said it, he regretted it. "I'm sorry, that's way too personal."

"I don't mind," she said. "It's kind of a sad tale, though. Right out of college I was mostly into my career and hanging out with friends. Wasn't really thinking too much about marriage and family. Then I met Greg. Thought for sure he was 'the one.' I met him at church, we dated for years." She shook her head as if in disbelief. "I mean . . . *years*. That should have been a clue he wasn't as serious about me as I was about him. We finally got engaged, but that dragged on for a few more years, until finally four years ago, he decided he'd met 'the one,' and it wasn't me."

"That's so sad."

"Yeah . . . so I never married and never had any kids." She sighed. "I really love kids too."

"You seem like someone who'd make a good mother."

Karen's expression suddenly changed. She picked up a napkin and began dabbing her eyes.

"Are you okay?" Dave asked. "Did I say something wrong?"

"No, I'm fine." She put the napkin down and blinked away the tears. "That was a sweet thing to say. I always thought I would too. Make a good mother, I mean. Maybe we should change the subject."

Dave wished he could comfort her somehow. The waitress returned with the check. Dave looked it over, then handed her the debit card. The interruption seemed to help. When he looked back at Karen, she'd regained her composure.

Karen led Dave to their next stop. She'd asked him to keep their cars close since it was totally dark out now and the traffic was fairly heavy. He reminded her his rental car had GPS. She turned off the Frontage Road beside 114 into the Southlake Town Square and up to the parking lot of the Barnes & Noble. On the way there, the rational part of her brain kept trying to convince herself this was a silly, stupid fantasy she was entertaining. He wasn't interested in her; he was just a genuinely nice guy.

A nice, good-looking guy.

A nice, good-looking guy who was the right age.

And a Christian.

And available.

And . . . he was flying back to Florida tomorrow to a life that did not, and could not, involve her. Besides, he wasn't even interested. That part *was* total fantasy.

He held the doors open for her as they walked in. It was nippy enough to be able to see their breath. The heat inside the store felt great. "I'm definitely ready for coffee," she said.

"Me too." They walked through the aisles toward the café. "This is still part of the dinner, so still my treat."

"You won't get an argument from me," she said. "I'm the realtor who's not selling any houses, remember?" He paid for their coffee, once again with a shiny gold debit card. She noticed how he looked at it, smiling as he handed it to the cashier. "So what's with this gold card, and why do you smile every time you look at it?"

He laughed. "It's just . . . I still can't believe I get to do this."

"Do what?"

"Be here with you, in Texas. That I could just buy a ticket without worrying about the price, fly here, rent a car, buy dinner, pay for my hotel. All of it." He looked down at her with his handsome face. "I don't usually have this kind of money. I'll tell you about it when we sit down."

As she sipped her caramel macchiato and he sipped his latte, he explained the origin of the gold debit card. Which led into a story about an oil executive named John Lansing and his search for her birth father, Aaron Miller.

She wished she hadn't asked. Because now the subject would shift to the real reason Dave wanted to meet her in the first place. She knew there was very little to say on that subject, and when they were through, he would probably need to leave. And walk right out the door and out of her life.

But she absolutely loved hearing him talk.

"I know it's probably hard for you to fathom, Karen . . . having a dad who won the Congressional Medal of Honor, when he wound up being such a disappointment after he got home. But I heard the story of what he did over there, and it was pretty amazing. He literally saved three guys' lives. They definitely would have died if it hadn't been for what he did. And from what John Lansing said, it sounds like Aaron got messed up on drugs because of all the pain from his injuries."

"I remember my mom saying something about him always having nightmares. I don't remember any details, though."

"Sounds like most of the guys who fought over there had them. It was a nightmare kind of war. The guys who come home from Iraq and Afghanistan have the same problems. The difference now is, there's all kinds of help available. Your dad didn't get anything like that when he got home. It didn't help that the general public treated the Vietnam vets like outcasts."

Karen didn't share Dave's passion for this. But she remembered his father had been killed in Vietnam. In a way, that war had taken both their fathers' lives. She sipped her coffee. "I'm

not really mad at my dad for leaving us. I was when I was a kid.
A lot, for the first few years. But when my mom remarried, well,
it wasn't long before I forgot all about my first dad. Mark, my
new dad, really treated us like we were his own. Actually, until
Steve called this afternoon, I hadn't thought about Aaron Miller,
probably for years."

"So you're okay with me trying to find him?"

"Sure, but I really don't see how I can help."

"You have no idea where he is?"

She shook her head.

"No idea at all?"

"From what my mother said, after he left us, things went from
bad to worse. He wound up living on the streets. My brother
went through a phase when he hit thirteen where he wanted to
find him. I remember him and my mom arguing about it. She
said Steve wouldn't like what he found. She was telling him that
he needed to be thankful. That he had a real dad now. Our first
dad, she said, was nothing but a homeless drunk. He deserted
us and never gave us a dime."

"Wow."

"That was pretty much the end of the discussion," she said.

"Did that conversation take place here in Texas?" he asked.

"Yes. And that was pretty much the last time we talked about
Aaron Miller." She thought about what she'd said. "I guess it
must sound strange, me calling him by his name. But I don't
think of him as my father."

"No, I understand," he said. "So, did he stay in Florida?"

"I don't know. That was so many years ago. He could be
anywhere by now." She didn't want to say the next part. "He
could be dead."

Dave sighed. "I know, I thought about that. I hope not for

these three veterans' sakes. They're really hoping to have this big reunion with him so they can thank him properly for saving their lives."

Karen was quiet for a moment. "I wish I could be more help," she finally said. "But Dave, I'm afraid your war hero book isn't going to wind up with a happy ending. Not if you make it about Aaron Miller."

He didn't know what to say. He took a long sip of his latte and looked at his watch. "I probably need to get back to my room. I want to call my son before it gets too late."

She knew their time would end once they started talking about Aaron Miller. She stood up, and Dave looked in her eyes, the same way he had before . . . before they'd gotten on this subject.

"Karen, I . . . I don't know how to say this. And if it wasn't for the fact that I'm flying out of here tomorrow, I'd never be this bold."

"What is it?"

"I'd really like to see you again."

"You would?"

"I really would. I'm not flying out till late in the morning. Do you suppose . . . would you consider meeting me somewhere for breakfast?"

"Yes."

"You would?"

"Yes, I definitely would."

He smiled a wonderful smile. But what was she thinking? This couldn't go anywhere. He was leaving tomorrow.

He gently took her hand, but not like a handshake, more like someone about to ask for a dance. "I've got to go. I'm really glad I met you, Karen, even if I don't wind up finding Aaron."

"I really enjoyed this too," she said.

He smiled. "If anything else about your dad, you know, Aaron Miller, pops into your head, will you let me know?"

"Sure, I can do that."

"And tomorrow, before I leave, I'd definitely like to get your email address."

"All right."

He turned and walked her out to her car. She thought about what her brother said about coming over at Thanksgiving, that she could "bring a friend" if she wanted. Thanksgiving was the day after tomorrow. How she wished Dave lived in town. She would definitely invite him. But he didn't. He lived in Florida, over a thousand miles away.

It might just as well have been a million.

29

The next morning, Dave drove to a nearby Cracker Barrel to meet Karen for breakfast. This trip was turning out better than he could have imagined. He still had no idea where Aaron Miller was, but he'd found Aaron's children. That was huge. And he was from Florida. That didn't mean he was still there, or even that he was still alive, but it was a solid lead. For now, it meant he could ignore all the other Aaron Millers in the remaining forty-nine states.

But the biggest deal by far was meeting Karen. He had the hardest time falling asleep last night, just thinking about her. And he woke up thinking about her. He was obviously attracted to her, but that was no surprise. She was beautiful. But this was something more. The longer he thought about it, the more certain he'd become—and he knew now it had nothing to do with the fact that he'd been thinking about Anne just before Karen walked into Chili's.

Dave hadn't felt these feelings for anyone else but Anne.

That had to mean something.

As he pulled into the parking lot, he was keenly aware that this breakfast—at least for him—was more a date than official business. Karen had already said she didn't know where her father was and couldn't remember anything significant about him. She had said yes to meeting Dave this morning without hesitation. And it had nothing to do with talks about Aaron Miller. She had to be interested in him on some level.

So . . . it *was* a date. He had no idea what they would talk about. He got out of the car and left his pad and pen on the front seat. He walked into the store side of Cracker Barrel, which was decorated for Thanksgiving, and found Karen standing in front of a display of bowls and platters. "Karen," he said from behind her.

She turned, and her eyes seemed to light up. "Hi, Dave."

They stood there a moment, as if unsure what to do next. Shake hands? Hug?

"Are you browsing or shopping?" he said.

"I'm trying to find something to bring to Steve's house tomorrow for Thanksgiving. Just a little present for his wife, Aileen."

"You need a little more time to decide?"

"No, we can go in. I know you've got to get to the airport. I can walk around some more after you leave."

They walked to the hostess. Fortunately, there was no wait. A waitress brought them water and coffee, and they small-talked awhile as they read the menus. She ordered oatmeal and an apple bran muffin. He ordered Uncle Herschel's Favorite. "Somebody's hungry," she said.

"I am, but I'm also not sure when, or if, I'll get to eat lunch."

"Do you like to travel?"

"I used to. Not anymore." Then he had an odd thought. Maybe that was the wrong answer. If they were going to have any chance of a relationship, he'd have to travel; they lived in different states. Then a more rational thought: *You're being ridiculous. This is breakfast; we're not in a relationship.* "I mean, I used to do it all the time in some of my other reporting jobs. Now I only travel a little." He thought something else and decided to just say it. "I'm very glad I made this trip."

She smiled. "I am too." She sipped her coffee. "Sorry I didn't have more to tell you about my dad. Steve called me this morning. He wanted to hear all about last night."

"What did you tell him?"

"That I enjoyed meeting you, but that there wasn't much to say . . . about our dad, I mean. He's so fired up about this Medal of Honor thing. He can't wait to tell his son Steven. He's a Marine in Afghanistan."

"Is he there now?"

"Yes, but he'll be on leave for Christmas. After that, he'll be staying in the States."

"I'm sure a soldier would find it pretty amazing to hear his grandfather won the Medal of Honor."

"That's what Steve said. I asked him if Steve Jr. even knew about his *other* grandfather. All he's ever known is Mark Rafferty, the father who raised us."

"What did he say?"

"My brother said he did talk about our birth father a little, back when his son signed up for the Marines. All he knew was that he'd fought in Vietnam and got seriously wounded. Not much else."

"I guess that must be a little strange."

"It is. We never talk about him. Do you ever think about your dad?"

"I have lately. Quite a lot. But before I got going on this book project, hardly ever. So, I think I understand what you're saying."

The waitress came with their food. Dave didn't think it wise to suspend the "don't talk with your mouth full" rule like he had with John Lansing, so they continued talking in between bites and swallows of oatmeal and eggs. The conversation shifted to more conventional topics. The kinds of things you talk about when you're on a date.

He loved talking with her; it was the easiest thing in the world. She wanted to know some more details about growing up in Chicago, what it was like being a reporter, did Jake have a girlfriend, did he know where Jake was going to college or what he wanted to do when he graduated. He wanted to know some more about her favorite books and movies, did she have any friends at church, what she liked to do on her time off.

When they had finished their meal, the question Dave wanted to ask most of all was: *When can I see you again?* If he lived in Fort Worth, that was what he'd ask. Or even better, *Can I see you again tonight for dinner?* But what could he say? He looked at his watch.

"I can't believe your time's almost over," she said.

It seemed she wanted to also say, *And you have to go.* He decided to be bold, at least a little. "Karen, I . . ." He looked right in her eyes then sighed.

"What?"

"I don't know how to say this, so I'm just going to say it. I only came here hoping to find a lead about your dad. But now . . . I don't want to leave. It almost feels like the real reason I came here . . ." It was way too early to say something like this. But it's what he felt, strongly.

"Was to meet me?" she said.

He nodded. "I really like you." He looked away. "Listen to me, it's like I'm back in fourth grade."

She laughed. "I like you too, Dave. I do feel like something . . ." Then she stopped, took a breath.

See, he thought, *she doesn't want to say what she's feeling either.* "We're both being so well-behaved." He smiled, glanced at his watch. "I really have to go."

"I know."

"But I really want to see you again."

"I'd like that. But . . . how?"

"I don't know." The waitress brought the check.

"Here," she said, and handed him a card. "It's my business card, but I wrote my cell number and personal email address on the back."

"That's a good start." He pulled a card from his wallet and wrote the same information on the back. He stood up and handed it to her, then grabbed the check.

"How will you spend Thanksgiving?" she said as she stood up.

"Just my mom, Jake, and me. Sometimes she invites a couple of friends from church. But my mom makes the whole spread. We eat leftovers for a week. Jake and I start the day off making fun of the Macy's Parade."

She laughed. "Oh, I almost forgot. It's probably nothing. But Steve reminded me this morning, he's got a bunch of boxes stored at his house from when my mom passed away. When she first died, we divided up the sentimental things each of us wanted. But there was a box with my father's name written on it that Steve took. He thought we could look through it together tomorrow when I come over. Maybe we'll find something you can use in your hunt."

"That'd be great. Call me if you do. Or . . . even if you don't find anything." He smiled. They walked through the double front doors, then stood on the sidewalk out front. "I gotta go."

"Well, bye," she said.

They stood there a moment, neither wanting their time together to end but not knowing exactly what to do, so he hugged her. It was more like two relatives hugging or two Christians hugging at church, though he wanted to convey more than that. He took a step back after and just looked at her. "I don't want to leave."

"I wish you didn't have to."

Without thinking, he leaned forward and kissed her forehead gently. As he pulled away, he said, "Sorry, I shouldn't have done that."

She smiled.

"Call me tomorrow," he said and waved as he walked away.

Karen walked through the front door of the model home. She was over thirty minutes late, but she'd already called Gail to let her know. She took off her coat, set her purse on her desk, and walked over to the coffeepot. Gail had been sitting at her desk reading some papers in a black notebook. As Karen carried her mug toward the desk, Gail was sitting back in her chair, staring at her.

"Are you going to tell me?" she said.

"Tell you what?"

"What that look on your face is all about?"

"What look?"

"C'mon, Karen. I know you. I haven't seen you look this happy coming into work for . . . years."

Karen laughed and sat down. "It's . . . nothing. Sort of nothing."

"Don't give me that. What's going on?"

"I may have . . . met someone."

"Really?" Gail closed the notebook.

"Yes and no. It can never work, though. I'm just being silly."

"Why can't it work?"

"It just can't."

"Why . . . is he married?"

"No."

"In jail?"

Karen laughed. "No."

"Is he . . . the right age?"

"Yes."

"Then what?"

"He lives in Florida."

"Okay . . . that's a wrinkle."

"It's more than a wrinkle. It's four states away."

"Four states . . . okay, a big wrinkle."

They looked at each other. "Well," Gail said, "you know we're not going to get a single thing done around here until you tell me the whole story, from top to bottom."

"Okay," Karen said. "But I don't see how this can work." She took a sip of her coffee as an image of Dave flashed through her mind. The moment he kissed her forehead, the look on his face as he stood in front of her. Then a strange thing happened. A deep stirring inside. A flash from someplace else, a memory from somewhere very far away. Far back in time. That's what her father—her first father, Aaron Miller—used to do before bed every night. Lean over and kiss her on the forehead, just like Dave had done.

"Karen? Hello . . . it's me, Gail."

Karen laughed. Her eyes refocused on Gail's face. "I'm sorry. Okay, the rest of the story."

"From top to bottom," Gail said.

30

The normal city buses didn't run on Thanksgiving Day, but the folks at the outreach center downtown had a fifteen-passenger van at their disposal. Aaron was sitting in it now, along with ten other volunteers who'd just served Thanksgiving dinner to over two hundred people. He looked at his watch. By the look of things, if he waited till the driver dropped everyone off in the right order, he'd be late getting back to the trailer park. He sat one row back from the driver so he leaned forward and said, "Hey, Joe, wonder if you can do me a favor?"

"Sure, Aaron, if I can."

"Any chance you could alter your route here and get me back home pretty quick? I've got this second Thanksgiving thing at my church I've got to get to, and I don't think I'll make it otherwise."

The driver looked at him through the rearview mirror. "Gosh, Aaron, I'd like to, but I'm not sure I can. The director gave me this route to follow, and I better stick to it." Then he leaned back in his seat and said quietly, "And I'm thinking some of these people might get upset if I drove right past where they live and skipped to your place. Your trailer park is the farthest out."

Aaron sat back in his seat. Another Vietnam vet named Drew sat next to him. "Say, Aaron, I wouldn't mind if you skipped my place if you're in a hurry. Our family dinner's not till five-thirty. What time's the church event?"

"Four-thirty," Aaron said. "Thing is, they're sending a special van to pick me and a friend up at four. He's a vet too. Lost his legs to a Bouncing Betty. I just got him talked into coming with me. There's no way he'd go on his own. So if our church van stops by the trailer park and I ain't there . . ."

"Let me see what I can do." Drew turned around to face everyone. "Hey, everybody, listen up. Aaron here's in a bit of a hurry. He's got a church event he needs to get to, another Thanksgiving dinner, kind of an outreach thing, and they're sending a special handicap van out to his trailer park. He's got a friend who's agreed to go to this thing, but he won't go if Aaron's not on that van. Anybody have anyplace they've got to be in the next twenty minutes?"

"You mean, are we okay if Joe takes him home first, then backtracks?"

"That's about it," Drew said.

"I'm okay with that."

In a few moments, everyone else weighed in the same. "Whatta you think, Joe? Can you head over to Aaron's place next?"

"Sure. I'm just here to serve. If that's what y'all want, I'm game."

"There you go, Aaron."

"Appreciate that, Drew." He turned around to face the rest. "Thank you, everyone, means a lot."

"What's this fellow's name anyway?" Drew said.

"Billy Ames," said Aaron. "He's a hard nut to crack, but he seems to be coming around."

"Well, I'll be praying for him."

About twenty minutes later, the van pulled into Bentley's Trailer Park and let Aaron off. He waved and hurried to his storage room. Didn't see the church van anywhere. When he got inside, he checked himself in the mirror. Wasn't much could be done; didn't see too many hairs out of place. He glanced over at the faded picture of his kids sitting on top of his little metal box. How were they spending this day? Did they spend it together? He didn't even know how many grandkids he had, if any.

Well, he needed to stop this right now. Thoughts like these didn't lead down a thanksgiving road. After washing his face and hands, he locked up and hurried over to Billy's trailer. "Lord," he muttered, "please don't let him chicken out." He knocked on the door just as the church van pulled up to the park office. Tess barked a few times.

"That you, Aaron?"

"It's me, Billy." The door opened. "Look at you."

"Whatta you mean, look at you?"

"Your hair . . . it's all . . ." He thought to say clean. And combed.

"Oh stop."

Aaron sniffed the air. "You wearing cologne?"

"Just a few sprays. Would you stop?" He looked to the side, around Aaron. "That the van?"

"It just got here." Aaron turned. "Let me go wave at him so he'll come over here."

"I don't mind riding there."

Aaron started walking. "Just come on down the ramp. He won't mind." Aaron got the driver's attention and motioned for him to head over. When he turned around he saw Billy had eased out the front door.

Billy was hugging Tess's neck, then patted her head. "You can't come this time, girl. You got to stay here and watch the place. I'll see if they won't let me bring you home something. Now, you go on." Tess backed up and Billy closed the door. He met Aaron at the bottom of the ramp. "Say, Aaron, you think they might let me take home a little bit of turkey and stuffing for Tess?"

The van pulled up. "I think they might. They usually have leftovers they let the workers take home. Tess can have mine. How'd your day go so far?"

"We had a good day overall. Watched the Macy's Parade together, and then it turns out they have this National Dog Show right after. She sat right beside me, eyes glued to the TV. I could tell she was watching."

Aaron smiled as the van door opened. He had never seen Billy so upbeat.

"Mom, you're killing me. This smell. When are we going to eat?" Dave Russo walked into the kitchen, peered over his mother's shoulder. She was stirring homemade mashed potatoes. The turkey had been roasting in the oven for hours.

Jake stood in the doorway. "Really, Grandma, we're starving. I haven't eaten anything since breakfast."

"You two go watch your game. In about ten minutes, I'll call one of you back to pull this thing out of the oven. It's way too heavy for me. Then I gotta make the gravy, and then we're ready. Here." She reached over and grabbed two dinner rolls. "Put some butter on this, one for you and your father, and go."

Dave looked at his son. A few weeks ago they were seeing eye to eye. "Come here."

"What?"

"Just come here. Stand here and look at me."

"What'd I do?"

"You didn't do anything." He looked down at Jake's feet. He was just wearing socks. "Look at this, Mom."

"What, I've got to stir this butter in here."

"Just look a second. You see this? I'm looking up at him. You see this?"

She turned. "Jake, you're bigger than your father."

"Taller, Mom. Not bigger."

Jake smiled. "Bigger's coming, Pop."

"Now, you two go on, go watch your game. I'll call you in a few minutes."

Dave's phone rang. "Where'd I put it?"

"It's over there on the hutch, Dad." Jake walked back and plopped on the sofa in front of the TV.

Dave looked at the cell phone screen. It was Karen. He picked it up before the third ring. "Hi, Karen, how are you? Happy Thanksgiving."

"Thank you. You too. I'm doing fine. Did I catch you at a bad time?"

"Not at all. We haven't eaten yet, but the smell is torturing me."

"I'm stuffed," she said. "We always eat around one. Then we go back and eat some more around six. Well, the men do. Aileen and I just have some coffee and pie."

"So what kind of pie is your favorite, pumpkin or apple?" he said.

"Pumpkin."

"Me too."

"Store-bought?" she asked.

"Are you kidding? Not in Angelina Russo's house."

"I'll bet it's wonderful."

"It's the best." Dave felt a presence behind him. He turned to find his mother standing in the kitchen doorway, staring at him, a funny look on her face. "Maybe I should call you back after we eat?" he said. "My mom's going to need me to pull the turkey out in a few minutes." He walked toward his bedroom.

"Sure, we're just sitting around recovering. Call whenever. Let me just tell you this real quick. My brother and I went through that box of my dad's stuff. It was just a bunch of odds and ends of his my mom kept. But we did find a stack of birthday and Christmas cards he sent us as kids. I'd forgotten all about them. There were a couple of envelopes in the stack. Unfortunately, at some point they'd suffered some water damage. The ink on the envelopes is smeared and faded. But on one of them I could make out that it came from Perry, Florida. Steve said that's the town where we lived before moving out here. I was too small to remember."

"Really? Perry's less than an hour from where I live." This could be just the break Dave was looking for.

"Do you want me to send them to you?"

Dave thought a moment. "I know, how about I fly out there tomorrow and pick them up?"

"What?"

"I know, it sounds crazy. But Karen, this is the biggest lead I've had so far. I could fly out first thing in the morning, have dinner with you, and fly back in the evening. Then I could start working on this over the weekend."

"I . . . I don't know."

"Do you have to work?"

"No. We decided to close the office down for the holiday. Tomorrow's the biggest shopping day of the year."

"Then let's do this. I'll go pull the turkey out of the oven, then get on the internet to book a flight while my mom makes the gravy."

She laughed. "Okay. I'd love to see you."

"You would?"

"I didn't think I'd see you again . . . so soon."

"Well, you'll see me tomorrow. I'll email you the flight info."

"Okay. How about this time you skip the rental car? I'll come pick you up and drop you off after dinner."

"Great. That's what we'll do. Okay, well . . . see you tomorrow."

"Bye."

Dave turned around to find his mother, now standing in the hallway, with that same look. "So what, you're flying out again tomorrow?"

"Yeah, Mom. It's about this guy I'm searching for, the war hero. That was his daughter. She's found something that might help me locate him. I'm going to go out there and get it and fly back here tomorrow night."

Jake walked up and stood behind her. "Are you going to tell us what's going on?"

"What do you mean?"

They were both smiling. "Who's this girl?" his mother said. "This . . . daughter?"

"What? It's nothing."

"C'mon, Dad. We're not stupid. You've been acting different ever since you got home."

"Is she somebody nice?" his mother asked.

"Yeah, Mom. She's nice. She's . . . real nice."

"See, there's that smile on your face. You like this girl."

"No, Mom, it's not . . . well, yeah. I think I do."

"Whoa . . . Dad. Is this for real? Did you meet somebody?"

"Maybe."

"What do you mean maybe?"

"I don't know. She's really nice. Her name is Karen. Her father's this war hero I'm looking for. But I don't think anything can come of it. She lives in Texas."

"Are we going to get to meet her?" his mother said.

"I don't know, Mom. It's way too early for that."

"Maybe so," Jake said. "But I haven't seen you like this before." He leaned down and said in his grandmother's ear, "I think your little boy's in love."

"I think you may be right. He's flying out there to see her."

"When?"

"Tomorrow," she said. "To pick up something. Something she could mail just as easy. What sense does that make?"

"It doesn't make any sense," Jake said. "That's how love is."

Dave shook his head, but he couldn't stop smiling. "You guys are making way too much out of this."

31

It was just after lunch, the day after Thanksgiving.

Bentley's Trailer Park was half empty from all the folks gone for the holiday and the people out shopping. But Aaron's chore list was still half full. Fortunately, none of them were marked urgent, and the day continued to promise few interruptions. It would give him time to get to some rainy-day projects and, hopefully, allow him to spend some quality time out on the deck as soon as he clocked out.

But all of that changed at 1:12 p.m.

Aaron had been riding his golf cart, towing a wagon full of dead palm fronds to a pile on the back side of the property, when he heard the loudest CRACK he'd ever heard. A moment later, a thundering BOOM.

He slammed the brakes on the cart. *Lord, what was that?*

He turned toward the sound behind him, then looked up. The sun was shining through the trees; it couldn't have been lightning. Shouts and screams rang out from the front end of the park. He got out, unhooked the wagon, got back in, and headed in that direction. As he drew closer, he saw a cloud of dust and debris rising up and spreading through several trees. *What in the world?*

It wasn't a fiery explosion; there wasn't any smoke that he could see. That was always a worry in trailer parks, with all the propane tanks people use. The shouts and screams were getting louder. *Lord, please let everybody be all right.*

His walkie-talkie squawked. "Aaron, you hear that?"

"On my way, Sue. Fast as this cart'll go. What happened?"

"I just called 911 to be safe, but we should be okay. It's that huge oak tree hangs over Irene Hamlin's trailer. The biggest limb just broke off. 'Bout scared me half to death. Squashed her trailer like a bug."

Oh no. Aaron wished this thing would go faster.

"But she's in Tampa for the holiday," Sue continued. "That's what she told me earlier this week."

"Sue . . . she got back late this morning. I waved to her not fifteen minutes ago while I was gathering up these dead palm fronds."

"What?"

"She said she was only going for Thanksgiving Day, because of her cat. She insisted her son bring her back this morning."

"Oh Aaron, that means . . . she's in that thing? I'm looking at it right now. Oh my word, you need to get here quick."

"I'm just around the corner." Aaron couldn't think straight. He just prayed some more. As he turned the corner onto the paved road, a small crowd gathered up ahead in the vicinity of Irene's trailer. Sue was off to the left, her hands covering her mouth. People were pointing, some crying.

"Where's the fire department?" someone yelled.

"Already called them," Sue said. "They're on their way. Has anyone seen Irene?"

"She's gone for Thanksgiving," a lady said.

"No, she's not," Sue said. "She came home a little while ago."

"You mean she's in *there*?"

"Has anyone seen her?" Sue yelled again.

People shook their heads no. Aaron rolled up and parked the cart. Then hurried over to Sue. Before he reached her, the devastating scene came into full view. If poor Irene was in there . . . he didn't see how she could be alive. The largest oak limb of Big Bertha, the one that arched right over the roof, had snapped near the trunk. The whole thing had fallen down the middle of Irene's trailer. It looked like a giant had stepped right on it with his boot.

Billy Ames rolled over on his scooter, Tess beside him on a leash. "That's just awful. I never knew Irene, but no one should have to die like that."

"We don't know she's dead yet, Billy," Aaron said.

Tess started barking and pulling at the leash, as if she wanted Billy to move away. "You smell that?" he said.

"Anyone smell gas?" someone else said. "I think I smell gas."

The woman in the crowd closest to Irene's trailer yelled, "I hear some kind of hissing sound."

"Everybody, get back," Aaron yelled. "It's a gas leak. This thing could explode." People instantly responded. Those who could, ran.

"Nobody smoke. Nobody light a match," Sue shouted. "Where's that fire department? We aren't that far out of town."

The circle widened now, till everyone stood maybe fifty yards away. Aaron wondered if it was far enough. If that trailer exploded . . . "I think we need to get back more," he yelled. "At least till the firemen get here. They'll know what to do."

Just then, a new sound. Everyone heard it.

A woman screaming from inside the crushed trailer. "Help me. Somebody. It's me, Irene. Anyone there?"

"Oh Aaron," Sue said. "What are we going to do?"

"Nothing we can do," Billy said. "That thing could explode any minute."

"But she's trapped."

Aaron ran toward the trailer. "Where are you, Irene?"

People yelled behind him.

"Aaron, come back!"

"What is he doing?"

"You're both going to die."

"Wait for the firemen."

The gas smell was strong. "Irene?"

"I'm in back. I don't know what happened. The whole trailer is tilting up."

"That big limb over the house snapped off, fell right across your living room. I'll be right there." Aaron ran down the length of the main limb. All the brush and branches near the trailer were too tall to get through. He climbed over and ran toward the back bedroom. It was off the ground about two feet higher than normal. "You in here?"

"In the bedroom. I was taking a nap."

"Are you hurt?"

"Banged my head pretty bad. Knocked me out, I think. My right leg is cut and bleeding. My walker's all messed up."

He ran around the back to the other side. A door hung open, the top half of the hinge torn off. The gas smell seemed stronger on this side. In the distance, he heard sirens, but he couldn't wait. Then Irene's cat leapt down to the grass. She looked dazed but otherwise unharmed. She ran off as he made his way to the steps. "I'm right here, Irene. We need to get you out, now."

"That gas is making me sick." She paused. "Wait . . . Aaron . . . you need to go now. I'll be all right till the firemen come."

"This thing could explode."

"I know," she said. "You go on. If this explodes, I'll see Jesus and Moe in the blink of an eye. I can't be the cause of you dying here with me."

Aaron walked up the metal steps and jumped into the opening. He was lying in the hallway. To his left about five feet, the ceiling and hallway floor joined together. It was hard to even make out what he was seeing. Her bedroom doorway was at the other end of the hall. Through it, he saw her arms on the floor. "I'm in, Irene. Can you move at all?"

"I can move my arms and legs, but I'm too weak to pull myself up to the doorway. The angle's too steep."

"Just stay there." The sirens were getting louder. He scrambled up the narrow hallway toward her door. When he reached the opening he looked to the left, saw her lying on the floor, pushed up against a built-in dresser. The bed had slid over her. "I'm going to pull you toward me by the arms. It might hurt a little."

"It's going to hurt a lot more if you don't. Go ahead."

"If your feet can push on anything," he said, "do it."

"All right. Have you seen Lucy?"

"She's fine. I just saw her jump out the back door."

"She's probably scared to death."

"We'll round her up, don't worry." He came through the doorway and wedged his legs between the jamb and the nearest wall and started pulling. It took quite a few moans from him and groans from her, but he managed to drag her toward him. He slid back through the doorway down the hall. Once her body passed the door opening, gravity began to lend a hand. He shimmied feet first down the hall until his legs were sticking outside. "You okay?"

"Keep going," she said.

When his feet touched the metal steps, he said, "This is going to be awkward for you, Irene, but to get you out and away from this trailer, I'm going to have to give you a piggyback ride."

"Do what you gotta do, Aaron."

He pulled her down the hallway some more as he backed outside. After coming down the stairs, he tossed them aside. Standing on the grass, he began to feel dizzy. If he didn't get out of here quick, he might just pass out. "As I pull your arms out, you grab hold around my neck. When you're out most of the way, I'm going to lift you up, and you just hold on."

"All right."

In a few moments, she was safely on his back. He thanked God she wasn't a big woman. He ran as carefully as he could away from the trailer. They were on the opposite side, running away from the crowd. The sirens now pierced the air, and red lights flashed throughout the area. But Aaron couldn't see the trucks just yet. He kept moving farther from the trailer.

Suddenly, the whole thing exploded. A roaring blast of heat and wind knocked them to the ground. He lay there a minute, his face in the dirt and leaves, Irene lying on top of him. He didn't feel hurt. "Irene, you okay?"

She rolled off to the side. "I'm alive."

People screamed and yelled things on the far side of the trailer. It dawned on Aaron: they probably thought he and Irene had just died in the explosion. He rolled over on his side the other way, turned his head, and looked at her. It was an odd scene. He'd never seen an old woman lying flat on the ground.

She looked right at him and smiled. "You just saved my life, Aaron Miller."

"I suppose I did." He sat up. "You stay put. I'm going to

walk around all this mess and get those paramedics to bring a gurney over here. They're going to want to give you a ride in their ambulance, check you out at the hospital."

"I'm fine here at the moment."

He stood up.

"But," she said, smiling, "whatever comes next won't be near as fun as that piggyback ride I just got."

32

Dave had enjoyed spending the day with Karen and didn't want it to end. After Karen picked him up at the airport, they had driven back to Southlake and eaten lunch together. She had brought the box of cards and envelopes with her, the ones written by Aaron Miller to her and Steve when they were kids. During lunch, he'd looked them over. They didn't yield many clues. Aaron had clearly written simple sentences that any child could read.

But a few lines had backed up the one clue Karen had found on the faded postmark: that Aaron had mailed them from somewhere in Florida.

It's very hot here, is it hot there in Texas?

I went to the beach yesterday, do you like to swim?

It never snows here, do you ever see snow?

Dave's mom had been right—it was pretty silly for him to fly out here like this; he could have asked her to scan them and send them as an email attachment and achieved the same result. He had flown out here for one reason. To spend more time with her.

Dave set the cards back in the box Karen had brought them in. He looked up and saw her coming back from the ladies' room. They were at a Starbucks a few blocks away from the restaurant where they'd eaten lunch.

She sat in her chair and picked up her cup. "I can't believe you have to fly back already."

"I know. I wasn't thinking about the extra holiday traffic. All the flights that leave later this evening were booked solid. This was the only one that had any open seats." He glanced at his watch. She would need to drop him off at the airport in two hours. He'd only brought a carry-on bag but still needed time to get through security.

She sipped her latte. "There weren't any flights you could take tomorrow? Or maybe Sunday afternoon? Then you could visit my church. I could drop you off after lunch."

Dave loved hearing her talk like this; she didn't want him to leave, either. "The thing is, my son has a basketball game tomorrow afternoon. I promised him I wouldn't miss any home games."

Karen smiled. "I'm glad. That's a good thing." She sighed. "I think I'd like to meet Jake someday."

"Hey," Dave said. "I never showed you his picture. I've got some on my phone." He pulled it out and flipped around till he found them. "Here, this one's pretty recent." He handed her the phone. "We were in Houston at a basketball tournament. Actually, flip through the next four or five. They're all of him in Houston." As she did, he watched her eyes.

She looked up. "Dave, that is one seriously handsome young man."

"Isn't he?"

"No, I mean . . . he's really a nice-looking guy. He doesn't have a girlfriend?"

"No one serious. Not yet anyway."

"I can see the resemblance," she said. "Especially in the eyes."

"You think?"

She nodded. "He doesn't seem very tall, for a basketball player, I mean."

"He's not. Just a little taller than me. He plays point guard, when he gets to play. He's on second string. But it doesn't seem to bother him. He's just happy to be on the team."

She handed the phone back. They sat in silence a few moments. Dave had a number of questions he still wanted to ask her about her childhood. He'd written them down on the plane ride here that morning, back when he was still fooling himself that the purpose of this trip was finding Aaron Miller. They were the kind of questions he thought might stir up some additional clues. But that's not how he wanted to spend their last moments together.

"What are you thinking?" she said.

He looked into her eyes, and an idea suddenly popped into his head. "Come back with me?"

"What?"

"Come back to Florida with me . . . tonight."

Her eyes lit up. "Tonight? You mean fly back with you now?"

"Yes."

"But I can't."

"Why?"

"For one thing, I can't afford something like that."

"Not a problem. Gold debit card. I'd pay for it."

"Can you do that?"

"Sure I can. It'll help with my research. You're the daughter of the man we're searching for. You used to live there. It's just an hour away from where I live. Maybe going back there in person will jog some fresh memories from your childhood. And . . . I'd get to spend more time with you."

"But he might not be living there, Dave. We don't even know if he's still alive."

"True. But that's the nature of a project like this. It's all speculation . . . hunting down clues, following up on leads. You never know which one might pay off. I've still got a list of questions I haven't asked you about your childhood. We could talk about it on the plane ride back."

"But Dave—"

"Give me another reason."

"I'm supposed to work over the weekend. Gail's expecting me."

She was resisting, but Dave could see in her eyes, she wanted to come. "Tell you what, call her now and ask. See what she says. If she's even a little hesitant, we'll drop the idea completely."

"Call her now?"

"Would you . . . please?"

She pulled her phone out of her purse, clicked a few buttons, then looked up at him. "It's ringing . . . this is so crazy. Hi, Gail? It's me."

Dave couldn't hear Gail's side of the conversation, but it wasn't hard to figure out what she was saying.

"We did," Karen said. "We had a wonderful Thanksgiving. How about you? Did you get along with Bill's family?" She listened a few moments, nodding, smiling. "I'm glad, I knew you would. Listen, I've only got a few minutes. I need to ask you something. It's going to sound crazy. It's not something I'd ever think to ask you, and I want you to feel totally free to say no." She listened a moment. "Well, let me tell you. Remember the guy I told you about who's trying to find my birth father? Yes . . . *that* guy." She looked up at Dave and smiled. "He's here, right now, sitting across the table from me. No, he didn't spend Thanksgiving with us. He just flew in this morning. But listen, he has to fly back to Florida tonight. Actually, I'm supposed to drop him off at the airport in two hours. He's following some lead about my dad, and, well . . . I'm just going to say it. He's asked me to fly back to Florida with him . . . tonight."

Dave heard some loud words coming from Karen's phone. But they sounded happy.

"It's not exactly like that," she said. "He wants to keep talking about my childhood, but we've kind of run out of time. And he thinks if I go back there, it might stir up some memories that might help him find my father." She listened some more. "Where would I be staying?" She looked at Dave.

"You could stay at my place," he said. "I mean, my mom and son would be there. Or I could put you up in a hotel."

She repeated this back to Gail. "But Gail, the thing is, I'm supposed to be working with you over the weekend. I don't want to leave you all by . . . what? Are you sure?" A big smile came over Karen's face. "You sure you don't mind?" Gail said some other things. "Well, okay. I guess I'll say okay then." She listened some more. "I'll call you when I get back, tell you everything. I promise." She hung up the phone.

"Sounds like Gail is okay with this," Dave said.

Karen put her phone away and looked up. "She's more than okay with it. She said it was a crazy idea, totally unlike anything she'd ever expect me to do. And she absolutely wants me to go."

"So . . . you'll come?"

"I guess I will. But what if they don't have any more seats left on the plane?"

Dave pulled out his phone. "Let's find out right now."

33

Karen was so excited, sitting in 26E, the window seat. Dave sat next to her in 26D, walled in by a middle-aged man in a suit occupying the aisle seat. His ample girth spilled over into Dave's seat, but that gave him a good excuse to lift the armrest between them and sit closer to her.

The captain had just announced they'd reached cruising altitude so people could turn on their electronic devices. Dave leaned toward her and said, "I'm so glad you agreed to come. You should have heard my mother when I told her."

"She was okay with it?"

"Are you kidding? She was ecstatic. I'm sure right now she's cleaning the condo from top to bottom. Then she'll sit down at the dinette table and make a list of all the food she needs to buy."

"But I'm only staying a day." They had tried to find a return flight on Sunday, but because of the Thanksgiving weekend, all the flights were totally booked.

"Doesn't matter," Dave said. "She loves company, a lot."

"Does she know . . . about us? I mean that we're . . ." Karen didn't know how to describe . . . *them.*

"She knew, after the first few sentences I'd shared about our first meeting. And I didn't say anything. In fact, I went out of my way to hide my feelings. It doesn't matter with her. If she were a Martian, her antennas would scrape the ceiling."

Karen laughed. And she loved it when he said "hide my feelings." Dave had feelings for her. She knew that by now. She certainly had feelings for him. Very nice ones. So, was that the stage they were at? Was he her boyfriend? Listen to her, she was talking like a high school girl. It had only been a couple of days. This whole thing was so foreign to her. She hadn't felt this way about anyone for ages.

She was sitting on a plane, flying to Florida with a man she barely knew.

She never did anything like this . . . ever. Another crazy thing was that the reasonable people in her life, the ones who should have tried to talk her out of saying yes, Gail and Steve, both had almost insisted she go.

"What are you thinking?" Dave said.

"I can't believe my brother."

"You mean, that he thought you should come?"

"Yes. I was sure he would say it was a terrible idea."

"I'm glad he didn't."

"Me too. He's just so excited about the idea of finding our dad. It's this whole Medal of Honor thing. I'm sure it has something to do with his son too."

"The one in Afghanistan now, right? Is he in any danger where he's stationed?"

"Steve says no, but they're worried all the time. I am too. Every time I hear about a soldier dying over there I hold my breath and pray we don't get that call. I'll be so happy when he comes home for good."

The flight attendants wheeled the refreshment cart by. "Do you want anything when they stop at our row?" Dave said.

"Maybe a Diet Coke."

"So . . . does your brother know . . . about us?"

"His antennas aren't as long as your mom's," Karen said. "But I think he knows something's up. He asked some questions that hinted at it in our last conversation. I guess my long pauses didn't help."

"Do you think he'd be concerned?"

"I don't think so." Karen always considered Steve a good judge of character. She was sure he'd like Dave instantly and even more as he got to know him. Steve's only concern might be the one Karen kept trying to suppress herself. How could she have a meaningful relationship with a man who lived four states away?

She noticed Dave reach down to get something out of his laptop bag. "Are you getting your laptop?"

"No," he said, pulling out a small notebook. "Going old school. My laptop battery is dying, barely gives me twenty minutes. I've got one on order but didn't want to get stuck, so on the plane ride to Texas I jotted down these." He opened the notebook and showed her a short list of handwritten questions.

"Those are about my childhood?"

He nodded. "Thought we should go through these now. My mom will pretty much dominate our time once we land."

She smiled. But also felt herself tensing up. She knew he wanted to talk about this but wished she didn't have to. She'd been telling herself, and Dave, it was because there really wasn't anything much to say. And that none of these things bothered her anymore. But for the last day or so, whenever they talked about her birth father or she thought about it, an unsettled, disturbing feeling would come over her. She'd finally figured out what it was. This man, Aaron Miller, had abandoned her and Steve when they were children. For a few years he had sent them cards. And then after that . . . they never heard from him again.

"Are you okay?" Dave said. The flight attendant wheeled the cart to their row. He looked up. "Two Diet Cokes, please."

"No, I'm fine. I know we need to do this."

"Nothing may come of it," he said. "And if any of it makes you uncomfortable, we can stop."

She liked that. "Well, fire away then." The flight attendant handed Dave the drinks, and he set Karen's on the tray.

Dave took a sip then said, "I know you were very young, but do you remember anything about where you lived in Florida before your father left?"

"I know we were living in Texas when he left for good. Steve would remember a few more details about our place in Florida. He was a year older. I remember it was a mobile home, and it had these rickety metal steps. I was afraid of them because I fell down them once and cut my leg. Steve and I shared this teeny bedroom, I remember that. We lived on a dirt road and there were lots of shady trees. I think we had a cyclone fence around our yard. I remember mosquitoes." She stopped a moment, noticed him writing. "Getting anything useful?"

"Not yet." He looked up and smiled.

"I don't know if we'll even be able to find the street where we lived. I doubt that mobile home is still there anyway."

"Probably not, but you never know what these trips down memory lane will turn up. You might remember something or see something that will create some new leads."

"Maybe," she said. "I have a hard time imagining it. It's just something Steve and I haven't talked about very much. After my mom remarried when we were seven and eight, Aaron Miller pretty much disappeared from the scene. He just never came up again."

"That's okay. Do you know why you moved from Florida to Texas? Did your mom ever say why?"

"I think it was because he joined the Marines. They met in Florida, not sure how. Fell in love, got married, and started having kids."

"Did you say he *joined* the Marines? Wasn't he drafted?"

"I don't think so. I remember Steve saying one time that mom told him our father couldn't find work for months. The war was going on, and he figured if he enlisted he'd get a steady paycheck. After he left for boot camp, she moved us back to Texas. That's where her family's from."

"So after the war, he came there?"

"No, we moved back to Florida for a few years, when he got discharged. Steve said he was pretty messed up. I think he was in a hospital for quite a while. I have vague memories of my mom leaving us with some neighbors a few times. Maybe she was visiting him."

"So did he ever actually live in your home in Texas? Were you ever there as a family all together?"

"I think for almost a year. Steve said we stayed in Florida for a while, but Mom wanted to move back to Texas. When we moved, our father came with us. I remember him reading books to me before bed, eating at the dinner table. I remember him even being there one Christmas. But I guess the whole time he was driving my mother crazy. She told us later he was constantly coming home drunk or stoned. He kept getting fired from one job after another. Some nights he'd go out and wouldn't come back for days. I don't remember any of this."

"Do you remember when he left for good?"

She shook her head. "But Steve said he does. I was asleep. He said he heard our parents yelling. So he got out of bed and stood in the hallway. He doesn't remember everything they said, but he remembers the last thing. She told him that we'd all be better off if he just left for good and never came back. My dad said, 'All right then, I will.' That was the last we ever saw of him." She looked at Dave; he was writing as fast as he could.

Karen wasn't sure how she felt about all this. Emotionally, she felt detached, like she was describing someone else's life. Back then she had felt plenty of emotions. She remembered crying a lot after he left. And she remembered something else: her first dog, Alfie. That's why she'd gotten him. Her mother bought her a puppy to help her stop being so sad.

The plane started to shudder. Then it began shaking violently up and down. The fasten-seatbelt light flashed overhead, and an alarm sounded. Karen's left hand grabbed for Dave's right. She turned toward him, ducking her head into his chest.

"It's okay, Karen. It's just some turbulence."

She felt his free hand reach up and stroke her hair.

"But you can stay here just as long as you want."

34

It was Saturday morning, just after 9:00. Dave and Karen didn't get in from the airport last night until 8:00 p.m. Dave hoped she wasn't overwhelmed by his mother's hugs and heaping bowls of salad, Italian sausage, garlic bread, and baked ziti (with "fresh ri-GOTT-a and motzu-RELL-a").

He'd offered to put her up at a nearby motel, but his mother wouldn't hear of it. "What?" she said. "Jake can sleep on the couch. I already changed the sheets." They'd sat around the dinner table talking for two more hours. His mother had asked Karen a barrage of questions, but she asked them so nicely and was so encouraging you'd hardly notice she was being incredibly nosy and occasionally inappropriate.

Karen had answered them all, even the inappropriate ones, and never lost her smile.

Jake had stayed at the table the entire time. That was saying something, because it was a Friday night. He didn't say much. But as they broke to get ready for bed, Jake caught Dave in the hallway and whispered, "I like her, Dad. Really."

Dave had walked Karen to Jake's room while his mother cleaned up the kitchen, quietly apologizing. Karen gently scolded him. "Don't worry about me. I love your mom. She's a little over the top at times, but I kind of liked it. My mom . . . she was more on the prim-and-proper side."

"You sure you're okay?"

"Totally."

He'd wanted to kiss her good night. After the conversation at dinner, she was almost family. But he'd held back. It was too soon.

He walked down that same hallway now to knock on Jake's door. "Hey, Karen, are you up yet? Believe it or not, it's time for breakfast. A big breakfast."

"Just a minute," he heard through the door. "Be right there."

He stood and waited. Jake was still asleep on the couch, but he heard his mom out there waking him. Karen opened the door.

"I'm already showered and dressed," she said.

And she had put on makeup and fixed her hair. She looked beautiful. "Did you sleep well? I wanted to let you sleep in. Well, as much as possible with my mom's breakfast plans."

"I slept fine. But I'm on Texas time. It's still an hour earlier for me."

Compared to her he felt like a slob. He'd washed his face, but that was about it. Put on a baseball hat. Hadn't even shaved yet.

"Did you sleep well?" she said.

"Slept great. This is how I always look in the morning."

She walked past him. "If that's as bad as it gets, I could live with that," she said quietly.

He returned the smile and followed her out to the table.

"My, Mrs. Russo. Look at all this," she said. "What time did you get up?"

"About seven," she said, over the dish towel on her shoulder.

"Same as always." She turned around. "You and Davey sit. Start filling up your plates. Those eggs are for you two. I almost got Jake's and mine ready."

When Mrs. Russo turned to face the skillet again, Karen mouthed the word *Davey* at him, then gave him a thumbs-up.

"Ladies first," Dave said, pointing at the food on the table. Besides the scrambled eggs, there was homemade Italian bread, toasted and buttered. Bacon and sausage links. Coffee, orange juice, tomato juice. Karen took bird-sized portions of each but passed on the toast.

Jake came out of the bathroom, almost presentable, and sat down. "Thanks, Grandma, I'm starving." After last night's dinner, Dave couldn't imagine how that was possible.

After she'd added another layer of eggs to the bowl, his mother joined them. "So what are your plans, you two?" She pointed at Jake. "Him? I know he's got a game this afternoon."

"Well," Dave said, "Karen's here to help me find her father." Jake shot him a look that said, "Really?" Dave was glad Karen didn't see it. "And . . . we've got reason to believe he might be living somewhere in Florida."

"If he's alive at all," Karen added.

"You think he might not be?"

"It's hard to know, Mom," Dave said. "He left Karen and her brother when they were kids. He sent some cards for a few years, then after that . . . nothing. Karen's mother told her that he wound up living on the streets."

"That's so sad," his mother said.

"Yeah, he had it really rough after the war," Dave said.

"A lot of men did back then." His mother finally put some food on her plate.

"The thing is," Dave said, "if he stayed out there too long, he probably didn't make it. The average life expectancy for home-less men is midforties."

"That's terrible."

"It's a hard life."

"So how you two going to find him?"

"It won't be easy. I've got a list of things we can check on the internet. Karen and I are going to take a drive over to Perry. They used to live there when she was little."

"You better leave some time to take a shower," his mother said. Karen smiled.

"I will," Dave said. "We're going to have to get a move on to get there and back in time. Karen wants to go with me to Jake's game."

"Really?" Jake said.

"I'd love to watch you play," she said. "Your dad's talked about you more than anything else since we met."

Jake seemed to like that. "He couldn't be talking about how I play. I mostly sit on the bench. Today, we're playing the Red Devils. It's only our second game, but the coach told us to expect a close one. I might not even get on the floor at all. Maybe you two should do something—"

"I don't mind," Karen said. "I'd still like to come."

"Okay." Jake shoveled in a mouthful of eggs.

Karen and Dave had finished eating. Karen brought her plate and coffee cup to the sink. "Can I help you clean up, Mrs. Russo?"

"No, you and Davey go do what you came to do. I'll have this all spick-and-span in no time."

———

A few hours later, Dave and Karen sat in a noisy, crowded gym watching a very close game between the Panthers and the

Red Devils. He looked down at the gym floor, trying to find his son. Jake had been right; the coach didn't seem to have any plans of putting him in. In the third quarter, the Red Devils had started to pull away. Dave secretly started rooting for them. If the Red Devils ran away with it, Jake still might see some action at the end.

But it was not to be. The buzzer sounded; it was Red Devils 68, Panthers 65. Jake's team had lost, and he had sat on the bench the entire game.

That wasn't the only disappointment of the day.

Before the game, Dave and Karen had gotten on the internet, worked through every item on Dave's checklist, tried every trick in the book. But nothing had worked. They weren't any closer to finding Aaron Miller than when they started. Then the time they'd spent in Perry that morning didn't really turn up any new leads. Karen had just been too young to remember anything specific. The only thing she knew for certain was how much smaller everything looked. "Well, it would," Dave had said, "you were only three feet tall."

Dave was clearly more frustrated about it than Karen. She reassured him that it didn't really matter. He knew what she'd meant. It didn't matter to her. She hadn't really come here hoping to find her father; she'd come for the same reason he'd invited her: to spend time with him. But it mattered to Dave. He didn't want to let John Lansing and his two Vietnam friends down.

But it seemed obvious: Aaron Miller was either not in Florida or not on the earth.

"Are you still thinking about my dad?" she said.

He looked at her pretty face and kind eyes. The noises and sounds in the gymnasium came back into focus too. "Yeah."

"It's okay. I'm still glad I came. Even to the game. It's sad

Jake didn't get to play, but it was so exciting. I loved watching how much Jake cheered his team on. He didn't seem to mind being on the bench at all."

"No, he's got a great attitude about it."

"I'll tell you one thing," she said. "He may not have a girl-friend, but there's a really cute brunette down there, about three rows up from the floor, who can't keep her eyes off him."

"Really?"

"She's right down there behind the cheerleaders, wearing a bright red sweater. Dark shiny hair. Do you see her?"

Dave followed her eyes. Sure enough, a very attractive young lady was sitting in the third row, staring right at Jake. Dave looked at Jake and noticed he wasn't looking at her. The players of both teams were on the floor in single file, walking past each other, nodding and shaking hands in a show of sportsmanship. "Did you see him looking at her . . . during the game?"

Karen looked back at Jake. "Not once. I don't think he has any idea. But I know that look. She likes him."

Dave would have never caught something like that. "Do you think I should tell him?"

"I don't know. You're his father. Would he want to know?"

"I guess. I think so." These weren't things Dave typically thought about. "But what if she's not . . . a nice girl?"

"I can't say for sure," Karen said. "But I've been watching her most of the game. You can tell by the way she's dressed, the way she carries herself and interacts with her friends. She's the quiet type. Not flirty. If Jake doesn't approach her, she'll never make a move."

"You can tell all that without even having a conversation with her?" He looked down to the gym floor and found Jake. Jake looked up into the stands, saw him and Karen, and waved for them to come down. "He wants to talk to us." They stood and started down the bleachers.

"How much time until we leave for the airport?" Karen asked.

"Maybe three hours."

"Will Jake have to stay here awhile?"

"Are you wondering if he'll be through in time to join us?" Karen nodded.

"When he doesn't play at all, he doesn't have to shower. But the coach usually gets the guys together for a quick meeting. I'll see if he has any plans after." Dave loved the fact that Karen thought to include Jake. They reached the floor level. "There he is, over by the first row." Dave yelled, "Hey, Jake, over here."

They weaved in and out of the crowd toward him. As they neared, Dave wondered what Jake was up to. He was bent over trying to reach something that had fallen between the bleachers. When Jake stood upright, he was holding a newspaper. He unfolded it and looked at the first page.

"Hey, Dad. I found this in the locker room before the game."

"What is it?" Dave said. Karen stood beside him.

"Didn't you say the guy you and Karen were looking for was named Aaron Miller?"

"Yeah."

"A Vietnam vet, right?"

"Yes," Dave said.

Jake nodded. "That's what it says right here. On the front page of the local section. There's this guy here, some kind of hero, named Aaron Miller, a Vietnam vet. Even got his picture." He held it up for Dave and Karen to see. "Could this be the guy?"

35

Karen was stunned.

Jake had handed the newspaper to Dave, who held it out for both of them to see. The headline read:

Vietnam Vet Saves Life of WWII Hero's Widow

There were two photographs. On the left, a trailer lay smashed under the weight of an enormous tree limb. On the right, an elderly woman and an old but slightly younger man stood next to a fireman in all his gear. Their names were listed below, left to right: Irene Hamlin, Aaron Miller, and Lt. William O'Donnell.

"This is him, Karen. It has to be!" Dave sounded so excited.

But Karen didn't need Dave to tell her. The man in the picture was so much older, and he looked as though life had worn him to the bone. But she recognized his face. A flash of that face appeared in her mind, the last time she saw him, bending down to kiss her good night on the forehead, smiling, telling her to "sleep tight."

Dave read the first two paragraphs aloud:

On Friday afternoon, Irene Hamlin lay down in her trailer for a short nap. She had just spent Thanksgiving Day with her children and their families in Tampa. "I was exhausted," Irene said.

A moment later, she heard a loud crack. Her trailer erupted like a volcano, flinging her across the room. "I didn't know what happened," Irene said. "I wondered if a tornado hit my trailer, but there wasn't any wind, and it was sunny outside." A large tree limb had just broken off from an aging oak tree next to Irene's trailer and fallen across her living room.

Dave continued to read in silence. Karen did too.

A few moments later, Jake said, "I've got to go. The coach always calls a short meeting after the game."

"Are you doing anything after?" Dave said.

"A few of the guys are heading out to the movies. I figured you two would be . . ."

"That's okay, Jake. You go have fun."

Jake looked at Karen. "You're flying home in a little while, right?"

"In just a few hours."

"Well, it was great meeting you. Wish I could stay longer, but—"

"You go on, Jake. I really enjoyed spending time with you and your grandma."

Jake gave his father a quick side hug, said good-bye, and ran off toward the locker room. Dave sat on the first row of bleachers and kept reading. Karen sat beside him. Every few sentences, she looked up at her father's face.

Still holding the paper, Dave said, "It says he's a Vietnam vet, but it doesn't say anything about him winning the Medal of Honor." He looked at her. "Maybe they don't know."

"I guess not." She wished she shared his enthusiasm, but she couldn't. "Isn't that the newspaper you work for?"

"Yeah, but this article was written by a paper two counties south of us. I know the reporter. He mentions the trailer park's name but not its address. I could call him right now. I have his number on my cell. Karen, do you realize what this means?"

Sadly, she did. With it staring her in the face like this, she felt her insides churning.

"We've been searching for your father all over the place, and here he lives just an hour away. And look, he's still saving people's lives." Dave's face was all lit up. He stood, still holding the paper, and looked at his watch. "We could drive there and back in two hours. That would give us almost an hour there, and we'd still get back in plenty of time for your flight."

"What?" she said.

"You could see your father. Right now. Well, an hour from now."

"He might not even be home."

"True. But let's start driving. Your bags are all packed and in the car. I can find the number for the trailer park on the way. He obviously doesn't have a phone or we'd have found him already. But I'm sure the park does."

She was still sitting on the bleachers. "I don't know, Dave. Maybe we should wait."

"Wait? It's like God just handed us a personal invitation. Don't you want to see him?"

Karen looked down at her feet. The truth was she didn't, not at all. For her, coming here was about getting to know Dave better, spending time with him. Meeting his mom and Jake. She never imagined anything would come of this search for her father. At the most, she thought Dave might turn up a few interesting leads. She stood up. "Actually, Dave, I don't."

"You don't?"

"No. If you want to see him, that's okay. I know it's your job. I can take a cab to the airport."

"What? No . . . Karen. It is my job, but I don't have to see him today. I didn't realize it would upset you. You seemed so—"

"So calm about it before?"

"Yeah. But I can see how this would be a shock for you. I never even thought about it that way."

She was relieved to hear him say it, but she still felt all tense inside. She didn't really know how to describe it. All she knew was she wanted to go back to Texas.

Now.

This old man she was looking at in the newspaper, almost a stranger . . . the man who'd read her stories and kissed her forehead before turning out the light, was also the man who'd abandoned her and Steve almost forty years ago. Her only connection to him was a handful of cards he'd sent a few years after that, and then . . . nothing.

He'd made no attempt to find her, was never there for her at any point in her life. It was easier when she'd imagined he was probably dead. But there he was in the photograph, alive and well. The big hero. All this time, he hadn't cared about her, hadn't taken any interest in being a part of her life. Why would she want to meet him now?

Dave reached out his hand, laid it gently on her shoulder. "Are you okay?"

"Yes, but I think I'd like you to take me to the airport. Could we go there now?"

36

Something had changed between them. Something had shifted.

Dave was sure of it.

When he'd dropped Karen off at the airport a half hour ago, she insisted she was fine. They were fine. She had just been taken aback by the suddenness of seeing her father's picture in the paper after forty years of silence. Then, confronted with the idea of seeing him, she realized she just wasn't ready.

But Dave could feel her pulling away. Maybe not back to square one, but in those last few hours together she seemed distant. Their conversation no longer flowed. It was more like what you'd expect between two people who barely knew each other. Choosing words carefully, keeping things to themselves. But that's not how it had been between them since their first dinner at Chili's. It was like they had been given a pass, allowed to skip all the necessities and formalities most couples wrestle with in those early weeks and months.

He'd asked her to call when she got home safe, so he wouldn't worry. He looked at the digital clock in his car. He still had several hours before then. Hopefully, when she did call, he'd discover he was making something out of nothing.

Dave drove south on a nearly deserted county road on his way to Bentley's Trailer Park. He was used to driving through these long stretches of nothingness now, just trees and farmland rolling by mile after mile. The towns in northern Florida were mostly small and spread far apart. The region had a beauty and serenity all its own. A place in the Sunshine State unspoiled by tourism or developers. This was especially evident when you got closer to the historic river areas like Steinhatchee and Suwannee. He got the sense he was seeing pretty much the same scenery the early Timucuan Indians saw hundreds of years ago.

Dave had called the reporter who'd written the story about Aaron Miller about fifteen minutes ago and gotten the phone number and address of the trailer park. He'd just gotten off the phone with Sue Kendall, the park's manager. He didn't tell her much, just that he was a journalist who'd read the story about their handyman who'd saved that woman's life yesterday. Sue said he wasn't the first reporter who'd called today. She'd taken quite a few phone calls on Aaron's behalf, including a producer from some cable news channel.

But Aaron had made it pretty clear, he wasn't looking to be famous and wasn't interested in doing any more interviews with any more reporters. Dave had assured her that wasn't his intention. He wasn't a reporter looking for a story. "Well, you can come on down if you want," she'd said. "He's here, but he's off today. I don't know if he'll see you or not." Dave had thanked her and told her it was definitely worth it to him, that he'd like to give it a try. "Well, come on down then."

Dave had one more phone call to make before he arrived. A big one. He dialed the private cell number for John Lansing. Dave wasn't supposed to call this number unless it was something significant. When he did call, John would try to answer it himself.

This was as big as it gets.

"Hello? That you, Dave?"

"It is, John. Did you have a nice Thanksgiving?"

"We surely did. We're actually about to sit down to some nice-looking leftovers. Most of the family's here. Can I call you back in about an hour or so?"

"No need. This will just take a second. Thought you'd like to know, I'm driving right now to meet Aaron Miller. I should be pulling into the trailer park where he lives in about twenty minutes."

"*The* Aaron Miller?"

"The very one."

"So he's alive?"

"He is."

"Thank God! I can't believe it. How did you find him? I figured it'd take you at least a month or more, if you ever did."

"It's an amazing story. I'm thinking you must be praying hard or living right, or something. Because I'd been trying all my tricks and getting nowhere. Then today, it's like God just dropped him down right in front of me. Turns out he only lives an hour away."

"You're kidding. So he's right there in Florida?"

"Lives and works in a trailer park on the Suwannee River. And you're not going to believe how I found him."

"I've got to hear the story. Hold on, let me talk to my wife."

Dave waited maybe thirty seconds. He came to the intersection that led west toward the trailer park, stopped, and turned.

"Dave? My wife said I can have five minutes. Can you talk fast? She's thrilled, by the way, but the whole family's here."

"I understand. I'll do my best, you cut me off when I run out of time."

Aaron cleaned up the remnants of the frozen dinner he'd just eaten, thinking that today had gone a whole lot better than yesterday. He was grateful God used him to help Irene out of that trailer before it exploded but felt like he was being made to pay for it now. He'd had a bad dream last night. He was back in Vietnam dodging mortars. Figured the sound of that gas explosion triggered it. Now all afternoon, his back was aching something awful from the piggyback ride.

"In everything give thanks," he repeated to himself. So he thanked the Lord Irene hadn't died. And he thanked the Lord he hadn't blown up either. And he was thankful it was only the one bad dream, no flashbacks all day like he used to get years ago.

He glanced out the lone window and saw it was almost dark. Wanting to spend some time out on the deck by the river before it got too late, he dried off his hands and headed out the door. Across the way, he noticed Sue talking to a young man, maybe in his forties. Didn't have a camper behind his car. She looked Aaron's way and pointed. The man turned, saw him, said something else to Sue.

Not another one of them reporters, he thought. He'd seen his picture in the paper first thing in the morning and now wished he hadn't agreed to that interview. He'd asked Sue to please say no to all of the others who started calling. She was happy to oblige. In fact, she had been treating Aaron pretty special ever since the explosion. This morning she'd told him Mr. Bentley called after he'd heard about it, said to give Aaron a dollar-an-hour raise as a reward. Then she mentioned she was sorry that was all he was getting. "You saved his butt and ours too when you saved Irene. If she died in that thing, her family would've sued for sure, probably cleaned Mr. Bentley out. Then both of us would be out of a job."

One more thing to thank the Lord for, he thought.

He looked in the direction of the river but saw Sue waving her hand at him out of the corner of his eye. She motioned for him to come over. The man was now looking at him, smiling from ear to ear. What in the world? When he got closer, he noticed a strange expression on Sue's face.

"Somebody here to see you, Aaron. I promise, he's not a reporter. He's just told me some amazing things. I think you're going to want to hear what this young man has to say."

37

"Aaron, you won the Medal of Honor?" Sue said as Aaron came near. "Well, I'll be."

This wasn't good. How'd this fellow find that out? "It was a long time ago, Sue."

"How come you never said anything?"

"Don't like to talk about it much."

"Guess I understand why you ran in that trailer after Irene, when everyone else was scared to move. You're a born hero, Aaron. You know that?"

He didn't know what to say to that. Didn't even know himself why he'd done it. He turned to face the young man, who held out his hand.

"Mr. Miller, I'm honored, sir. I mean that sincerely."

Aaron shook his hand. "Most folks call me Aaron."

"If that's what you prefer . . . Aaron. My name is Dave Russo. I'm writing a book about the heroes of Vietnam, and I—"

"I don't wanna be in anybody's book."

210

"Well, Sue here tells me you're kind of a private guy. I can appreciate that. And whether or not you let me interview you for my book isn't the reason I came. Though, I hope after you hear me out you might reconsider."

"I don't follow you," Aaron said.

"Is there someplace we can talk?"

Aaron looked toward the river. "I was just heading out to the wood deck. Suppose we can talk there."

"I'll follow you. I'll explain a little more as we walk."

Lord, why are you doing this to me? I was only trying to help Irene out. I don't want all this fuss. He silently apologized for complaining as he walked toward the deck.

"See, Mr. Miller—Aaron—I'm not really here about the book. I'm really here representing three friends of yours."

"Three friends?" He couldn't imagine.

"Three of your war buddies from Vietnam."

Aaron didn't know he had any war buddies. Whatever was this fellow talking about?

"They still get together every few years for a reunion of sorts. They've been doing that since the war ended. But they've been trying to find you for the longest time. One of the men in particular. He's given me a good deal of money to do whatever I need to do to find you."

None of this made a lick of sense to Aaron. He kept walking.

"You remember that battle in '69, in Song Da Krong Valley?"

"Course I do. It was my last."

"You remember the three men you saved that day?"

Aaron hadn't thought about them for years. "Tex, Hammer, and Redman." They were the reason he'd received that medal. "I haven't seen them since . . ."

"When you were in the field hospital?"

"That was it." Such a long time ago. They reached the wooden walkway. Aaron stepped up and kept walking.

"I saw the picture of you in the hospital, with them standing around the bed."

"You did?" He didn't even remember anyone taking a picture that day.

"Tex showed it to me himself. His real name's John Lansing. He's the man who hired me to find you."

"Tex hired you to find me?"

"Yes, sir. He, Hammer, and Redman want very badly to meet you. Well, to see you again. Of course, they don't go by those names anymore. The other two men are Allan Summers and Paul Patterson."

Aaron wouldn't have known those names from any three names in the phone book. "Can't understand why they'd want to see me. I don't recall we were ever what you'd call war buddies."

"John said something about that, and he feels pretty bad about it. The thing is, all three of these men have done real well since the war. Especially John. He's actually an oil executive, a millionaire several times over."

"You don't say. Well, good for him."

"Man, this is really beautiful back here."

Aaron nodded. Though he wasn't aware of the sights and sounds this evening. This young man had stirred all kinds of feelings and memories inside him, talking about all these matters.

"John asked me to ask you if you'd consider flying out to Texas for a reunion."

"I don't know about that. I don't think that's a good idea." They reached the deck. Aaron walked toward the railing, looked out over the water. The sun had set, but you could still see pretty well. The river was dead calm.

"Is that a no?"

"I guess it is."

"May I ask why? I'm sure John's going to ask me."

How could Aaron say this? "Well, for one thing . . . I'm glad they've all done well. But things didn't go so well for me."

"John knows that. I think the others do too. They don't care. I mean, they care about the hard times you've been through. But it doesn't matter. I'd say that seeing you again has become extremely important to John. Wouldn't you—"

"But I don't have the kind of money folks need to travel. Airplanes and hotel rooms. I'm just a handyman. I can't even afford to—"

"But it won't cost you a cent. John's going to pay for the whole thing. The airfare, the hotel room, your food."

"That don't sound right," Aaron said. "For him to do all that. I don't even have decent traveling clothes."

"They want to thank you properly, Aaron, for saving their lives. You should have heard John go on about you. He told me everything that happened that day, what you did for them at the creek. He's willing to spend whatever it takes to make this thing happen."

Aaron looked out over the water. This was too much. He wasn't ready to face something like this. Not after all this time. "I don't think so, son. You go on back and tell John and the other fellows thanks. Really, I'm grateful they'd even want to do all that for me. But I think we should leave well enough alone."

Dave and Aaron walked back along the wooden walkway, mostly in silence. Dave had gently challenged Aaron to reconsider. Would he at least take a day or two to think and pray about it? Dave already knew a little of Aaron's story from talking with Sue. That he'd gotten his life cleaned up sometime in the late eighties. And that faith and church had a lot to do with it. "Aaron, he never misses church," Sue had said.

As they stepped off the walkway and strolled across the grass, Dave kept trying to think of some angle, some way to get Aaron to open up. He'd talked with a lot of Vietnam vets before, but he realized now that the men he'd spoken to were guys already willing to tell their stories.

Aaron just wanted to be left alone.

It was growing darker now. The park's streetlights had come on, and the lamps were on in most of the trailers. They stepped off the grass onto the main paved road. "So what got you interested in writing a book about Vietnam?" Aaron said, breaking the silence.

"I wanted to do it for my dad," Dave said.

"He's a vet?"

"No, he didn't get the chance to become one. He was killed in the Battle of Ripcord in 1970. I never got to know him. I was only three." For some reason, Dave didn't know why, but saying this out loud in the presence of this man, someone who'd fought hard, had almost given his life in battle, stirred emotions deep inside him.

"Men like your dad," Aaron said, "they were the real heroes. Not men like me."

Unintended tears rolled down Dave's cheeks. He quickly wiped them away, tried to blink them back, but Aaron saw it. They stopped walking.

"It's okay, son. Nothing to be ashamed of. A lot of good men didn't come back. I don't know why God let me survive." Aaron looked down at the ground. "'Cause I wasn't a good man."

"That's not true, Aaron. I know what men like you went through when you got home. All tore up. Not just your bodies but on the inside. My mom told me about it, and I've talked with a lot of vets already. You didn't get any help, nothing like our guys get now. People hated the war, so they treated guys like you terribly."

Aaron released a deep sigh, started walking again. Dave followed.

"But none of that explains what I did to my family," he said. "Betty and the kids didn't deserve what I did to them. I let 'em down something awful. It's like I was a different man then. Dead inside. My soul was black as night."

Dave suddenly remembered who he was talking to . . . this man was Karen's father. From what Karen had said, Aaron probably had no idea where she was, what had happened in her life. But she and Steve were "the kids" Aaron had just mentioned. Did Aaron even know he had grandchildren, a grandson stationed in Afghanistan in harm's way? He had to find a way to bring this up. When they reached the parking area in front of the main house, Dave said, "Aaron, do you still have the medal?"

Aaron nodded. "Keep it in a metal box in my room."

"Could I see it? I've never seen one, just in pictures."

"I suppose. It's this way." He walked across the parking area toward a storage shed.

Is this where Aaron lives? Dave thought. A single lightbulb dangled from a rusted metal fixture illuminating the doorway. As Dave stood there watching Aaron bent over, unlocking the door, it dawned on him that he was standing next to a national treasure. A living, breathing national treasure. A man who had won the highest medal for bravery and valor this country bestows in a time of war. And yet, there was nothing about Aaron that would ever draw attention to this fact.

He was a handyman in a trailer park, living in a shed.

The door creaked open. Aaron flicked a switch; a lamp came on. Except for a small cot, an aging armchair, a tiny refrigerator, and a microwave sitting at the end of a crowded workbench, Dave was looking at a storage room that doubled as a workshop. It didn't seem possible someone lived here. A memory flashed into his mind. The intimidation he'd felt, standing in the foyer of John Lansing's mansion in Houston.

It would break John's heart to see this.

"It's right over here on the shelf," Aaron said. "I don't think I've opened this box in ten years."

Dave watched as he moved something aside on the workbench and reached up for a plain metal box parked on a wooden shelf. The lamplight faded this far away, but Dave saw a picture frame sitting on top of the box. Aaron lifted it carefully, looked at it, set it on the workbench, then reached for the box.

Curious, Dave stepped up behind him to look at the picture. *Oh my*, he thought. *It had to be.* "Is that Karen and Steve?" he asked.

Aaron set the unopened metal box down. "Why . . . yes. It is. It's the only picture I have of them. My wife sent it to me just before Christmas, the last year I was in Vietnam." He stopped talking, and a puzzled look came across his face. "But how do *you* know about them?"

Dave froze. This wasn't how he intended to bring up the subject. "Uh . . . I've met them."

"You've . . . met them? Karen and Steve?" Aaron suddenly seemed so frail and weak.

"Yes, well, Karen. I've only talked on the phone with Steve. But Karen and I, we've actually become . . . good friends."

"Karen?" he said. Tears instantly filled his eyes. "You . . . know Karen?"

"Yes, I do," Dave said. He wanted to mention she had been with him just a few hours ago, but how could he? "She's a wonderful woman . . . Karen." He looked down at the fading picture of a baby smiling at the camera, squinting in the sun. He wanted to say, "And I'm in love with her."

Aaron seemed to wilt right before his eyes. He backed away from the workbench and sat on the armchair. His head all but fell into his hands as he began to sob.

38

Dave had waited patiently for Aaron to get through whatever was breaking loose inside him. It had taken almost fifteen minutes. Dave thought he should leave, just slip out quietly and give Aaron some privacy. Before he got halfway to the door, Aaron had asked him to wait.

"I want to hear more about Karen and Steve."

For the next thirty minutes, Dave had shared everything he knew about them with Aaron, including how he and Karen had begun to see each other and Dave's hopes that their relationship would continue. That conversation led to this moment, one Dave had been dreading. Aaron had just asked, "How do they feel about me—Karen and Steve? Do you know?"

"I can't share anything about Steve," he said. "I really only spoke with him briefly. I know from what Karen said, he was very excited when he heard about you winning the Medal of Honor. Neither of them knew that."

"I guess Betty never told them," he said, still sitting in the

218

armchair. "I don't blame her. Wasn't any kind of hero when I got home."

"You have a grandson in the military," Dave said. "He's stationed in Afghanistan right now. His name's Steven Jr."

Aaron smiled weakly. "I'll bet he's a fine boy. I'll have to start praying for him. What about Karen?"

Dave paused, trying to think of what to say. He'd wondered the same thing. He noticed a clock on the wall. She should be home now. "I'd say Karen is struggling." He'd already told Aaron all about his family, how his ex-wife Betty had remarried, and the way Karen talked about her stepfather as her real father. Aaron seemed to know all this. The only thing he hadn't heard was that Betty had died four years ago from colon cancer. It clearly saddened him.

"Karen's got a right to struggle," Aaron said. "They've got good lives now. They don't need me coming around messing things up." He looked down at the floor. "I've missed out on so much, though. For so many years."

Dave was sure he was about to lapse into another bout with tears. "Can I ask you something, Aaron? You don't have to answer if you'd rather not."

He looked up.

"I'd say one of the things Karen is struggling with—maybe the main thing—is why you never tried to contact her all those years. She thought you must be dead. I know your life got straightened out quite a while ago. How come you never tried to reconnect?"

"I did try. Several times. But Betty told me no."

"When was that?"

"Back in 1987, after I got off the streets and turned my life over to God. I even waited for six months to make sure I was really free and I knew I'd left my old life for good."

Aaron talked for the next ten minutes, pouring out his heart. It was abundantly clear how much he loved Karen and Steve, and it grieved him deeply that they'd been apart all these years. It was equally clear that his ex-wife, Betty, had shut the door, locked it, and bricked it over. Aaron had told him what she'd said in their last conversation together. Dave could understand why Aaron had given up hope of ever being allowed back in their lives again.

Karen didn't know this. He had to tell her.

Dave left things with Aaron on good terms. Knowing he'd have to call John and update him on the visit, he'd asked Aaron one more time to reconsider John's offer to fly out to Houston and meet him, Allan, and Paul. Aaron still said no, but he did agree to pray about it, maybe even talk to his pastor about it at church tomorrow. Aaron had thanked him several times for telling him about Karen and Steve's lives since they'd been apart.

As Dave walked across the parking lot toward his car, he looked at his phone. Still no call from Karen. She had to be home by now, probably even home from the airport. He wanted to call her but thought he should give it a little more time. He called John instead.

John answered the phone in an excited tone. "So did you meet him? Did you meet Aaron? How did it go?"

"I did," Dave said. "I just said good-bye for the night."

"So is he coming? I'm going to need a few weeks to set this reunion up."

"I'd hold off on making any big plans just yet." Dave spent the next ten minutes filling John in on his conversation with

Aaron, including what he did now for a living and where he lived.

"Saddens me to hear that," John said when he finished. "But I am glad to hear he got straightened out and off the streets. Did he seem healthy?"

"As far as I can tell. Still working with his hands every day. Folks around this trailer park love him, according to his boss."

"We've got to find a way to get him to come. Did you get any sense from talking to him why he's saying no?"

"First it was the money. When I told him everything would be covered, he still said no. My guess is, it has something to do with not feeling worthy of all this attention. He's an extremely private man, and he doesn't see himself as a hero, on any level. After his picture got in the paper for saving that woman, he turned down every other interview request, even from a TV station. When I mentioned about my book being about the heroes of Vietnam, the first thing he said was he didn't want to be in anyone's book. No one in this trailer park even knew he'd won the Medal of Honor."

"I know a lotta guys don't feel worthy of their medals. I sure didn't, and mine's a few notches below his. I imagine he feels even more unworthy after the way his life turned out when he got home."

"Losing his family the way he did," Dave added, "all the lost years between then and now . . . it really eats at him. I'd say he doesn't feel worthy of winning the medal back in Nam or worthy of wearing it ever since."

"We've got to find a way of changing his mind on that. I really want him with us this time. You said you think he might be softening up a little?"

"Maybe."

"Well, how about this," John said. "You stay there overnight and try again after he gets home from church."

"I was actually thinking the same thing."

"Then let's do it. Call me back tomorrow afternoon and let me know."

Dave hung up the phone and walked into the office. Sue was still there, but she looked ready to lock up for the night. "Excuse me, Sue. I'm thinking of staying over tonight. Know of any motels nearby? Didn't see any on the way in."

"Don't stay in a hotel, stay here."

"Here?"

"I've got a few trailers empty. Unoccupied rentals. Electric's on. They're furnished. Aaron's cleaned 'em all up."

"Well, I guess I can do that. How much per night?"

"Just tonight?"

"That's the plan."

"No charge, then. My treat."

"That's very kind of you. Say, did you hear me mention the book I'm writing?"

"The one about Vietnam heroes? Heard you tell Aaron that. Did you get him to change his mind about being in it?"

"Not yet. But I'd like to talk to some of the people who know him. That's one of the reasons I'd like to stay over. I bought this little video camera, and—"

"You making a documentary?"

"No, it's just for me, to help with my research. Think you could recommend anyone here in the park I could talk to?"

She thought a moment. "I bet Billy Ames will have some nice things to say. He's a Nam vet in a wheelchair, lost his legs in the war. Aaron's been helping him out a lot lately. And you might want to interview Irene Hamlin, the woman Aaron rescued when that limb crushed her trailer. She thinks the world of Aaron. Course, she's down in Tampa now staying with kin. I'm sure she'd be willing to talk to you. Either on the phone or you could drive down there."

Dave wrote all this down. "Anyone else? I'd like to have three." He was just about to suggest her.

"You know, I just thought of someone. A young teenage girl used to live here, up until a few weeks ago. She got pregnant, and her boyfriend came after her with a knife. Right over there in the trailer on Lot 31."

"Oh my."

"Aaron saved her life too, come to think of it. The boy came after him and he used some of his old combat moves to take him down."

Dave could hardly believe it. "I'd love to talk with her. Know where she is now?"

Sue shook her head. "Aaron helped her reconnect with her parents up in Georgia somewhere. She wanted to get as far away from that boyfriend as possible." Then a look came over her face. "But you know what?" She walked over to her desk. "I think I saved her parents' phone number." She opened a drawer, moved some things around. "Here it is."

Dave walked over, and she handed it to him.

"She'll be a great one to interview," she said.

"I agree. You've been so helpful. I guess if you're locking up for the night, maybe I should get that key to the rental trailer."

Sue got that for him, then gave him directions so he could find it easily in the dark. He said good-bye and walked out to his car. He glanced at his watch under a streetlight. Karen still hadn't called. He needed to call his mother, let her know he was staying over for the night, but he couldn't wait any longer.

He dialed Karen's number. It rang four times. He heard a click, expecting it to be her voice mail message.

"Hello?"

"Karen?"

"Hi, Dave."

She didn't sound good. "Are you all right? You make it back to Texas okay?"

"I did."

"I was getting a little worried. I thought you were going to call when you landed safely."

He heard her sigh on the other end. "I know . . . that's what I said, but . . ."

She didn't say anything for a few moments. "Is everything okay? I met your father, by the way. We actually talked for over an hour." He waited a moment. She didn't respond. It dawned on him, that probably wasn't a good thing to say now. "Karen?"

"Dave, I'm sorry. I had a lot of time to think on the plane ride home. I've decided we should back off for a little while. A few weeks, anyway. This whole thing is just moving way too fast for me."

"You're not talking about your father, are you?"

"No, I'm talking about you and me."

His heart sank.

"But this thing with my father hasn't helped any. It's all just too much for me right now. I need some time to catch my breath. I hope you understand. I do . . . care about you. But I really think I need a break."

"You said a few weeks?"

"Yeah, at least a few."

"How will I know when it's okay to call you?"

"How about I call you?"

That old saying ran through his head: "Don't call us, we'll call you." This wasn't good at all. "I guess that's okay."

"I'm really sorry, Dave. I don't want to hurt you or your mother or Jake. I just need some time."

"I understand." But he didn't. He didn't understand.

She said a polite good-bye and hung up.

39

It was a quiet night of sleep for Dave in the trailer, compliments of two Benadryl. He had to take them. Before he did, he'd tossed and turned for over an hour trying not to think about how he'd messed things up with Karen.

It was Sunday morning, and he normally went to church back home on Sundays. He thought about asking Aaron which church he attended but thought that would come across as being pushy, like he was trying to butter him up into changing his mind about Houston. Instead, Dave made himself a cup of coffee, found a church service on television that seemed relatively safe, and slept right through it (also compliments of the Benadryl).

When he awoke on the couch, he got cleaned up and walked over to the park office to ask Sue which trailer Billy Ames lived in. She'd said she was pretty sure he wasn't a churchgoer and that Dave could mention she had recommended him. Dave also got the phone number of Irene Hamlin's son in Tampa, thought he'd call her next, after stopping in to see Billy.

He walked over to Billy's trailer and heard a dog bark as he walked up the ramp. Rapping gently on the metal door, he heard a humming sound on the other side in between the dog barks. "Who is it?"

"My name's Dave Russo. Sue, the manager, suggested I talk to you. It's about Aaron Miller. She said you two were friends."

"You a reporter?"

He was, but . . . "Not exactly, more like a friend."

"Aaron doesn't want to talk to any reporters. Since we're friends, I'll respect his wishes, so I don't have anything to say to you."

"I'm not here as a reporter."

"What kind of thing is that to say? You're either a reporter or you aren't."

Dave laughed; the man had a point. They were still talking through the closed door. "I came here to find Aaron. One of his friends from the Vietnam days hired me to find him, to try to get him to come to a special reunion. And I'm also a friend of Aaron's daughter Karen." That was still true, he thought.

The door opened. A happy-faced retriever greeted him. Behind the dog, Billy Ames sat in an electric scooter in a blue terry-cloth bathrobe. "Pretty dog," Dave said.

"Yes, she is. Okay, Tess, let the man in." Billy backed his scooter up, and Tess followed. "Aaron's probably still at church."

Dave walked into the living room. "I know. Could I sit down a few minutes? I'd like to explain why I'm here."

"Guess I got a few minutes."

Dave sat on the edge of an old plaid sofa. He had his little video camera in his coat pocket but didn't want to scare Billy off with that just yet. Dave explained the situation as quickly as he could. Billy listened then interrupted him when he got to the part about Aaron's medal.

"Say what?"

"Aaron won the Medal of Honor," Dave said. "Back in Vietnam."

"You're not serious."

"I am. I've seen the picture of Nixon pinning it on him at the White House in 1970. The guys who hired me to find him, they were there in the battle where he won it. Aaron got it for saving their lives."

"That's incredible. Aaron never said a word." Then he thought about it. "But you know, I'm not surprised. That's the kind of guy Aaron is. You shoulda seen the way he went right in that crushed mobile home to save Irene."

"See, that's exactly why I wanted to talk with you. I'm writing a book about Vietnam War heroes. I'd like to make one of the main chapters about Aaron, maybe the first one. I think you could help me. Not about the battle scenes, obviously, but I'd love to hear what he's like now. What it's like to be his friend. Would you be willing to do that?"

"I'd consider it a privilege. Isn't that something?" he said, more to himself. "Aaron got the Medal of Honor."

"Is it okay if I record you? It's just a lot easier than taking notes."

"That's a video recorder? Such a small thing."

Dave said it was, and Billy said he needed a few minutes to spruce up. Dave waited until Billy came back looking just about the same, except he'd swapped out the robe for a gray T-shirt and had combed his hair. Dave fronted him a few questions, then pretty much listened as Billy talked about Aaron nonstop for the next forty-five minutes.

He'd offered a lot more information than Dave could use, but mixed in there was at least five minutes of gold. Including a jaw-dropping secret that Billy said he'd never told a soul. It was about the day Aaron had come over to fix his ramp. Billy said he had a gun lying right there on the table beside him and was all set to pull the trigger. Aaron's care and friendship, not just that day but every day since, had pulled Billy out of his depression, gave him a flicker of hope again.

After they parted, Dave walked down Billy's ramp with an even deeper respect for Aaron Miller than before.

He was glad he got all this on tape.

Later that day, just after sundown, Dave was traveling back to Bentley's after spending the better part of the afternoon in the car, driving to and from Tampa. In between, he'd met with Irene Hamlin for an hour. She was delighted to talk about "my good friend, Aaron. He saved my life, you know."

Once again, Dave was glad he got it all on tape. And once again, he was even more in awe of this man, Aaron Miller. It was sad that Aaron viewed himself so poorly, as if he had never done anything worthwhile with his life. Billy Ames thought the world of Aaron, and so did Sue, the park manager. And like Sue, Irene said everyone at Bentley's loved him. She didn't know a soul who'd say a cross word about him, thought he was the kindest, nicest, most thoughtful man she'd ever met.

On the way down to Tampa, Dave had called the number Sue had given him for the parents of Heather, the pregnant teenage girl. He left a voice mail. On the way back, Heather's father had returned Dave's call, and after hearing Dave out, he put Heather on the phone. She was happy to tell him all about Aaron. She got choked up and started crying halfway through the story. Dave couldn't take notes on the road, so he asked her if she had any way to video her story. She agreed to make a video and send Dave the memory card.

When Dave pulled into the trailer park, it was almost dark outside. He was so tired he couldn't imagine driving all the way home tonight. A light was on in the park office. Maybe Sue would let him stay in the trailer one more night.

As he got out of the car, he felt pretty satisfied about the day's efforts. He couldn't wait to call John with his updates. First, he wanted to take one more try with Aaron, see if he could give John a glimmer of hope that Aaron might change his mind. He glanced over at the storage room where Aaron lived.

A light glowed from the lone window. He decided to go there first.

Walking across the parking lot, he tried to think of a way to break the ice. Then it dawned on him. He hadn't gotten a chance to see the actual medal last night. Aaron had reached for it, but then the whole conversation shifted when Dave had seen the picture of Karen and Steve.

Karen. *No, don't go there.* He had been doing his best to not think about her all day. That was the one thing he'd dreaded about the car drive to Tampa. All that time alone to think. The phone call to Heather and her parents had helped, but it had only covered a fraction of the time. An audio book saved his sanity and kept him from drifting into full-blown depression.

He tapped lightly on Aaron's door. Heard some noise inside, then the door opened.

"Oh, hello," Aaron said. "I thought you'd gone home already."

"Not yet," Dave said. "Think I might stay one more night. I wanted to ask if I could see your medal. Remember last night you were just about to show it to me, then we started talking about your family and never got back to it."

"Oh, that's right. Well, you better come in then."

Things looked pretty much like they had last night. Aaron walked over to the shelf, lifted the picture frame, and set it on the workbench. Only this time he didn't look at it. He reached for the metal box and slid it carefully from the shelf and set it down. "Been a long time," he said.

Dave guessed he meant since he'd looked at it.

Aaron pulled the lid off, and there it was. He stood aside so Dave could come close. "The Congressional Medal of Honor," Dave said reverently. Aaron had been in the Marines, so this was the navy's version. A collar of light blue ribbon formed a circle. In the middle, a small blue octagon with thirteen white stars. Hanging from this, a gold five-pointed star. "Aaron, it's beautiful. Can I bring it over to the light?"

"I guess. But be careful. I haven't let that thing touch the ground all these years."

"I will." Dave wanted to say "You must be so proud" but knew Aaron would struggle with that.

The medal was even more remarkable under the lamp. Dave was struck with the realization that he was standing next to the man who'd earned this highest honor in battle, dodging a hail of machine-gun fire and mortar to save three men.

Aaron had no idea who he was or how much he mattered.

Dave thought of something he could ask. "What was it like being at the White House, having the president put this around your neck?"

"Wish I could remember. It's all a blur. I was so high on pain meds that day. Well, every day back then." Dave handed the box back to Aaron. Aaron took the box and said abruptly, "Oh, I guess I'll go with you to Houston."

"What?"

"Changed my mind. I'll go with you. You go ahead and call John for me, and the guys. Tell them I'll come, and thank them for their kind offer."

"Aaron, thank you. I don't know what to say. John will be ecstatic. What changed your mind?"

"Something my pastor said this morning after church. I could tell, he thought I should go. After I explained things, he said, 'Aaron, sometimes people need to experience the blessing of thanking others for the kind things they've done, and the people who've done those kind things need to let them.'"

Then Aaron smiled. It was the first time Dave had seen him smile. "What else did he say?"

"He said that when I die and go to heaven, and the Good Lord says to me, 'Well done, my good and faithful servant,' well, he feels pretty sure I'll struggle hearing that too."

They talked a few more minutes. As they shook hands at the door, Dave told him he'd find out the details about the Houston trip from John and let Aaron know.

When Dave stepped into the night air, for a few moments he was excited about this new development and couldn't wait to call John. Then he thought about Karen. He wanted to call her and share the good news. It was so nice having someone in his life again to talk with about everything, big or small. And this was a big deal.

But he couldn't call her. He was in exile.

Besides, the last thing she wanted to hear was news about the father who'd abandoned her as a little girl.

40

A week later, Dave was back home trying to keep himself busy and his mind off Karen. It wasn't working. He should be happy. John certainly was. He couldn't believe how effectively Dave had pulled off his assignment. In just over a week he'd found Aaron, met with him, and got him to agree to come to Houston. Allan and Paul were happy too. The three men couldn't wait to see Aaron again and had set December 18 as the date for the reunion.

Now less than two weeks away.

Another reason Dave should be happy . . . it was the first week of December. Christmas was in the air. The stores and government buildings in town were all decorated. Houses were trimmed with Christmas lights. And of course, Christmas music dominated the radio stations.

Dave had never noticed before how many Christmas songs had depressing themes. He used to hum or sing along with them, blissfully unaware. Now he heard them differently. They were written for the heartbroken.

"Blue Christmas" was one, seemed like he heard it at least once a day. And "Have Yourself a Merry Little Christmas"—he used to really like this one but now understood that it was about someone having a lousy Christmas, hoping next year might be better. Even the Charlie Brown classic "Christmastime Is Here." The lyrics sounded nice, but now Dave heard all the minor chords, the glum, haunting melody, and the children singing sadly in the background. Were they singing about him or Charlie Brown?

All week, Dave had done his best to put off his mom and Jake when they asked about Karen. At first, he'd give a vague answer or change the subject. Then he felt guilty, so he sat them down and told them the truth. Of course, they were encouraging and sympathetic. He was especially touched by Jake's efforts to comfort him. "Doesn't sound like she dumped you, Dad. She just needs a little time."

So Dave busied himself by working on his book, mostly Aaron Miller's part. Aaron hadn't agreed to be interviewed yet; Dave was waiting for the right time to ask. A large part of his time was spent reviewing the videos of Billy Ames and Irene Hamlin. Heather had also sent her memory card in the mail, as promised.

Dave was almost finished editing and splicing, reducing over two hours of tape to a solid five minutes. But the end result was priceless. He couldn't watch it without getting choked up. The next step was to transcribe this into text for the book. But the video turned out so good, he decided to hold on to it. Maybe he'd upload it to YouTube when the book came out.

When the book came out. As if he already had a contract.

He tapped the play button and watched the video once more, thinking through different music tracks that might work. The front door of the condo closed hard. Had to be Jake coming home from school.

Dave called out as Jake walked by his bedroom door. "No practice today?"

Jake backed up, stood in the doorway. "No practice on game night."

"I forgot you had a game tonight."

"You coming?"

"Of course."

"How are you doing?" Jake said. "About this Karen thing. You seemed a little sad at breakfast."

"It's just hard to sit around and wait until she calls. *If* she calls."

"I'm kind of surprised how much this bothers you, considering how short it was. I mean, the two of you—"

"I know what you mean." Dave swiveled in his chair. "I wish I could just snap out of it. The thing is . . . I've only felt like this one other time in my life, about one other woman."

Jake nodded. He knew Dave was talking about his mom.

"I just can't believe God intended us to meet, for me to feel all these things again, only to let it slip away so fast. But I don't know what else to do."

"What else? You're not doing anything, Dad. You're just . . . waiting."

It felt odd to Dave, getting dating advice from his seventeen-year-old son. "But she asked me to give her some space," Dave said. "She even said not to call, to wait and let her call me."

"That was over a week ago. I think maybe it's time for you to do something, to fight for her. Maybe you should just fly there and show up at her front door, try to win her back. It'll show her how you really feel."

Dave thought about it, then realized where this advice was coming from. He and Jake had sat through a number of romantic movies with Dave's mom the last few months. "I appreciate what you're saying, Jake. Really. But I don't think it's going to work out like it does in the movies. The girl has to totally love the guy, and she's heartbroken they're not together anymore. Then she walks away from the relationship because she thinks he loves someone else. So someone tells the guy, 'Go after her. Don't let her get away.' If I do that here, it's going to come off like I'm some kind of stalker."

"Yeah," Jake said, "I guess you're right. I don't know, Dad. You're in a tough spot." He smiled. "Maybe you just need to give her some more time. She'll come around."

"Thanks. And thanks for trying to help out your old man."

"Sure, Dad." He headed toward the kitchen.

Dave had only known Karen a short time. Before that, he'd been perfectly happy day after day, just having Jake back in his life. Besides, who gets to have a conversation like this with their teenage son? He sighed.

But then a thought came . . . Karen did need to hear something he'd planned to say the last time they'd talked. He reached for his phone and dialed her number before he chickened out.

Please, Lord, help me not to come off sounding desperate.

Karen set her purse down on the desk. When she pulled her cell phone out, she saw she had a missed call. It was from Dave, maybe twenty minutes ago. Her heart began to beat faster. She quickly checked and was disappointed he hadn't left a message.

Before she talked herself out of it, she hit the send button. She waited a few rings, then heard that wonderful voice saying hello on the other end. "Hi, Dave, sorry I missed your call."

"That's okay. I didn't leave a message. I know you said to wait until you called me, but—"

"Actually, I had a good talk last night with Steve and Aileen. They're helping me sort out some of the things I'm going through."

Dave didn't respond for a moment. "Are you doing any better?"

"I think so," she said. "And I want to thank you for not calling me all week."

"It was hard."

She was relieved to hear him say this. "It was hard for me too," she said. "But to be honest, I've needed the break. Talking it over last night helped. I can really see this is more about my dad than you. I guess I'd been fooling myself. It bothers me way more than I realized . . . why he left us, why he never came back, or even tried. I thought I was completely over it, but when I saw his face in the newspaper like that, all these things just started floating up."

"Did I make it worse? I've been trying to think of things I said or did all week, the only thing I can—"

"It really wasn't you, Dave. Other than I really do think we were moving too fast. At least for me. I've barely dated anyone since Greg left four years ago, and here I was flying to Florida and meeting your mom and Jake already."

"I'm sorry, I shouldn't have pushed you into that."

"You didn't push me. I went willingly. But that's just not who I am. I don't just get up and fly away with some guy on a moment's notice." She thought that sounded a little harsh. "I'm not saying you're just 'some guy.'"

"That's all right. Have you thought about a pace you might be more comfortable with?"

"A little bit, but I'm not sure I want to talk about that just yet, if that's okay. I still think I need a little more time. Is that what you were calling about?"

"No, but just know I'm ready to go whenever you're ready, at any pace you want. I was calling about something you just mentioned a moment ago, about how much you've been struggling with the way your dad left and him never trying to reconnect with you. Turns out, he did."

"What do you mean?"

"You never knew about it. Your mom never told you."

"When?"

"In 1987, six months after he got off the streets and got his life straightened out. He called your mom and told her he didn't want to cause any trouble for her and had no intentions of making any legal claims, but he really wanted to start having a relationship with you and Steve again."

"He did?" Karen felt her heart stirring inside.

"Your mom turned him down flat. Karen, I know you loved your mother a lot. I'm sure she was a wonderful lady and had very good reasons for doing what she did. And I don't want to make any judgments here, but—"

"What did she say? Why did she turn him down?" Karen suddenly felt a rush of anger come over her.

"I'm making you upset. Look, I can call back—"

"I'm sorry, Dave. I'm not upset at you." She had to calm down. "Did he tell you why she refused him?"

"He told me what she said. It was . . . well, to me, it was pretty harsh. I'm sure she thought she was just protecting you guys."

"I want to hear what she said." There was that edge again. "I'm sorry."

"That's okay. I know this is deep water."

She heard Dave exhale.

He continued. "She made it clear you all wanted nothing more to do with him. She said you had brand-new lives now. A real father you even called Dad. He provided a normal family life and had been doing it for years." Dave paused. "Are you okay? You sure you want to hear the rest?"

"Yes."

"Aaron remembered one quote word for word. I wrote it down. Here, let me read it." A brief pause. "Your mom said, 'It's too late, Aaron. Much too late. I'm glad you're feeling better about yourself now, and you finally got off the streets. But this isn't your home anymore, and this isn't your family anymore, either. It's best you leave well enough alone. The kids don't even ask about you anymore. Haven't for years.' He was all broken up talking about this, Karen. He cried, almost uncontrollably, for twenty minutes, talking about how sad he was that he missed out on so much of your lives."

Karen began to cry. "I'm sorry," she said. "I just need a minute here." She pulled a package of tissues from her purse and tried to get control.

"I'm sorry, Karen. I hate hearing you so sad."

"This is all pretty hard to hear," she said as she wiped her eyes. "But I'm glad you told me. Really."

"Listen, I won't keep you on the phone much longer. But I have an idea. Don't answer now, just talk it over with your brother, pray about it, and let me know. The man who hired me to find your dad set up a reunion in Houston for December 18th. I'll be flying there with Aaron, so they can spend some time together.

I know Aaron—your dad—would be wide open to the idea of heading up to Fort Worth to visit you and your brother after." He waited a few moments.

She wasn't sure what she thought about the idea. She wasn't sure of anything at the moment. "I'll talk with Steve about it."

"That's great. Take your time. I'm not going anywhere. And Karen, I don't know if this helps, but . . . I've gotten to know your dad some. I'm hoping to get to know him a lot more. He's actually quite a remarkable man. If you don't mind, I'd like to send you something."

"What?"

"A little video I've made. It's not him talking but what others here at the park are saying about him. It's only five minutes long."

41

Aaron looked at himself in the mirror. It was about nine-thirty in the morning. He barely recognized the man looking back at him. Apparently, Dave Russo, the young man who'd set up this whole reunion affair, had called Sue two days ago, asked her if she'd take some time to help Aaron get a makeover.

That was the word she used when she'd taken Aaron out yesterday—a makeover. The day started with a new haircut, and not at his regular barber's but some fancy hair salon. Made Aaron cough, all the perfume in that place. And he wasn't too sure about the fellow that cut his hair. Especially when he'd tried to talk Aaron into coloring his hair darker and giving him a manicure. Aaron thought he was kidding. Aaron passed on that one. He wasn't about to let anybody play with his hands.

But he had to admit, he kind of liked the way his haircut turned out.

He also liked all these new clothes: shirts, trousers, belts, socks, and shoes. Dave even insisted he get a suit, a nice dark

241

blue one. And a long-sleeved white shirt and matching tie. Then Sue bought him a suitcase with wheels to put all these new duds in for the trip. She wouldn't let him see what any of it cost. She said Dave had given her a budget to work with, and by day's end, she'd come well under that.

But it didn't seem right, getting all these things for nothing.

Aaron walked to his armchair, picked up his Bible, and zipped it inside the front flap of the suitcase. It was tucked neatly on top of his metal box, the one holding the Medal of Honor. Dave had insisted he bring it, told Aaron they'd be putting the suitcase in a compartment right over his seat while they flew. No chance of it getting lost or stolen that way.

Aaron lifted his new brown jacket off a hook and put it on. It was only a little nippy outside, but Dave said it was considerably colder in Houston, where they were headed. He was picking Aaron up this morning to take him to the airport, supposed to be here any minute.

Aaron sat in the armchair, ready to go. When Dave arrived, Sue said she'd call on the walkie-talkie. He looked over the place. Guess everything would keep; not like the world would stop spinning if he took a few days off. *Thank you, Lord*. He had to admit, now that this day was here, he was mostly looking forward to it. He hadn't flown on a plane in over twenty years. Probably hadn't bought any new clothes since before that; he only shopped in thrift stores.

"Okay, Aaron, you can come on out. Dave's here." Sue's voice startled him. He slid the suitcase off his cot, wheeled it to the door. Hard to believe that before the sunset, he'd be four states over in Texas.

The same state where Karen and Steve lived.

He opened the door, saw Dave in the parking lot in front of

the main house. Already had the trunk open. He was talking with Sue. Aaron took a few steps, then remembered. The picture. He hurried back to the workbench and grabbed his picture of Karen and Steve, still in its frame. He unzipped the top of his suitcase and carefully laid it inside.

Now he was ready.

When Dave saw Aaron coming, he waved. "All set, Aaron?"

"Guess so."

"You look mighty fine in your new clothes."

"I don't know how to thank you, buying all the stuff in this suitcase. I—"

"You can thank your friend John when you see him. I'm just the messenger."

"You think that old heart of yours can take all this excitement?" Sue said as he reached the car.

"Guess we'll find out."

As Dave took his suitcase, they heard a familiar humming sound. Aaron turned to see Billy and Tess heading their way.

"I know you didn't want no big send-off, Aaron," Sue said quietly. "But I had to tell Billy."

"That's okay, Sue. Meant to tell him myself."

"He's still the only one in the park knows about your medal," she said. "I don't know why you don't want anyone knowing about it, but I'll keep my trap shut. Can't promise Billy'll do the same."

"Hey, Billy." Dave closed the trunk lid.

"Dave . . . Sue . . . Aaron," Billy said when he reached them.

"They gotta be on their way now, Billy," Sue said. "Or they'll be late for the airport."

"I didn't come to give a speech. I just wanted to say good-bye to my friend."

"You know I'm coming back in a few days," Aaron said.

"I know . . . but I also came to say . . ." He let go of Tess's leash, and with the same hand gave Aaron a full salute. "Aaron Miller, I'm proud to know you and proud to be called your friend."

Aaron just stood there, didn't know what to say. He started getting choked up. He saluted back. "It's been my honor to know you, Billy."

"And I want you to know . . ." Billy picked up Tess's leash again. "Everything you hear me say on that tape Dave has . . . I meant every word."

They shook hands again, said their good-byes, and Aaron got in the car. As they drove off, Aaron turned to Dave. "What was Billy talking about?"

"You mean the tape?" Dave said. "Just some things he told me, to help me with my book research. I'll let you hear it later."

42

Three hours later in Keller, Texas, Karen got her things together at the model home where she worked and headed out to meet her brother for lunch. Last night they'd had a big welcome-home party for his son, Steven. He'd just gotten home from Afghanistan that afternoon. His leave allowed him to stay home through New Year's. Karen was so excited.

She was sure having Steven home would revive her Christmas spirit. After the party, Steve had stopped her at the door, asked her to meet him today for lunch. She had a pretty good idea why. Sometime last week, Dave's video had arrived, the one he'd made about Aaron Miller. Karen couldn't bring herself to watch it. She'd given it to Steve, asked him to watch it first. He probably wanted to discuss what was on the tape.

"Hey, Karen, before you leave, can I talk to you a minute?"

Karen looked up. It was Gail. She had just hung up the phone. "Sure, I've got a minute. What's up? You need anything while I'm out?"

"No." Gail stood and walked over, a serious expression on her face. "I'm going to feel awful if you find this out from Steve instead of me."

That didn't sound good. "Find out what?"

"You asked me a couple of weeks ago to stop hounding you about Dave. I bit my lip at least a dozen times since, but you know I did my best to stop."

Karen nodded. She really had.

"Well . . . your brother called me yesterday."

"Why?" Steve never called Gail.

"He asked me all kinds of questions, about you . . . and about Dave."

"What kind of questions? Did Dave call you?"

"No. But Steve is concerned about you. That's why he called. He just wanted my honest impressions on some things, and you know how he is. He asks really good questions, and I—"

"What did you tell him?"

"It'll take too long if I get into all of it. Just know, I gave him permission to tell you anything I said." A worried look came over her face. "Please don't be mad at me. I'm just trying to be a good friend."

Karen didn't like the sound of this. She glanced at her watch. It was time to go. "Don't worry about it, Gail. I'll be fine." She hurried out the door, now wondering if she really did know why Steve had asked her to lunch.

Karen walked into Steve's favorite Tex-Mex place, not far from his law office. He was already seated. When she got to the booth, he'd already ordered her a Diet Coke. He was munching on chips and salsa.

"Hi, Karen. I already ordered you that chicken strips salad. You seem to always get that here. But the waitress just left if you want to change it."

She sat across from him. "No, that's fine. I'd probably look at the menu for five minutes and order that anyway. Guess you're in a bit of a hurry."

"I am. I have to scoot in about forty-five minutes."

She took a sip of her soda. "So how's Steven doing? It was so great seeing him last night. I guess you guys are going crazy having him home."

"We are. That's partly why I'm in a rush. I've got one more client I have to see today, then I'm taking the rest of the afternoon off to do some Christmas shopping with him."

"That ought to be interesting, the two of you men on a shopping spree." She wanted to keep asking him questions about her nephew but realized he was in a hurry. "So, what's up? I thought you might want to talk about that video I gave you, but Gail just told me about your phone call yesterday."

"You sound a little upset."

"Not upset . . . well, maybe a little. She said you were asking her all about Dave."

"That was the main reason I called."

"So . . . why didn't you just call me?"

"I did better than that. I asked you to lunch. I just called Gail to get her thoughts. You consider her a friend, right?"

Karen nodded. "A good one."

"I just wanted to see if she'd made the same observations about you that Aileen and I have."

"What are you talking about?"

"About you and Dave."

"There is no 'me and Dave.' We're still on hold for now."

"I know, and I know you asked us to stop bugging you about it when you came back from Florida. Gail said you asked her to do the same thing. But you've got to know, when Aileen and I talked with you last week, I was doing my best to gently nudge this situation."

Karen thought a moment. "I recall you were helping me sort things out about our birth dad."

"I was, mostly. But I really wanted to talk more about you and Dave. Last week, you didn't seem ready."

"I'm just . . . I just wanted to slow things down. There's nothing wrong with that."

"Seems more like you've shut things down."

"No. I just thought I'd take some time off, give the whole thing a rest, see how I felt after that. Thought maybe I'd wait until after Christmas or New Year's. If I still feel strongly about him then . . . I'll give him a call."

"You said 'still feel strongly.' So you do have strong feelings for him?"

"Well, yeah. I guess I do. But we were just moving way too fast. And then this whole thing with our dad came at me out of nowhere. So, why are you bringing this up now? Is it because of what you saw on Dave's video?"

"Probably. I'm sure that stirred the pot. And I do want to talk about it. But I keep thinking about what happened between you and Dave. And from listening to Gail, she said almost the same thing Aileen and I were thinking."

Karen waited, but he didn't continue. "So . . . what is it?" Karen said. "Do you really like Dave or something? I thought you guys only talked once or twice on the phone."

"I don't know him well." He took a drink of his iced tea. "But I think I know you pretty well, as well as anybody does."

"Okay, so what have you, Aileen, and Gail figured out about me?"

"I guess it's just . . . we haven't seen you *that* happy for such a long time."

"You mean when I was with Dave?"

"Yeah. I couldn't believe it when you called me and said he'd asked you to fly to Florida with him, and you wanted to say yes."

"I couldn't believe you thought I should go," she said. "You're my big brother. Why did you?"

"Because I could see the effect he was having on you. I've wanted you to be happy for so long. That's what I saw in your eyes and heard in your voice when you talked about Dave. I knew Greg had hurt you so badly and so deeply. And I knew you haven't opened your heart to any other man since. I knew how closely you've been guarding that heart against being hurt again. So I figured, if you were willing to open up so quickly to Dave, after all you've been through, you must have seen something very special in him. And I guess I believed God must be in it, because I knew you wouldn't dare open your heart to love again for just anyone."

Karen set her glass down. Steve really did understand her, maybe better than she understood herself. She felt her emotions beginning to stir, as if they were starting to break out of the box she'd locked them in the past few weeks.

"Let me ask you something," he said. "You've put yourself, me, Aileen, and Gail on this moratorium. Nobody can talk about Dave Russo. But be honest, have you stopped thinking about him?"

"What?"

"How often do you think about Dave?"

"Some."

"How much is 'some'? Once a day, every few days? Once a week?"

She looked away. The truth was, she thought about Dave all the time. When she caught herself, she'd force her mind to think about something else.

"That's what I thought," Steve said. "Karen, you're in love with the guy. Gail thinks it. Aileen thinks it. And I do too."

"I can't be in love. We hardly know each other."

"Well . . . knowing someone does take time. But you can't turn your heart on and off like a switch. I knew I loved Aileen within two days after we met." The waitress walked up with their tray of food. "By the way, I also want to talk with you about Dave's video."

She was glad the waitress had come and that Steve had changed the subject. They both stopped talking while the waitress set the food down. After, Karen said, "So you watched it?"

Steve nodded. "Yeah. And . . . I couldn't stop crying."

Oh great, she thought. Now she knew she didn't want to see it.

"After Steven and I finish Christmas shopping this afternoon, I'd like to stop by your apartment. I want to play it for you."

"I don't think I can do that." She felt a rush of tears, but she shut them down. "I'm not ready."

"I'll be there. Just you and me. Karen, look at me." She looked up. "You need to see this video. I think we need to see it together."

"Okay," she said feebly, reaching for a napkin.

"And after we watch it," Steve said, "there's something else I need to ask you about. Something pretty important."

43

Dave and Aaron sat together in the first-class section on a nonstop flight to Houston. Dave had briefed John Lansing earlier on the somewhat fragile hold Aaron had on things most people take for granted. Like flying. Like staying in hotels. Like eating food in restaurants. Like buying brand-new clothes. John had given Dave the green light to spring for the first-class tickets, mostly to honor Aaron. Dave was glad because it also gave them a better atmosphere to talk.

On the car ride to the airport, Dave had kept the conversation light, drawing Aaron out on day-to-day life at the trailer park. Aaron wasn't a big talker, but he had some good stories. Now on the plane, with almost three hours together, Dave hoped to get into some deeper conversations. They were at cruising altitude now. Aaron was just getting back from the restroom. Dave got up to let him slide by into the window seat.

"They cram a whole lot of bathroom in that little space," Aaron said.

"They sure do."

"Could live the rest of my life never using that toilet again." Dave smiled. "But I don't mind these seats one bit. Way more comfortable than I was expecting, and there's plenty of room. You always hear people complain about that."

"Actually, the whole plane's not like this, Aaron. This is first class. You probably didn't see the rest of the seats, since we came in right up front. Back there, they cram three seats in the same space we've got here. And see all this leg room? Back there it's about half."

Aaron looked over his shoulder, then whispered, "I suppose these seats cost a little more money then."

"A little bit," Dave said.

"I can't get over all the trouble John and the other men are going to on my account. Do you remember Hammer and Redman's names? I know you told me once."

"Hammer's name is Allan, and Redman's name is Paul. Allan and Paul."

"Hammer is Allan, Redman is Paul," he repeated. "I need to get it straight. I'm going to be seeing them tonight, right?"

"I'm not sure. I don't think so. The get-together is tomorrow. John's the only one who lives in Houston. Allan and Paul are probably traveling there today like we are. The plan is for me to rent a car once we land, then drive to the hotel. We'll all meet at the hotel tomorrow."

Aaron repeated their names again. "Do you know if they changed much since the war?"

"I've only met John. But I did see that picture of the four of you at the hospital in 1970."

"That's how I see all three of them in my head," Aaron said.

"John's face looks much the same. He's a little heavier, got a little less hair. And it's gray like yours. I have no idea how much the other two have changed. But I'm sure you'll be fine after a few minutes. None of these men were with you when you received the Medal of Honor, right?" Dave thought he knew the answer to this. He was hoping to get Aaron talking about the war.

"No, the hospital was the last time I saw them. It was months later I got the medal, after they shipped me to a hospital in the States."

They looked at each other, Dave hoping Aaron had more to say. But he didn't. He smiled, turned, and looked out the window. Dave watched him a moment, trying to think of something else to keep the conversation going. The flight attendant came by, asked if they wanted something to drink. After she took their orders, Dave said, "Aaron? Can I ask you something?"

He turned from the window. "Sure."

"It's something about the war. If you're uncomfortable talking about it . . ."

"Is it something for your book?"

"I might like to include it in my book someday, if you ever change your mind." He smiled. "But right now, I'm just curious. John told me what he remembered that day in the creek. He said he was certain he was going to die that day. Allan and Paul too. He still has no idea why you saved them. He especially feels bad considering how they treated you before then. It wasn't like you were saving good friends."

"No, I suppose not."

"So why'd you do it?"

Aaron thought a moment. "They were going to die if I didn't."

"But . . . you almost died when you jumped in."

"Yeah, I suppose that's true."

"Weren't you afraid of dying?"

"Wasn't thinking about it right then."

"John told me he lived in constant fear, every single day."

"He said that? I don't recall him ever looking like he was afraid."

"He was. He said it about drove him crazy. How did you overcome it?"

"Not sure I did. I remember being that afraid. All the time. Every hour of every day. Got so bad I thought of killing myself a number of times, hoping to get relief."

"That sounds like the kind of fear John talked about."

"Fear's an awful thing."

"But you got control of it."

"I think I just buried it awhile. Actually, fear's why I started volunteering to be point man all the time, on patrol. I knew I couldn't kill myself, figured I'd let the enemy do it for me. It's a weird way to think, but it's what I did. The guy on point was often the first to get it. When I wasn't on point, I'd just sit around being worried sick about how many days I had left till it was my turn again. I finally decided, the heck with it, I'm just going to be on point every chance I get. That way I didn't have to live in fear all the time. I figured if my number's up, it's up."

"Did you ever get shot or wounded before that day in the creek?"

"Nope, never did. An odd thing, considering the chances I took. I started thinking, maybe God was looking out for me. Maybe my number wasn't up till he said it was up. That's why I had to help Tex, Hammer, and Redman. It was supposed to be me out there on point that day. It was my fault they got pinned down."

"You blamed yourself?"

Aaron nodded. "See, after a while, being on point so much

got my senses trained to spot things. I never would've walked into that big open area of the creek. I saw Redman heading right into a trap. I shoulda spoke up, tried to stop him. It was my fault, what happened."

"So you don't think you deserved the medal?"

He shook his head no.

"But Aaron, you saved three men's lives. And got hurt pretty bad in the effort."

"Maybe, but doesn't seem like a man should get a medal for doing something he should've been doing all along. And I wasn't being brave. I was scared to bits running out in the open like that."

It was extraordinary hearing how Aaron's mind worked, but Dave felt he had to speak up. "Aaron, I've interviewed a lot of men who won medals in battle, and read a whole lot more interviews in books. Most of those men were just as scared, and most of them didn't feel like they were worthy of the honor they received. But believe me, from what I've heard, they gave the right medal to the right man this time, and for the right reasons."

Aaron seemed puzzled, like he couldn't absorb what Dave just said. The flight attendant came back, set a Diet Coke in front of Dave, a cup of coffee in front of Aaron. She mentioned she'd be back in a few minutes to take their orders for lunch.

"They're going to feed us lunch?" Aaron asked.

"Looks like it. Usually something nice in first class. As good as some restaurants."

"Billy told me all they give folks anymore is peanuts. Some airlines don't even do that. Guess I'll wait and see what they've got on the menu. Decide if I'll eat that or my sandwich."

"You brought a sandwich?"

"It's up there in my suitcase."

"That's fine, Aaron. You eat whatever you want. And when you're done, this airline even brings around these nice hot towels to wipe your hands with."

"Hot towels for your hands?" He sat back and looked out the window, then repeated quietly, "Hot towels. Well, I'll be."

44

Aaron opened his eyes, but he could have sworn he was still dreaming.

He normally awoke to the dusty rafters in his storage room at Bentley's, the pine knotholes from the underside of the roof staring back at him. What his eyes beheld now was more like a palace. He lifted his head and scanned the room, even more amazing in the daylight than what the lamps and chandeliers had revealed last night.

He lay in a king-sized four-poster bed, big enough for three people. A whole living room sat right there inside his bedroom. But that was nothing compared to the even bigger living and dining area just outside his door. This hotel room was as big as a house. A whole family eating Thanksgiving dinner could fit around the dining room table. Dave said it was an antique made of mahogany.

The whole place was decorated for Christmas, but not like the things he set out at Bentley's. Seemed more like the set of a

Hollywood Christmas movie. Not just in this room but in the hotel lobby, even the streets downtown. And it was much colder here than in Florida, but Aaron didn't mind; made it feel even more Christmassy this way.

He sat up and looked over toward the bathroom door, smiling as he remembered soaking in the whirlpool tub last night. Like nothing he'd ever experienced. Dave had to help him figure it out, but he insisted Aaron had to take a bath in it. Not because he smelled bad. Dave said people took baths in these things just to relax, for no other reason than how it made them feel.

It felt very good.

Dave called this the Governor's Suite. They were staying at the Four Seasons Hotel on the twentieth floor. Dave stayed in a smaller second bedroom at the other end of the suite. But even that room was bigger and nicer than anything Aaron had ever slept in. Aaron looked over at the clock. Felt like he'd slept till noon, but it was only eight-forty.

He got up, put on the terry-cloth robe that came with the room, took a moment in front of the mirror, raking a brush through his hair, then walked into the next room. Figured they must have a coffeepot somewhere in a place this nice.

"You're up." It was Dave, sitting in one of the fancy armchairs in the living room. Looked like he had a Bible open and a nice cup of coffee sitting on an end table beside him.

"You fixed a pot of coffee?"

Dave smiled. "Didn't have to fix it. In a hotel like this you just call room service. Over there on the counter, there's a carafe of coffee. They just brought it about twenty minutes ago. I already had breakfast. I didn't know what you'd want, but there's a menu right next to the coffeepot. Just mark down anything you like, and I'll call it in for you."

"Room service," Aaron said. Hard to imagine. He'd never had room service. He looked over at the dining room table, a big basket of eats sitting in the middle. All kinds of nice stuff in there. Beef jerky, made right here in Texas, pretzels, cashews and peanuts, little packages of crackers and different cheeses in fancy wrappers, some chocolate bars. Aaron had thought he'd be eating breakfast from what he saw sticking out of that basket. Maybe he should get some nice scrambled eggs and bacon then. As he walked through the room toward the coffeepot, it felt unreal.

"Quite a view, isn't it?" Dave was standing by the window now, looking out.

"So high it makes me dizzy." Aaron poured his coffee.

"Did you read the note John left you last night? It was in that basket on the table. He was very apologetic that he couldn't meet us when we got in, said he had a bunch of details he had to nail down yesterday. But he said Allan and Paul got in okay, and they can't wait to see you."

Aaron couldn't fathom why. "I'll give it a look right now." He took his coffee cup and the menu and sat at the table. He reached over and slid the beige envelope out of the basket and opened it up. Inside was a note and a photograph. He smiled as he looked at it. There they were: Tex, Hammer, and Redman, smiling at the camera. Three old men. Just like him. Hammer—Allan—might even have more wrinkles on his face.

He picked up the note and read:

Dear Aaron,

I'm so glad you agreed to come. Allan, Paul, and I have said it so many times over the years when we'd get together. "Aaron should be here." I can't believe the four of us will finally be together again. This will be our best reunion ever. I'm really sorry I couldn't be there to greet you. Sounds like Dave's doing a great job in my place. Hope you enjoy this basket of snacks. It's the stuff we always munch on at our reunions.

Feel free to hang out at the hotel today, or if you want, Dave can take you around the city, show you the sights. Whatever you do, eat a light lunch. We've got a big dinner planned. I'll meet you and Dave in the lobby around 4:30, then take you up the elevator to meet the others. Thought we'd have more privacy, so I've arranged for us to eat in a separate room instead of a restaurant.

So looking forward to this,
John

Dave and Aaron sat on a couch in front of a massive Christmas tree in the hotel lobby. Elvis Presley sang "Blue Christmas" through the house speakers, reminding Dave that Karen had not called him before they'd left for Houston. He'd hoped she might have watched the video he'd made, that it might have softened her heart toward meeting Aaron in Fort Worth after this Houston trip, and that he might still have a chance with her.

It didn't happen. He was still in exile.

He did a pretty good job blocking such depressing thoughts, most days. If it weren't for all these depressing Christmas songs on the radio, he might have this situation licked. He looked at his watch; John should be here any moment. "You look real nice in that new suit, Aaron."

Aaron looked up, attempted a smile.

"You nervous?"

He nodded. "Not sure why. Everyone's been so nice to me. You especially. I want to thank you for that, Dave, before we meet the others and I forget to say it."

"You're welcome. But really, I've enjoyed every minute. No reason for you to be nervous. You're going to like John, I can—" Dave looked up. John had just stepped out of the elevator. "There he is." Dave stood up; Aaron did too.

John looked around by the tree, saw them both. A big smile came over his face. He walked right to them. As soon as he recognized Aaron, tears welled up in his eyes. He picked up his pace. "Aaron, I can't believe it. It's really you."

Aaron smiled, put out his hand. John took it, used it to draw him into a big Texas hug. He was almost a head taller than Aaron. Dave smiled but nearly laughed out loud at the expression on Aaron's face. Especially as John's hug went on a bit long.

John pulled back but now had both hands on Aaron's shoulders. "Thank you so much for coming all this way. I've been waiting for this day for so long." He let go and wiped the tears from his eyes.

"Good to see you too . . . John." Aaron smiled. "It's going to be hard calling you and the others by your real names."

"Don't worry about it," John said. "You can call us whatever you like." He turned to Dave, held out his hand. "You did it, Dave. You brought Aaron to us. I knew you would."

"Thanks, John." Dave shook his hand.

John turned back to Aaron, a puzzled look on his face. "Aaron, you're not wearing your medal."

"Well, I . . . I uh . . ."

"I'm sorry, John," Dave said. "I texted you, guess you didn't get it. Aaron didn't feel comfortable wearing it around his neck. But he did bring it, right?"

"Got it right here." Aaron held out the metal box in his left hand.

"Well, look," John said. "We better get upstairs, the others are waiting for us. Don't worry about it, Aaron. Whatever you're comfortable with. Follow me." He turned and headed back to the elevator. "It's just on the third floor."

The three men walked through the lobby then headed up the elevator.

"So what's for dinner?" Dave said.

"Three choices. All of them good, you ask me," John said. "A nice filet mignon, broiled lobster tails, or some fancy chicken dish. Can't remember what just now." He looked at Aaron. "But Aaron, you can have some of each if you can't decide." The elevator door opened. "It's just down this hallway here, a couple of doors down."

"You lead the way," Aaron said.

When they reached the door, John stopped. "Dave, can I have a brief word with you?"

Dave nodded. They walked a few steps away, just out of earshot. "Aaron's about to get quite a shock in just a moment. I should have mentioned it to you before now. Got so busy I just forgot. You stay close to him tonight, all right?"

"Sure, John . . . I can do that." Dave had no idea what he was talking about. They walked back and joined Aaron waiting by the door.

"You ready, Aaron?"

"Guess so."

John put his hand on the door latch. Aaron spoke up. "John,

before we go in . . . I just want to say, thanks for all you've done for me here. The clothes, the suitcase, the airplane ride. Then this fancy hotel room. I really—"

John looked into Aaron's eyes, and the tears welled up again. "Aaron, all that? It's just . . . stuff. I owe you my life."

45

The door opened.

Before it reached the halfway mark, Dave knew something was up.

He'd expected a room the size of a small suite, but the back wall was at least fifty feet away. On the left, a stage had been set up. Two men in suits were standing on it, off to one side. Two familiar photos shone on a movie screen hanging from the ceiling. On the left was a grainy photo of a young Aaron lying in a field hospital bed. Around the bed, younger versions of John, Allan, and Paul stood in military fatigues. The other picture was of President Nixon draping the Medal of Honor around Aaron's neck at the White House.

"What is this?" Aaron's eyes opened wide, trying to process the scene.

"I'm not sure," Dave whispered. As the door opened the rest of the way, Dave saw that the right side of the room was filled with people sitting at round banquet tables set for a fancy dinner. Like the rest of the hotel, the room was fully decked in Christmas décor. The lights were dimmed over the tables. At first glance, he didn't recognize a soul. No one said a word.

John led them inside. "Sorry to do this to you, Aaron. This part of the reunion's a surprise." He leaned over and whispered, "People wanted to jump up and yell 'Surprise!' when you came in, but I told them not to. Wouldn't do to have our guest of honor drop dead of a heart attack."

"Who are all these people?" Aaron asked. He looked like he wanted to be anywhere else right now.

"I'll tell you in a minute, Aaron. But first, let's go up on stage here and see Allan and Paul. Dave, would you join us?"

Dave nodded. They led Aaron up three steps on the side of the stage. The bright lights made it even harder to see the crowd, but Dave noticed they all stood as Aaron reached the center. Dave recognized Allan and Paul from the picture. Both men's faces were filled with emotion. They rushed toward Aaron then all four men shook hands and patted each others' backs. Paul pulled Aaron into a bear hug. "I can't ever thank you enough, Aaron," he said, tears filling his eyes.

The crowd erupted in applause.

John stood back from the others as the applause continued. He walked up to a microphone and motioned for everyone to let him speak. "Thank you all. You can be seated . . . at least for a few moments." He turned to Aaron. "We've set some chairs over there on the stage for you men. Please have a seat. Aaron, we'd like you to sit on the chair closest to the front, please."

Dave looked at Aaron, unable to read his face. He seemed a little better, but he had tears in his eyes. He squinted and leaned forward, trying to see the people sitting at the tables.

"I don't think you know most of the folks sitting out there, Aaron. But they know all about you. Allan, Paul, and I told them who you are. Especially what you did for the three of us that day back in February of 1969, in a muddy creek in South Vietnam. They know what the three of us knew that day . . . it was the day we were supposed to die."

John paused to regain his composure; a few started to clap again. John lifted one hand to quiet them, wiped the tears from his eyes with the other. "If you all clap every time I say something nice about Aaron, I won't be able to get through this." He took a deep breath. "But see, we didn't die. Bullets were flying not ten inches over our heads. Mortars blowing up all around us. Paul over there—we called him Redman then—was all shot up. We couldn't move. We just lay there out in the middle of that creek, covering our ears, waiting for the end to come. But . . . it didn't come."

There wasn't a sound in the room.

"In the middle of that nightmarish scene, one man pushed past his fears and rushed in to save us." He got choked up again, pulled out a handkerchief to wipe his eyes. "Tell you what, I'm just going to let Paul come up here and read what the U.S. government said Aaron did that day."

John and Paul nodded and exchanged seats. Paul came up to the mic, holding a sheet of paper up with a shaky hand. He looked over his shoulder at the photograph of the four men at the field hospital. "Until this evening, that moment was the last time I saw the man who'd saved my life." He turned and looked back at Aaron. "Aaron, I was grateful then. But now?" His eyes filled with tears. He wiped his face with the napkin. "I'm so much more than grateful for what you did for me that day. There aren't . . . there just aren't words to explain . . ." Paul blinked back a new onset of tears.

He took a deep breath, exhaled slowly. "I'm just going to read this or I won't make it through." He held the paper up again. "These are the words from the official citation read aloud the day Aaron Miller was given the Medal of Honor, this nation's highest award for bravery."

Dave looked up at the picture of Aaron with Nixon.

For conspicuous gallantry and intrepidity in action at the risk of his life above and beyond the call of duty. Private Aaron Miller, as part of the 3rd Battalion, 9th Marines, distinguished himself during the defense of Fire Support Base Cunningham. Members of his company were on patrol in the Song Da Krong Valley looking for enemy units that had attacked the base the night before. A firefight erupted in a creek below. The patrol had walked into an ambush. One Marine was instantly killed, three others were cut off from the rest of the patrol, pinned down in the middle of the creek. One of them was seriously wounded. The enemy attack intensified. Hundreds of rounds poured in from well-defended positions. A barrage of mortar attacks began falling into the area with increasing accuracy. Pvt. Miller ran through a hail of machine-gun fire toward his three brothers-in-arms. He was knocked down and wounded by a mortar round, got up, and began firing a grenade launcher with great effect at the enemy positions. More enemy mortars fell, exploding within a few yards of Pvt. Miller's position. Disregarding his personal injuries, he made a one-man frontal assault, fully exposing himself to enemy fire, launching additional grenades which effectively silenced the enemy mortar units. Inspired by his courage, the entire patrol rushed forward, pouring effective fire into the enemy's positions, causing them to fall back in full retreat. During this second assault, Pvt. Miller was shot in the abdomen. Ignoring this, he tended the wounds of a fellow Marine until relieved by a medic. Then he collapsed from his wounds. Pvt. Miller's gallantry and extraordinary heroism are in keeping with the highest traditions of the military service and reflect great credit on him, his unit, and the United States Marine Corps.

Paul dropped the hand holding the paper to his side. "I am here, alive and well, forty years after the events I've just described, because of this man, Aaron Miller." He pointed toward Aaron, then looked back at the crowd. "I was that wounded soldier lying facedown in the creek that day. The one Aaron rushed out to save. But my wounds weren't half as bad as the ones he sustained while coming to my rescue." His voice began to crack and shake. "I was . . . so afraid. But Aaron came. Everyone else in the patrol froze, but Aaron came. Even after he was knocked down by a mortar round and received over a dozen shrapnel wounds, still he came." Paul wiped the tears from his face. "Who does that?"

The words were so powerfully spoken, but no one even thought to clap or make a sound. Dave had experienced this before while interviewing a number of vets. But never in a crowd this size. Someone would say something, describe some moment in battle, and suddenly it was as if you were standing on holy ground. Dave felt it strongly right now. So did everyone.

Paul backed away from the microphone. Allan stood up, and they exchanged seats. Allan came to the microphone. He looked back at Aaron. "Aaron, would you stand next to me? I want to introduce you to someone. Well, to a lot of people."

After Aaron came up, John and Paul stood and walked toward him. Dave got up last and stood behind them. He looked out toward the crowd. He still couldn't see anyone's face clearly beyond the bright lights.

"Could we lower the lights up here," Allan said, "and bring up the lights over the tables? I want Aaron to see everyone's faces when I tell him who you all are." Allan turned to Aaron. "Aaron, these are our wives, our sons and daughters, their spouses, and our eighteen grandchildren. They drove and flew here from all over the country for one reason. To thank you. They know, and we know . . . none of them would be here if it weren't for you. And none of us . . ." Allan started to lose it. "Tex, Redman, and I would not be here. We wouldn't have lived the lives we've enjoyed these last forty years apart from the sacrifice you made for us that day in that bloody creek. Jesus said, 'Greater love hath no man than he lay down his life for his friends.' That's who you were, what you did for us that day. But the three of us know, we weren't friends to you."

Allan wiped his eyes. "The truth is, we treated you pretty badly sometimes. But still . . . you came. In the moment that mattered most, you treated us as friends." He put his right arm on Aaron's shoulder and just cried.

John once again came forward. "Aaron . . . Allan, Paul, and I wish we could have been there the day the president gave you the Congressional Medal of Honor. But that didn't happen. So, with your permission, would you grant us the great honor of placing the medal where it rightly belongs?" As John spoke, Dave stepped forward and presented John with Aaron's little metal box.

Aaron's eyes filled with tears again. He nodded, then looked down toward the stage floor. The three men gathered around him. Aaron lifted his head, allowing John to place the medal around his neck. As soon as he'd finished, John, Allan, and Paul instantly stood at attention and saluted. The whole room erupted into applause. Aaron's eyes moved back and forth throughout the room, tears rolling down his cheeks.

Dave looked over the crowd and noticed many were crying too. Then he saw something that took his breath away. At the very last table, in the farthest corner of the room. It was Karen, standing, wiping her tears with a linen napkin. His heart instantly began beating fast.

A man about her age stood next to her, arm around her shoulders, crying. Had to be her brother Steve. He was holding a woman's hand; Dave figured his wife, Aileen. Beside her, a young Marine stood ramrod straight in full dress blues.

She came. Karen came.

He looked at Aaron, who was crying, trying to take in all this attention. But it was clear to Dave, he had no idea who they were.

Dave's heart broke. He could see nothing more through his own tears.

46

The first time their eyes met across the room, Dave was still on stage. But Karen had her eyes on him from the moment he'd walked through the doorway. All her doubts were gone. Steve, Aileen, and Gail had been right. She did love him! She lifted her napkin, wet with tears, smiled, and waved at him. He waved back.

But these tears were for her father. She could freely call him that now. Something in her heart had melted last night as she'd watched Dave's video with Steve. She no longer resented him. How could she? He'd suffered through so many things alone, abandoned by the government, cut off from the care and comfort of family. But as Steve put it, the same God they worshiped each Sunday had not cast him aside. The Good Shepherd had gone after him, had found him and restored him. Then when Aaron had tried to come back, seeking to reconnect with her and Steve, he had been turned away.

But not anymore.

After a little time had passed, Karen had been able to let go of the resentment she felt toward her mother for making that decision. It hadn't been her mom's call to make. She hadn't even asked them what they thought. They were no longer children at that point, needing to be sheltered and hidden from the harsh realities of life. She had, essentially, robbed Karen of over twenty years of relationship, hundreds of moments she and her father might have spent together.

He had wanted that, and now so did she. She was willing to give this relationship a new start. Watching that video, listening to three total strangers talk about Aaron with such love, admiration, and respect made her realize . . . she wanted to know this man. She didn't want to miss out on any more moments. When Steve had suggested she drive down here together with his family, she'd instantly, tearfully, said yes.

Karen looked up at the four aging soldiers onstage, Dave right behind them. He had no idea what was about to happen next.

"Can we go see him now, Dad?" It was her nephew, Steven.

She turned to catch Steve's response. "I think Mr. Lansing's about to call us up. Now, remember, after we go up on stage, we agreed to let your grandfather eat dinner with his war buddies. But we'll have plenty of time together after that."

Karen looked up again at Dave standing next to her father. He was looking right at her. She smiled, acknowledged him with her eyes.

John got everyone's attention again. "Hey, folks, we've got another surprise in store for Aaron tonight." He looked at Aaron. "You might want to take a seat for this next one. There's another group of folks here tonight who drove a long way to see you." John looked toward the back of the room at Karen and Steve and nodded.

"Okay," Steve said. "Let's go."

"Just you two?" Aileen asked, meaning him and Karen.

"No, all of us."

When Dave saw Karen and Steve and their family making their way toward the stage, he instantly figured out what John had in mind.

John looked at him and said quietly, "Dave, would you mind taking it from here?"

"Not at all." Dave looked at Aaron, his eyes fixed on this small group of strangers climbing the stage steps. "Aaron, these are . . . some special people I'd like you to meet. Well, *meet* isn't exactly the right word, for two of them anyway."

Aaron stood by his chair. "I suppose we can do that." He smiled, but he looked so nervous.

Dave noticed the handsome young Marine in dress blues leading the way. It had to be Steven Jr., Aaron's grandson. Behind him stood Karen. Tears welled up in her eyes. Behind her were Steve and Aileen, and at the end, he guessed, their two teenaged children, a boy and a girl.

A huge smile appeared on the young Marine's face as soon as Aaron looked his way. He hurried across the stage, walked straight up to Aaron, and stood at attention and saluted. Tears filled his eyes as he held the salute. "Grandpa . . . it's an honor."

Instinctively, Aaron returned the salute. Then he thought . . . *Grandpa?*

Aaron looked back at Dave, whose face was beaming. Still holding the mic, Dave walked in front of the small group of people, stood next to a woman at the end, and reached for her hand. She quickly took it. What was going on? Aaron looked at her face. She was crying. The man standing next to her was crying, and the woman next to him too. The Marine ended his salute then stood off to the side, blinking back tears.

Can this be . . . ?

"Aaron," Dave said, "this is Karen, your daughter. And this is your son Steve and his wife Aileen. You've just saluted your grandson Steven Jr., just in from Afghanistan. And these are your other grandchildren. They've all come down from Fort Worth to see you."

Karen . . . Steve?

His face suddenly felt hot. Tears filled his eyes. He didn't know what to do, what to say. They had come here? To see him? "I . . . I'm so . . ." Tears poured down his face. "I never thought I'd see you again." He felt faint and collapsed in his chair, then buried his face in his hands and cried.

Karen and Steve rushed to his side. He felt their arms around him. "We're here, Dad," Steve said. "We're here." They were crying nearly as hard.

Through his tears, Aaron heard Dave address the crowd, his words filled with emotion. "I guess you all are wondering what's going on up here. This is Aaron's daughter and son, Karen and Steve, who he hasn't seen since they were children. And Steve's family, who Aaron has never met until right now." The room erupted in applause. Everywhere people reached for napkins to dab their eyes.

Aaron finally found the nerve to lift his head. When he did, Karen's beautiful face was right there. She handed him a linen napkin. He took it and wiped his face, then leaned forward and kissed her on the forehead, like he'd done every night when she was a little girl. But maybe it was a mistake. It made her cry even harder. "I'm sorry," he said. "I didn't mean to—"

"Don't apologize, Dad," she said. "I'm so glad you're here." She threw her arms around his neck.

———————

Dave stood a few feet away and let the moment play out. He was so happy. The scene before him was beyond anything he'd hoped for. Steve finally stood, then Karen. Dave walked beside her and took her hand again.

Steve handed his father a fresh napkin. "If you can pull it together, Dad, there's some others here who are dying to meet you."

"Okay. Not sure how much more excitement this old heart of mine can take." He wiped his face and rose to his feet.

Steve introduced him to his wife Aileen and his two other children, Kate and Andrew. They were a little shy, but both came over and gave him a hug without being asked. Then Steve turned back to his son, now standing at ease, who gave Aaron a warm, very non-military hug. He looked down at the medal around Aaron's neck. "I'm so proud of you, Grandpa."

Aaron had to fight back a new wave of tears.

"Can I get a picture with you?" Steven asked. "I'm going to put it on Facebook tonight, let the guys back in Afghanistan see it."

"Okay, if you'd like."

Steve, Aaron's son, looked down at the medal. "It's beautiful, Dad."

Aaron nodded his thanks. Everyone took turns getting pictures with Aaron wearing his medal, including John, Paul, and Allan. Afterward, as everyone began leaving the stage, Aaron's grandson Steven walked up to the three Vietnam veterans. He stood at attention, saluted them, then held out his hand. "Thank you, gentlemen, for your great service to our country . . . and all you've done tonight to honor my grandfather."

"Doing this has been one of the greatest joys in my life," John said. He waited till everyone had cleared the stage and started down the steps himself. Then he stopped. "Wait, I almost forgot." He walked back up to the mic. "Folks, I know you're all probably hungry and, like me, emotionally exhausted. But we've got one more small group of people who have a few words they'd like to say to Aaron. If you'd all take a seat, we'll dim the lights. This will only take five minutes."

47

Aaron took a seat at the guest-of-honor table with John, Paul, Allan, and their wives as the lights in the room dimmed. Dave slipped back to sit next to Karen, but he could still easily see Aaron's profile at the front. "I can't believe you're here." He reached for Karen's hand.

"It was your video," she said. "I think they're playing it now."

"Really?"

Steve leaned over and whispered, "Uh, I beg your pardon. I think I deserve some credit here."

"Okay," Karen said. "Your video and some things Steve said."

"And Aileen . . . and Gail," Steve added.

"Okay," Karen said. "I had some help."

"Thanks, Steve," Dave said. He looked at Aileen. "And thank you too. For whatever you said to get her here."

The video began to play on-screen. Dave turned, recognizing the intro music. Then his face appeared on-screen. *Oh man*, he thought. This close-up was way too . . . close. He'd have to redo this intro bit.

Karen squeezed his hand. "It's you."

He looked at her. She was looking up at him on-screen, smiling.

"Hi, Aaron, Dave here. I've put this little video together for you. Not sure what I'm going to do with it. Initially, I made it just to get some input from a few of the people at Bentley's Trailer Park. You know, you've got some serious fans there. In fact, everyone I talked to had nothing but good things to say about you. Sue Kendall said everyone at the park thinks the world of you."

Dave looked at Aaron, who had a puzzled look on his face, then back at himself on-screen. "I've narrowed the list to three people who've each taken a little time to record their thoughts. The first is Heather, a young lady you helped reunite with her folks in Georgia. Then there's Irene, whose life you saved the day after Thanksgiving. And then Billy Ames, your friend and fellow Vietnam vet. Well, I'll shut up and let them talk. Sit tight, Aaron. This won't take long."

The scene shifted, and the background music disappeared. Dave saw Heather's face appear on-screen. She looked so happy, like the youthful teen she was supposed to be. "Mr. Miller—I mean, Aaron—I'm so glad I get the chance to do this. Things were so rushed the day I left the trailer park. I know I thanked you then, but there's no way it was near enough. I'm back with my mom and dad, and things are going great, way better than I ever imagined. You saved my life that day when . . . well, you know the day I mean. He really was going to kill me, but you stopped him. You could have gotten hurt or killed yourself, but you jumped right in. I was amazed at what you did. But even more than that . . ."

Heather reached for a box of tissues. "I put these here because I knew I'd need them. I want to thank you even more for pushing me to get back with my folks. You were right. They really do love me . . . just the way I am, and . . . they had totally forgiven me." Tears rolled down her cheeks. "You saved my life in so many ways, Mr. Miller. I . . . excuse me." She wiped her face.

A man's voice said in the background, "Can I say something, Heather?"

"Sure."

She shifted her chair to the side, and her father got in the picture. "Aaron, we never met, but we talked on the phone. Heather's mom and I want to thank you ourselves. You didn't just save Heather that day. You saved our family. For the first time in years, we're whole again. You have no idea . . ." He started choking up. "There aren't words to express our thanks for what you did. Maybe someday we'll get a chance to come down there and tell you in person." He looked at Heather. "I have my little girl back again. Thank you, Aaron. Thank you so much."

He backed away from the camera, and Heather leaned over to appear once more. "Thanks, Mr. Miller. I mean, Aaron."

The screen shifted to Irene Hamlin sitting at a dining room table. "Is this thing on? It's working? It's on now?" Dave remembered the moment. She was looking at him offscreen. He heard people laughing quietly throughout the room.

"Okay, then. Hey, Aaron. It's me, Irene. I'll be staying down here in Tampa for a few months with my son, till we figure out what to do. I suppose the workers have already come and hauled the debris from my old trailer off to the junkyard. But thanks to you, that's all they're hauling away. I'm here, alive and kicking, because of what you did that day. I was all set to go home and be with Jesus, you know that? See Moe again. I'm still looking forward to that day, but I wasn't too keen on seeing them after getting blown to pieces. That was a very brave thing you did, coming after me like that. Wish I had a big reward to give you. Not just for what you did for me then, but really, almost every day. You were more like a friend than a handyman. And that's the God's-honest truth."

She sighed. "Well, I better sign off before I start getting emotional." She looked offscreen. "Will anyone besides you and Aaron be hearing this?"

Dave heard himself say, "I don't know."

Irene looked back at the camera. "Well, either way, I want you to know. That piggyback ride you gave me as we fled that trailer was the most fun I had in years." She sat back with a big smile.

Everyone laughed. Dave looked at Aaron, watched John pat him on the back. The scene shifted once more. This time to Billy Ames, sitting on his electric scooter, Tess sitting by his side.

"Hey, Aaron. This here fella says he knows you. He's writing some book about Vietnam heroes. Man, why'd you never tell me about getting that Medal of Honor? Well, I guess I know the answer to that. You hardly ever talk about yourself. So, I guess I don't know what you did to earn that medal, not the whole story anyway. But I'll tell you what . . . you're a hero to me." Billy started blinking back tears. "I haven't had a friend as nice as you since . . . well, I don't remember when."

Tess leaned over and rested her head on Billy's lap. "That's a girl." He patted it and continued. "And I want to thank you for setting me and Tess up here. I haven't had a dog since I was a kid, and that old hound wasn't anything like Tess here. Between her and you, I ain't ever lonely anymore. And believe me . . . that was a problem. A big problem." He was getting choked up again.

"I never told you this, Aaron. But you didn't just save the lives of those three vets back in 1970, or whatever year it was. You saved this vet's life, the day you came knocking on my trailer to fix that old ramp. You remember that day? I let you in for a drink after. I was listening to old Bob Dylan songs, remember that? Well, before I opened the door to let you in, I had to hide a loaded pistol sitting on an end table. I was all set to end it that day. Felt I had no reason to keep going." He looked down at Tess, offscreen toward Dave for a moment, then back at the camera. "Thanks to you, Aaron, I do now. You *are* a hero. Don't you ever forget that." He smiled as a tear slipped down his cheek. Then he sat up straight and saluted.

Some nice closing music began to play. Dave looked up at Aaron, who was saluting the fading image of his friend on-screen. People everywhere were reaching for tissues again.

John stood up and walked to the center of the room. "Could we have the lights up, please?" When they came on, he looked over at Aaron. "Guess you never quit, Aaron, do you? Still saving lives in your sixties. Three more, to be exact. Just like back in Nam." He looked out to the crowd. "I'm sure you're all hungry as I am. I'm going to ask Allan's nephew Sam to come up and say the blessing. He's a pastor in Tulsa. When he's done, we'll dig in."

John looked to the back of the room and said over the mic, "Dave, when Sam's finished praying, can I have a word with you?"

48

Dave wondered what John wanted. He didn't look upset. "I think he wants me to eat dinner up there with Aaron," he said to Karen. "But I'll be back as soon as I can."

"That's okay," she said. "John and Steve talked about this. John was a little concerned that our coming might be too much of a distraction for my father. But Steve told him we don't want to ruin their time with him. So we agreed, he'd eat dinner and dessert with you all at the big table, then we'd see him after. Please tell him that, so he can relax."

"I will."

"And tell him we're staying over till tomorrow afternoon, so we could spend more time together. John told us your plane wasn't flying back until tomorrow night."

"He'll love that," Dave said, and so would he. "Gotta go." He hurried over to John. They walked over and stood near a large Christmas tree. "What's up, John?"

John looked back at Aaron, who was chatting with Allan and Paul at the table. "Tonight I get to play Santa," he said, looking back at Dave. A big smile appeared. "The guys and I wanted to do this privately. I'll let you decide how and when to tell him. But after hearing about Aaron's financial situation, we didn't feel like this party here goes near enough to express our gratitude. So we pulled together our resources. We want Aaron to be able to retire as soon as he's ready, in a little bit of style."

Dave couldn't believe what he was hearing. "What did you have in mind?"

"My accountant will go over the details with you, but here's a card you can give Aaron from us that explains the idea and the amount. We were able to pull together just a tad over four hundred thousand dollars."

Aaron sat back in his chair, listening to the wonderful Christmas songs, his belly full, his heart overwhelmed.

After finishing off an eight-ounce filet mignon and the biggest lobster tail he'd ever seen, he'd spent the next thirty minutes receiving more handshakes, hugs, and words of praise than a man has a right to this side of heaven. He couldn't even think about dessert, so John had the waiter box it up for later. When John first opened the door to this room just over an hour ago, and Aaron saw this big crowd instead of just Allan and Paul, he'd felt trapped.

But not anymore.

On the plane ride, he'd worried about the conversations they might have over dinner. After they had gotten all their thank-yous out of the way, whatever would they talk about? The three of them were best friends, had been back in Nam and forty years since. They had lots in common, then and now.

Five minutes into the dinner, Aaron realized he had worried

for nothing. They made him feel like he belonged right there with them. John had even said, "Aaron, you need to be a part of all our reunions from now on." He had no idea how he'd afford something like that, but it warmed his heart that they had offered. They mostly talked about how their lives had gone over the years, but none of it came across like bragging, and none of it made him feel like the gap between them was anywhere near as big as it really was.

"Say, Aaron." He looked up. It was John.

"Why don't you go on back and spend a little time with your family before the night's over?"

Dave had told Aaron that he'd get to spend tomorrow morning and part of the afternoon with them. "You sure you don't mind?"

John shook his head. "Not a bit. You head on back there too, Dave. We'll be all right up here. The guys and I've got some family we need to get with anyway. By the way, in about thirty minutes, I'm going to change the Christmas music playing now to some of those old classic Christmas dance songs."

John gave Dave a wink. "If you get my drift."

49

Dave led Aaron back to Steve and Karen's table. They were still finishing up dessert. They all got up and hugged him again. Then sat down and started talking. At one point, Steve mentioned them getting together tomorrow morning.

"You all can come over to our room," Aaron said. "Dave's and mine. We're on the twentieth floor. It's as big as a house."

Dave looked at Steve. "John put us up in the Governor's Suite."

"That sounds like a great idea, Dad. Then that's what we'll do."

Dave noticed how Aaron smiled each time they called him Dad. He was so happy for Aaron. The family continued chatting. Steven Jr. was filling him in on some of his adventures in Afghanistan. Dave tapped Karen's shoulder. "Can I talk to you for a few moments?"

"Sure."

One of the families with small children had already left for the night, leaving an empty table. Dave pointed to it. "Let's sit over there." He reached for her hand then led the way. Dave realized something a little while ago. The Christmas songs that had been playing in the background included all the ones that had depressed him for the last few weeks. But he wasn't depressed tonight.

As he and Karen sat, Elvis Presley started singing one of the most depressing songs of all, "Blue Christmas." Whenever that song would come on, Dave would actually turn off the radio. Now, looking at Karen's smiling face, he felt no pain. But he was feeling a little anxious about what he was about to say. "Karen, I might be making a big mistake here. I know you wanted to slow everything down, take this break to think everything over, but I've got to tell you . . . I've been dying the last few weeks. Not being able to talk to you at all is like—"

"I've thought everything over, Dave," she interrupted.

"What?"

She reached for his hands. "What I figured out during my 'break' is something I knew almost from the first moment we met. I didn't really acknowledge it then, just went with my feelings. But I think that's what tripped me up. I'm not used to doing that. I just got carried away when we met, and it felt wonderful."

"Felt wonderful for me too."

She looked down. "Then I got afraid. For some reason, when I saw my father's picture in the paper that day, it was like I was standing next to a ledge and it suddenly gave way." She looked at him. "So I ran home, where I felt safe."

"But you're here now."

"I am."

"Okay, then, I'm just going to say it, Karen. I don't care what kind of trouble I get in." He looked deep into her eyes. "I love you. I don't want to chase you off again, but something's happened to me. I don't know how. It wasn't something I planned. The logical side of me says to feel this strongly about someone has to take a long time. But I've loved you from the first moment I saw you at Chili's. I can't stop thinking about you. These past few weeks have been like torture for me. I can't—"

"I love you too, Dave."

He looked in her eyes, her lovely brown eyes. "You do?"

She nodded.

"You love me?"

She nodded again, then picked up a napkin and dabbed her eyes. "Steve helped me see it."

"I love Steve," Dave said. She smiled. He stroked the side of her face with his finger. They stared at each other a moment. He looked in her eyes, then at her lips. *Just do it.* He slid his finger tenderly down her cheek and placed it under her chin. Then drew her close and kissed her.

The first kiss was short, until he felt her kiss back. Then he kissed her again, expressing all the love he felt so strongly inside. Their lips parted a moment. He kissed her once more as Elvis sang his final chorus of "Blue Christmas." "Listen," he said, "I know we need to spend time to get to know each other better. I don't know how we're going to make it work, being so far apart, but couples do it all the time now. We can find a way . . . until somehow we're both in the same place."

"We could get on each other's cell phone plans," she said, "so the calls are free."

"We can do that and both get phones that allow us to see each other when we talk. And we can text and email every day."

"But we need to see each other in person too," she said. "How are we going to do that?"

"I don't know. But we will. We'll make it work. Getting some time together tomorrow is a nice start, but it's going to be horrible going our separate ways." Another Christmas song began to play. Rascal Flatts sang that romantic classic "I'll Be Home for Christmas."

Karen turned and looked at the table where her father and Steve's family sat. Aaron was still talking with Steven Jr. while the others listened in. "I just had a great idea," she said.

Aaron did his best to listen to his newfound grandson talk about Afghanistan, but he was a little distracted. Across the way, he had just watched Dave kiss his newfound daughter, Karen. Dave had become his hero, so this made him very happy.

Then *the song* began to play. "I'll Be Home for Christmas." He didn't recognize the singers, but they were doing a beautiful job with it. His mind instantly went to the faded picture of Karen and Steve as toddlers, the only picture he'd had of them all these years. He remembered holding it in his trembling hands, raindrops falling on his poncho, artillery explosions booming in the distance. Then this same song began to play.

Listening to it while looking at that picture had become his simple, lonely Christmas tradition every year since.

But look, he thought. *The song is playing, but the photograph is back in my room.* He was looking at Karen and Steve face-to-face. It was so wonderful. And yet, a wave of sadness was crouching at the door of his heart. He knew in a little while this magical evening would end. He didn't want to leave.

He was so glad he'd get some time with Karen and Steve and the rest of his family tomorrow, but what about after that? How could he see them here—something he had longed for all these years—then head back to Florida and be all alone again? There had to be a way to see them more often. One day was not enough. But he didn't have the kind of money people needed to travel. He didn't own a car, couldn't even afford a cell phone plan in his monthly budget.

Just then Karen got up and headed his way. She tapped Steve on the shoulder, then whispered something in his ear. Steve got a big smile on his face and nodded. He leaned forward and said something quietly to Aileen. She smiled and nodded. Steve stood up. Karen motioned for Dave to join them. He did.

The three of them stood in front of Aaron.

Karen looked at Dave. "I want you to hear this too." Then she looked at Aaron. "Dad, listening to this song gave me an idea. We're really excited about tomorrow, but Steve and I wanted to know if you'd consider flying back to Texas a week from now. Only this time to Fort Worth. We'd like you to spend this Christmas at home, with us. At Steve's place. And Dave, we'd like to invite you, your mom, and Jake."

Tears rolled down Aaron's face. "I'd love that . . . more than anything in the world." He looked down. "But I don't have . . . I can't really afford . . ."

"Aaron." It was Dave.

Aaron looked up. Dave pulled an envelope out of his coat pocket. "You can afford to make this trip. And a whole lot more trips after that. Here, read this card."

Aaron opened the envelope and read the card. When he'd finished, he couldn't speak. The classic song ended with the memorable words "if only in my dreams." No one said a word. Aaron looked up into the faces of his children, then his grandchildren. He was here, with them. He felt as if he were already home.

And it wasn't a dream.

AUTHOR'S NOTE

While this book is entirely a work of fiction, as with several of my books, the inspiration behind *The Reunion* was drawn from real-life events. As I researched my first two novels, *The Unfinished Gift* and *The Homecoming*, I came across two stories that astounded me involving World War II vets. Both of these men had fought in horrific battles and had won this nation's highest award for bravery and valor, the Congressional Medal of Honor.

After the war, they came home to live in quiet obscurity. Both men worked as janitors. The people whose buildings they cleaned, whose floors they mopped and bathrooms they sanitized, walked past them every day and had no idea who they were or the amazing things they had done during the war.

One of the men's lives ended in tragedy (you can read about Bobbie E. Brown at http://en.wikipedia.org/wiki/Bobbie_E._Brown). The other man's life had a much happier ending (read more about Bill Crawford at http://www.homeofheroes.com/profiles/profiles_crawford_10lessons.html).

As I read their stories, I began thinking about all the people we pass by every day, who work in menial jobs (like Bobbie E.

Brown and Bill Crawford did). People whose life stories we never give a second thought. I wondered how many of them might have accomplished amazing things or had fascinating stories to tell . . . if we only took the time to listen, to take an interest in them.

As a Christian, I also began to think of my Savior's example. In the Gospels, Jesus routinely stopped to take an interest in ordinary people. A woman at a well, a blind beggar, a nameless leper. I want to be more like him in this way. And if you look at the Scripture verse I quote at the beginning of the book, it's obvious God will measure people's worth and value on judgment day very differently than how we measure people's worth here on earth.

From Christ's example in the Gospels, and the stories of men like Bobbie E. Brown and Bill Crawford, the beginnings of *The Reunion* were born. But I decided to make my hero, Aaron Miller, a Vietnam vet. This satisfied a strong desire I've had to honor these real-life heroes of my childhood, young men whose lives had been plunged into a dark hour in our nation's history, an hour from which my own life had been spared.

I wrote *The Reunion*, in part, as a tribute to all the military veterans of this country. The men and women who've served this great nation of ours throughout the years, sacrificially putting themselves in harm's way so the rest of us could live in freedom. But I especially wanted this book to honor Vietnam vets.

I am not a vet. I have never served in the military.

None of us can control the timing or circumstances of our birth. That decision is always left in God's hands. The Vietnam War ended before I became old enough to be eligible.

My *Leave It to Beaver* childhood of the late fifties and early sixties was brought to an abrupt halt by a number of national events, starting with the assassination of President John F. Kennedy. Then I watched the Civil Rights Movement unfold on the network news and listened as my parents talked about "how terribly these poor black people are being treated" (as a child, I had never even met an African American). A few years later came the assassinations of Martin Luther King Jr. and Bobby Kennedy. It seemed like the nation was spinning out of control.

But nothing affected me as much as the Vietnam War.

I was terribly afraid of the draft. Year after year, it hung like a Big Clock over my head, ticking down to the moment when I would be forced to join all the other unfortunate young men who'd been thrown into this terrible war. I didn't understand it. The whole nation seemed to turn against it. There were riots about it on the news, seemed like every night (along with constant reports on how many U.S. soldiers had been killed that day in Vietnam). My parents talked about the war around the dinner table as a horrible mistake some crooked politicians had made (they talked this way even though my father was a patriot, a veteran of the Korean War).

When the war finally ended, it was obvious . . . after all those years of bloodshed and dying, America had lost. But to me, the way we had treated the Vietnam veterans at home, during the war and after, was another national tragedy.

For the next fifteen years or so, until the first Gulf War in Iraq, people hardly ever talked about Vietnam, and when they did, it was rarely in a positive light. The veterans of that war continued to suffer neglect, mistreatment, and humiliation, as if they were somehow responsible for what happened.

I'm so glad this has changed, so grateful the men and women who fought and suffered through this time can now hold their heads up high and be properly honored for the sacrifices they made.

So . . . to all the Aaron Millers out there, the unsung warriors whose actions have made it possible for the rest of us to live free, not just in the Vietnam War but in all the wars our country has been engaged in, please accept this author's heartfelt thanks and unending gratitude.

Acknowledgments

This is now my sixth novel with the same team. It's a comfort when I write to know I'll have the best support any writer can have. Starting with my wife Cindi, who provides me with so much love, encouragement, and excellent advice. I wouldn't want to do this without you.

And Andrea Doering, my editor at Revell. I prize your insights and instincts more with every book. To Karen Solem with Spencerhill Associates, the best literary agent in the business and also a dear friend.

And to the management and staff at Revell who work so hard behind the scenes to get the book ready for the shelves and into readers' hands. Special thanks to Twila Bennett and Michele Misiak; also to Kristin Kornoelje for keeping me on track. And thanks to Claudia Marsh and Robin Barnett for your zealous support in spreading the word. It's so great working with you all.

I'd also like to thank Bill Gilliland, a friend in Daytona Beach and retired firefighter, for his help getting some important details right. And my good friend Larry Leech, a fine writer and executive chairman of Word Weavers, for the "inside scoop" about life in a newspaper office. And speaking of Word Weavers, thanks to my local chapter in Volusia County, Florida, for their encouragement and support, as well as their critiques of several chapters in this book.

Dan Walsh is the bestselling, award-winning author of *The Unfinished Gift*, *The Homecoming*, *The Deepest Waters*, *Remembering Christmas*, and *The Discovery*. A member of American Christian Fiction Writers, Dan served as a pastor for twenty-five years. He lives with his family in the Daytona Beach area, where he's busy researching and writing his next novel.

www.danwalshbooks.com

Meet Dan Walsh at www.DanWalshBooks.com

Learn more interesting facts,
read Dan's blog, and so much more.

Connect with Dan on
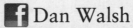 Dan Walsh
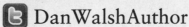 DanWalshAuthor

"Dan Walsh's books grab your heart and don't let you go until the last page. I look forward to reading every novel Dan writes."

—Dr. Gary Smalley, *bestselling author and speaker on family relationships*

Laced with suspense and intrigue, *The Discovery* is a richly woven novel that explores the incredible sacrifices that must be made to forge the love of a lifetime.

 Revell
a division of Baker Publishing Group
www.RevellBooks.com

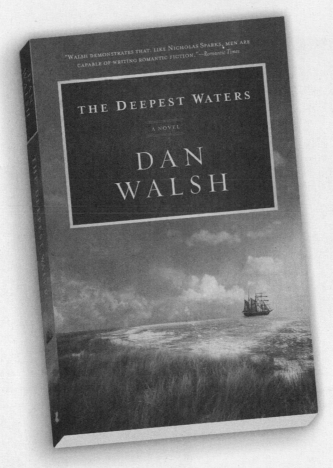

Heartwarming Tales of
Love and *Loss*

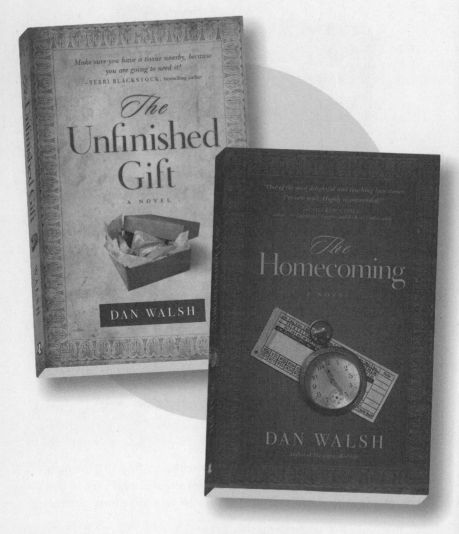

Coming Soon from
Dan Walsh and Gary Smalley

The Dance

Book 1 in the Restoration Series

New series following the Anderson family through
their family troubles, love and heartbreak, and the
legacy the family will leave.

Revell
a division of Baker Publishing Group
www.RevellBooks.com